Teaching Frankenstein:

A Cautionary Tale

Viktor James

For Wilson, my brother in arms

A Word of Caution

I am no longer a teacher.

By the time you finish reading these pages, you'll understand why. This is a cautionary tale, a warning. It is not for the faint of heart nor is it for the easily offended. While I have changed descriptions, names, and locations to protect those involved, I done my best to recount the events that happened as accurately as possible. The core of the story echoes the truth. However, as with all tales retold, imagination fills the gaps.

My goal is not to sway you one way or another, only to show you how things were. I believe you're wise enough to come to your own conclusions.

They say the best example is a non-example.

A fitting epitaph…

Yours,

A Nameless Mister

Prologue - Hold onto Your Apples

"The directions are on the board," I repeated.

To be fair, they were trying not to laugh. Trying and failing. I couldn't blame them. If I were fourteen, I'd be laughing too.

In my defense, I had tried to scrub it away, but that only made it worse. It wasn't my fault the image on the whiteboard wouldn't erase. They hadn't even needed to use a permanent marker because the board somehow absorbed everything written on it. And now it had absorbed a penis, a penis drawn in black ink that wouldn't erase... just in time for observations.

Was it a sign?

It looked like one.

It was a pretty crude drawing, two orbs and a long elliptical. I tried to scrub it off, but it only added shading, turning it into a kind of ghost dick. Fitting, I suppose, considering the approach of Halloween, horror, and all things macabre. I bit my tongue to keep from smiling. The Neolithic drawing of a floppy cock continued to curve like a jellied finger towards the daily lesson plan projected onto the board.

I stumbled through attendance, feeling sweat ooze behind my collar. Suddenly, there were sounds: the unzipping of backpacks, the shuffling of papers, the slamming of binders. It should've been quiet. All they needed to do was sit there and read the board. There was even a phallus pointing right at the instructions, and yet that didn't seem to help.

"Read the directions," I said for the third time.

Why was that so hard to understand?

Teaching literature was 85 percent pretending to be a hard-ass, 10 percent reading at least one entire book without SparkNotes (maybe), and the other whatever percent was having... What? Patience? Wherewithal? The ever-elusive "it" teachers in TED Talks bragged about? You mean the fantastical manifestation of ability that surpasses a rational sense of observation? You mean the pathologically developed, anxiety-induced continuous distrust forged after years of experiencing teenagers trying to get away with absolutely anything? *That* "it"?

That's not talent. That's PTSD.

And if there was an "it" to teaching, I definitely didn't have it. I could barely remember to read my emails.

I continued taking attendance, something much harder that day because I had to eyeball who was in my class and who wasn't. Normally, I had a seating chart. A body behind a desk meant "here" and an empty one, "not here." It was easy. And because I still didn't know everyone's name, it was also convenient. At two months into the school year, I probably should've learned them weeks ago, but... anyways.

I had decided to look cool and show off my teaching "skillz" for the bossman and had overlooked the whole "no seating chart" thing. There were a lot of things that happened that day, that year even, that I had overlooked.

And the dong was definitely on the list.

The nervous sweat seeped underneath my suit as growing murmurs betrayed the waning attention spans.

It looked like most of them were there, so I submitted the attendance and logged out. It wasn't like anyone gave a shit anyway.

"As you might've guessed—" my voice was awkward, choked off by nerves "—we're doing something a little different today. Before we start the novel next week, we're going to take a look at Mary Shelley's world. This way you get a feel for—"

A click drew eyes to the slowly opening door.

A trail of students entered. I waited.

Tardy.

I glared at them. "Grab any seat. We're just getting started." I walked back over to my computer and tried to log into the system again to adjust the attendance. A spinning hourglass appeared in the middle of the screen. *Not now.* The suit itched. I could feel the sweat pooling in my pits. I looked up at them from behind my computer; awkwardly standing by the door, checking out their options, calculating how to sit next to their friends.

"Just grab any seat. You won't be there for very long."

The computer was still loading as two of them walked towards the empty chairs. The other stood there, staring at me.

Grinning.

From my desk, I picked up where I'd left off. I wasn't in the mood to waste any more time, especially on that kid. "We'll be taking a look at Mary Shelley's world. To understand the novel, you have to understand what was happening around her during the time that she—"

He started scooting over to me like one of those toy robots in every Christmas movie. Slowly, he raised his hand from his side, revealing an apple. His face puckered red with restraint.

I looked at it, trying to hide my annoyance.

"Here you go, Mister. I got it for you."

I thought of telling him where he could stick that apple. Even better, I wanted to throw it in the trash and say something street like, "Fuck yo apple, bitch." But the

4

principal was recording everything I said and did for my formal evaluation, and "keeping it real" wasn't one of the graded categories.

"Thank you," I said through clenched teeth.

He had found out that I hated apples and decided to hand me one periodically just to annoy me. It would continue until he found another way to get on my nerves. My passing daydream of launching the apple at his head like some kind of medieval warlord laying siege to a castle faded.

I took the deformed apple and carefully placed the dull, lopsided thing on my desk, making sure it wouldn't fall to the floor.

The computer was still loading. *Fuck it*, I thought. I pretended to click some buttons and then closed it shut.

"Today, we begin a journey into a very familiar and very dark tale, *Frankenstein*." I took my place center stage. "Many of you may think you know the story, but you're mistaken. For the next eight weeks, you'll enter into a world of despair, anger, betrayal, and death. Our goal will be to answer a very specific question. That question is this: When pursuing scientific knowledge, is any action justified?"

There it was, the big question. Boom. I had hoped for piqued interest, imagined some kind of reciprocal "oooh" or "ahhhh." Instead, confused faces stared back at me while the sound of rapidly clicking computer keys continued in the background. Sweat still itched across my skin.

"Yes!" apple boy suddenly shouted sarcastically.

"Shut up," Anita said, pushing back her crimson bangs as she gave him a sideways glare.

"What? I answered the question," Joaquín fired back.

The sudden desire to throw the apple at his head appeared again.

"We're not supposed to answer it now," she said, then added, "dumbass."

"We're supposed to answer what now?" a girl asked.

"Wait, what does that even mean?" another said.

"Try thinking for one fucking second and you'd know," Anita said.

"Anita, be respectful," I said, hinting a reminder with my eyes that the principal was in the room.

"Sorry, Mister," she said, then turning to the principal added, "Sorry, Nimitz" for good measure.

"You'll begin by reading the article that's in the center of your table and—no. Put it down. Don't touch it yet. Just wait. All of this is on the board—never mind. I'm going to put you into groups," I said, and as requests to choose groups erupted: "It's on the board! No, I'm not letting you pick your group. I'll number you from one to five. Then you will—no. Put it down. Thank you. Once I number you, get up and find your new group. Got it? Okay.

"One. Two..."

I'm going to take a step back and say that despite what you may have heard, teachers aren't "unfireable." It's just harder to be fired the longer you've served. The district puts new teachers on probation for three years. Tons of observations, hours of coaching and training, pounds of useless information printed off in packets that you glance over while nodding only to throw in the shit-drawer of your desk and never look at again. All this just to make sure you do your job. And that's after years spent at university.

You spend your first three years as a teacher basically in a working interview. After that, getting fired becomes a process, but it's still very possible. Up until the end of the three-year trial period, if your principal says, "Duces hombre," your basic bitch-ass goes back to Bag 'N' Save or wherever you worked before you picked up a dry-erase marker and stood at the front of a class for the first time.

After three years of constant anxiety, you can't hear a door click open without your asshole tightening. It's Pavlov. Look it up.

While they may tell you that these observations, meetings, and other forms of "help" exist to improve your teaching, it's more to make sure you don't lose your mind and start bitch-slapping students. Hopes and dreams die in the first three years of teaching. It happens because you're thrown into the trenches, forced to build a functioning set of skills after you realize that everything you learned at university is useless.

Two years in and I still had hope, but it was dwindling.

I needed that observation to be a success. Especially after my first year. I had learned that there were a lot of ways to make sure teachers didn't return.

New year. New school. New start.

"Get in your groups," I said after numbering the students.

"Wait, am I a one or a two?"

"You're a two."

"No, I'm a two."

Confusion erupted. One group had eight kids, another only had two. One boy was standing by himself near the door, leaning against it, staring at his shoes. And there was another group that was just a horde of kids arguing about which numbers they were supposed to be.

"No. He said you're two."

"Nuh-uh. He told me I'm three. You're five."

"Your mom's a five."

"Let's try this again," I said through a forced smile. "One. One," I looked at her. "Repeat it back to me. One."

"One."

"Two," I waited. "Two."

"Two," the next student said.

Once that was over, I again asked them to find their groups.

"Where's group two?" someone asked.

"How can anyone be so fucking stupid?" Anita said, just barely loud enough for me to hear.

"Look up." I pointed to the ceiling where, during my planning period, I had balanced precariously on top of the desks to put up paper signs with numbers on them.

"Oh."

I checked the clock on my phone. Almost ten minutes had passed, and we hadn't even started.

Nimitz sat in the corner, pounding computer keys in a fury.

I pushed a shaking hand into my pocket and said, "Begin reading your articles."

Making sure teenagers are on task is what I imagine guiding cracked-out chimpanzees through a quilting class feels like.

I walked from group to group.

Eventually, I was standing by a table of students, listening in on what should have been a juicy bit of gossip about Mary Shelley's life. One of them read out loud to the rest of the group. I waited for a reaction. Nothing. They just continued to the next paragraph.

"Wait," I stopped them. "What do you think about that?"

"What?"

"What? What do you mean, 'what?'" I asked.

Shrugs.

"Reread that paragraph," I said.

"We already read it."

"But what happened?" I asked.

"I dunno."

"Exactly. You're missing something."

"What?"

"Reread it," I nearly shouted. *How hard is it to do what I say?* They reread it.

Still nothing.

I waited for someone to say something. Nothing. "What

happened?" I goaded.

"Oh," something clicked. "She ran away with that Percy guy?"

"Why's that interesting?" I asked.

"I dunno."

"What's wrong with Percy?" I asked.

"He's gay!" one of them shouted.

"Your mom's gay!" a boy in another group jeered.

"Focus," I snapped. "No. He's not gay."

"Oh... he's married?"

"Poses a problem, no?"

"What a slut."

"Interesting response," I said. "Write it down."

"Really?"

"It's what you think, isn't it?"

She wrote it down.

I instinctively glanced up at the wall, looking for a clock before remembering that there were classrooms inside Chernobyl's exclusion zone with more resources and in better condition. The bowing brown stain on the ceiling tile from the recent rain served to underscore that notion. A quick glance at my phone revealed that it was time for them to switch groups.

They weren't ready.

I gave them more time.

Still not ready.

More time.

Still not ready.

They weren't going to finish.

The principal was moving around, watching students work.

I had envisioned something vastly different. I should have known better. On paper, it looked great, but in practice my students were struggling to read simple news articles.

It was like watching them take the goddamn SAT.

CHAPTER ONE

Desperado

"We started five minutes ago," Principal Nimitz boomed from the front of the library.

Everyone turned to stare at us. Nimitz took a sip of coffee from his thermos. It didn't take a lot of effort for him to be intimidating. Although his youth had faded, his physique had not. A slight puff of his chest was enough to remind you that he was the alpha, and that you had fucked up.

The air conditioner hummed out refrigerator levels of cold air into the darkened room. The main screen glowed with a slide from the current presentation. Another lecture. We had spent the morning in training, the topic was "The Benefits of Avoiding Lecture in the Classroom." It had been presented to us at a lecture in a classroom. Like most things in education, there wasn't much follow-through.

Once we found seats, he turned toward Ritz, the assistant principal, and said, "Please continue."

She clicked to the next slide.

Scarfing down a mountain of carbs before sitting through another presentation had not been a good idea. The dim lights, the chill of the AC, the food settling heavily in my stomach, I wondered how Nimitz would react if I fell asleep.

Some days I was so sure I wanted to give teaching another chance. Others, I was ready to be fired so I could move on.

It was the infamous Teacher Workweek. You know the one you laughed about as a kid because you knew your teachers had to go back to school and work while you got to do nothing for an extra week? Yeah. That's the one. It was the first day back from the break for everyone except me.

I was already in week two. New teachers had to start a week earlier for even more meetings and training. I wasn't a "new" teacher in the district, but a previous clerical error had allowed me to dodge that training in my first year. They had realized that when they had hired me back. It was paid though, and $20 is $20. So, I had attended.

It had turned out to be a week-long PowerPoint presentation with breaks to sleep, eat, shit, and shower (in whichever order you preferred). I couldn't tell you what it was about. I had scribbled during most of it, or had daydreamed, or had checked out a couple of the hot new teachers, anything to pass the time.

The worst part of it hadn't been the useless meetings or the presentations. The worst part was that it had been held at the school I had taught at, the place where my former boss had asked me not to return. Yet there I had been, like an ex-boyfriend showing up in the rain, begging for one more chance.

My colleague Wilson had suggested lunch. Veal had picked Thai. And Paige had taken us over in her Jeep. My new team was different: an awkwardly dressed man who was way too cheerful for my taste – Wilson; a Hispanic woman in her early forties who was always texting – Veal; and an older woman with thin blonde hair and a sardonic smile who always seemed ready to rebel – Paige. Different, but at least I wouldn't get called out in the front of a class for having a crush on one of them. Of all the reasons to blush and leave the room, crushing on your teaching partner, your *married* teaching partner, was probably the worst.

If you haven't picked up on it by now, teachers refer to each other only by their last names. To utter one's first name, especially in front of students, is an unspoken cardinal sin.

I glanced around the room, attempting to stay awake. The library would have been outdated when I was in elementary school. Many of the shelves were empty, and others held copies of old, boring books, some splayed out on the shelves like drunk sorority girls trying to earn points with the neighboring frat. The staff of a school in a war-torn, developmentally delayed country with inconsistent access to drinkable water would scoff at its poor condition.

Earlier that day, they had taken us over to the new library at my old school, the one that had kicked me out. Going on a tour of a library as a person with two degrees, one that focused specifically on reading books, annoyed me. Having a guide show us how a library worked had been even more special. But the kicker had been watching Wilson pull books off the shelf to check out before we had even finished the tour. I didn't think he had been serious until we had to help him carry them back to his car. He had told me he lent them out to kids. Looking at the state of my new library, I understood why.

It wasn't all dreary. There were several stuffed animals on top of the shelves, very friendly and plushy. Paige had arranged a turtle and a dragon to look like they were fucking.

I'll let you guess who was the bottom.

I felt a familiar, fuzzy feeling slip over me as the room slowly went dark.

My head snapped back, and I shot up in my chair, looking around to see if anyone had noticed. I leaned forward and tried to pay attention, writing down notes I would never use. I felt every plastic contour pressing into me from the hard chair as the presentation droned on and on.

"Why are we here?" Veal whispered.

"Is that an existential question?" I offered, goosebumps spilling out over my arms.

"It's a reminder to teach reading and writing in your classroom," Paige whispered, her arms across her chest. The light from the projector caused streaks of gray to glisten in her blonde hair. "Don't forget to do that."

"That's the whole point of our job." Veal rolled her eyes.

Wilson leaned back with a leg crossed, hands holding his knee. He continued to smile. Chirpy.

"How about a meeting where we learn something we can actually use?" Paige asked. "I should say something."

"I'd rather be setting up my classroom," Veal said.

Wilson shrugged his shoulders and smiled.

"I thought this was an AA meeting," I whispered. "I think I'm in the wrong room."

Paige snorted a little, causing people to look back at us. I pretended to scribble down some notes (something I had learned from my students).

The assistant principal looked over as she spoke, drawing out each word.

Suddenly, a woman raised her hand.

What she asked doesn't matter. What mattered was that for each question she asked, there was a follow-up question, and we were running out of time. A quick side note, if you're the kind of person that asks questions during meetings, people don't like you.

"Is she serious?" Veal whispered.

There I was fighting off a cataclysmic crawl towards narcolepsy, and this woman couldn't shut up long enough for the meeting to end so we could all leave.

Veal's lips curled in disgust. She stopped doodling, put her pen down, and picked up her phone. As she was texting, she said, "We should do our drinking game."

"The one where we have to take a shot every time she asks a question?" Paige asked. "Who's in? I'll keep track. Wilson, you in? New Guy?"

"You're going to corrupt him before he even has students," Wilson said.

"Does she talk a lot?" I whispered as I watched her slowly start to choke up.

Veal stifled a laugh. "You tell me."

"Here she goes again," Paige said.

This time it was more of an opinion filtered through trickling tears. I couldn't believe she was crying. *Who cries during a meeting?*

"Is this a support group?" I asked.

They laughed and again the lecturer paused. This time the principal looked over at us.

Again, I pretended to take notes.

I watched the clock as the sharing continued. By the time she ended her run at a free counseling session that was bookended by more sharing and tears from other elementary teachers, we were all beyond ready to leave. That was the problem with working at a K-12; we all had different priorities.

"Drinks?" Paige asked, after the lights flickered to full brightness.

"I gotta go to work," I said.

"Work?" Paige asked. "We have shots to take. That's how the game works."

"I got a shift tonight. Sorry," I said. "Next time."

"At the restaurant?" Paige asked.

"Until eleven," I said.

"Are you going to do that during the year?" she asked.

"Probably," I said. I didn't want to wait tables, but $20 is $20.

"Next time," she said. "Drinks on me."

I heard my name and turned to see Nimitz looking at me. My comrades gave me a consoling look before leaving the library with everyone else.

"Yes?" I said, walking over to him. I felt small in his presence. I may be tall, but Nimitz was a beast. I heard he had been a monster on the field back in the day, and I didn't doubt it.

"How are you finding everything so far?" His salt and pepper five o'clock shadow bristling as he spoke.

"It's going well."

He stared at me in a way that instantly brought up the moments that led to my being there in that library.

My first year had been a disaster. I had started summer by walking away from the pile of smoldering remains that had been my dream of teaching.

The summer hadn't been any better.

I had spent so much of my life trying to become a teacher that I had had no idea how to do anything else. You can only bullshit your resume so much. And after endless rejections, I had sat there on the floor in my living room, looking down at sun-soaked resumes littering the carpet, listening to the faint trickle of the community pool outside that only existed to remind me that I had lived in a place I couldn't afford. I had needed to figure my shit out fast, or I would've been homeless.

Meanwhile, my girlfriend had been running out of patience. It had been bad enough that her friends all had husbands and boyfriends with careers leading to six-figures. I would've only ever been a teacher. *That* had been my reality. And then suddenly it hadn't been, and I had been left with nothing. She had wanted a better life, not an unemployed boyfriend who couldn't afford to make rent.

I had been nearing the end of another frustrating day of

trying to figure out how to lie my way into a job interview when I had received yet another rejection. It had been full of the typical responses: "We had such a great pool of highly qualified candidates and after careful consideration..." In a fit of desperation, I had searched for jobs on my old school district's website, hoping that a last-minute position had opened up and that maybe, if the gods allowed it, there would've been a principal eager enough to look beyond my clusterfuck of a first year and hire me.

There had been one vacancy.

I had applied.

I had even arrived at the school before the interview, sweating in a worn-out suit, ignoring the fact that every bit of gravel and grass pushed its way up through a hole that had long ago eaten into my only decent pair of shoes. I had wanted to meet the principal. I had wanted to hand him my resume and introduce myself. I had wanted to show him my dedication (*desperation?*).

I had caught him as he had been leaving. We had talked briefly in the parking lot.

I couldn't believe it when he had asked me to come in for an interview.

Later on, with laughter echoing from behind me through the open door, I had left the office and had walked past a row of young, suit-clad professionals nervously waiting in line. I had looked past them, feeling sorry for them.

The assistant principal had called a couple of hours later and had offered me the job.

Nimitz had called a few days later. "I heard an unsettling story, and I want to ask you if it's true."

Word travels fast in small school districts.

"I can explain."

He had listened and afterward had decided to take me on board anyway.

Looking at him there in the library, he gave me a nod as if to reaffirm that decision, but also to remind me why I was there. "This isn't going to be an easy year. Make sure you're ready for it," he said. "I'll see you tomorrow."

In other words, "don't fuck this up."

CHAPTER TWO

Accouterments

When you imagine a classroom, you probably picture rows of clean white desks, a whiteboard (if you picture a blackboard, you're either old or from Eastern Europe), a large teacher desk full of markers, yellow stickies, and a big metal stapler. Even right now, you can almost see the motivational posters covering the walls and bookshelves bowing heavy with stacks of literature eagerly awaiting young minds. Maybe you're a little excited, and you even imagine a pencil sharpener.

Tone it down a bit. Tone it down a lot, actually. You're at an 11. Dial it back.

My "new" school didn't have any of that.

My first school had been new when I had started, clean, shiny, perfect. It even had that new-school smell. The best thing had been the lockable faculty bathrooms on every floor. Nothing screams professionalism like being able to isolate yourself from students when the coffee hits you.

That wasn't the case at the school I started working at that year.

If last night's poor decisions decided to reverberate in my lower bowels, my options were either to risk embarrassment

19

blowing out the student bathroom down the hall that echoed every squeaker, or pray someone could come to relieve me so I could rush back to the main building, clenching, hoping I made it to the finish line in time.

That also described my classroom: a shitty situation.

The infamous "dry erase" board had a huge black gash through it that I would later cover up with Wite-Out. There was a partially destroyed corkboard in the back-right corner. At my old school, I had huge bay windows that provided a view of the entire campus. At this school, I had two windows that exposed shrubs covered in litter and a railing with chipped paint. Occasionally, someone would cry on the steps behind the band hall, but other than that, there wasn't much to see. I pulled the blinds down and left them that way nearly all year.

The other accouterments weren't any better.

The only thing about my desk that was impressive was the massive dent in the side of it. There were two broken bookcases held together with, no joke, blue painter tape. The carpet looked like something that would line the floor of an addiction treatment center. It was this kind of raw brownish gray color that begged for vomit. There was a mismatched collection of student desks. Some were porcelain smooth; others had worn wooden tops. Over the years, students had meticulously undone the screws to several of them (out of boredom, no doubt), and they were comically unstable. One had a swastika carved into it despite the school being nearly all minorities.

Resting in the center of the room there was this monstrous, black metal cart on wheels that held my projector. It was always in the way and running into it was like having a Razor scooter hit you in the ankle. Everything would stop until the pain subsided. Only then could you continue teaching.

And perhaps the most depressing sight was that there was no teacher chair.

A firefighter should have his hat, a doctor his stethoscope, and a teacher his swirly, oversized teacher chair.

No chair.

I looked around the room, sighed, and decided to talk to the other English teachers.

When I had found out that I had got the job, I had called a former team member at my old school, a guy I had thought of as a friend, and had told him. He had started laughing. "Good luck, man. That's the worst fucking school in the district."

I was beginning to see why.

Wilson was right across the hall. His room was much different than mine. While the only decoration was a Patriots poster that I wanted to rip off the wall (Tom Brady shining his bastardly beautiful smile at me in that mocking tone that ate away at the very fabric of my soul), his back wall held seven towering bookshelves stacked full of books. He had other furniture as well, cabinets and shelves and cubbyholes full of supplies, but it was the mountainous collection of books that twisted a pang of jealousy in me.

He had already finished setting up his classroom with the desks in neat rows ready for the first day and was sitting at a large, kidney-shaped table looking over something on his computer. The stack of books from the library expedition balanced precariously next to him.

"How are you already set up?" I asked.

"I came in last week with some students."

"I didn't know we could come in early."

"I didn't ask. I just showed up and had the janitor unlock it. We won't get time this week."

"They said we would."

"They always do."

"Do you…" I hesitated, "know if there's anything for my room?"

He put down his computer and shot up out of his chair, revealing a wardrobe that looked like he took styling tips from reruns of *Friends*. "You should talk to Veal. The teacher before you left all his stuff with her."

"What about all those?" I pointed to the books on his back wall.

"Oh, those? Those are mine. All bought with my own money. There's probably a couple thousand dollars' worth of books back there." He spoke with pride, placing a foot on a chair and resting an arm on his knee as he leaned towards the bookcases.

"You spent your own money on books for students?"

"Our library isn't great, so I figured why not make my own."

"Don't you worry about them?"

"One year, this asshole kid destroyed about a thousand dollars' worth of books by drawing dicks all over them. I fucking hate that little bitch." He paused and recollected himself, then shook it off. "It's the risk I take."

Some kids are assholes.

"I'll talk to Veal," I said.

"Good luck! If you need anything, let me know."

What I needed were books, and spending my own money wasn't an option.

I didn't have any to spend.

We didn't teach in a traditional high school. Instead, the "campus" was spread out over several annexes behind a larger elementary school. I found out later that it was only supposed to be temporary, but they had given up on waiting for the funding to build a new school and had ended up leaving it the way it was. It had the urbanized look of one of those colonial villages that you visit on a field trip when you're seven, except there was no maid churning butter outside.

Veal was in another building adjacent to ours, and I instantly felt the hot August air the moment the metal door rattled open. It was less than a minute before I was back inside the other building, walking toward her classroom.

Veal was at her desk and looked up from her phone when I walked in.

"Can I bother you?" I asked.

She continued texting. "What do you need?"

"I was told," I started apprehensively, "that you have some of the materials the previous teacher left from his classroom last year. I was wondering if I could grab them?"

"Materials?"

"Like classroom sets of novels or a curriculum?"

"Don't use the 'C' word."

"The 'C' word?"

"They hate that word here. Structures. We use structures to teach and assess the results."

Every year, some hotshot looking for a way out of education comes up with a "new" way to teach and then sells it to districts like a snake oil salesman. It's just different vocabulary for the same thing. Districts, eager to meet federal standards by improving their test scores so they can get more funding, bought in and force-fed it to their employees.

By the time it failed, the seller was long-gone.

Same shit, different school year.

Call me lazy, but after five years of studying in a university only to make less than most other professions, I wasn't exactly inspired to spend any additional time outside of work to improve my class. And knowing that my district was several years into a pay freeze didn't help either.

"What do I do about getting books?" I asked, already knowing the answer.

"Use your budget."

Aye-oh! There it was. Except five hundred dollars doesn't go far, especially when there wasn't a dried-up whiteboard marker in my room or even a goddamn stapler.

"There's nothing else?" I asked.

"Like what?"

"Lesson plans, classroom sets of books, maybe a year outline, you know, whatever you could spare from last year to guide me in the right direction."

"You can pretty much create your curric— I mean structures. Use what's familiar. As far as resources, I may have a couple of things, but I need most of it for my classes. You'll have to use your budget for the rest. Give me just a minute."

She glanced down at her phone and continued texting while I awkwardly slunk against one of her desks and waited in silence. When she finished, she stood up and went through some nearby boxes that were spread out over her room. She began moving things around in them, pulling out stacks of papers, magazines, a few books, until she found a purple folder. "I can give you this. It has a couple of activities that you might be able to use."

I feigned enthusiasm, took the folder, and headed out.

"Oh. I do have one class set you can have." She hesitated. "I taught it before. It's a great coming-of-age novel about a minority girl overcoming struggle and finding her place in the world."

"Thanks," I said again. "I really appreciate that."

In the back of my mind, I was hesitant about being the white teacher that showed a bunch of minorities a story about a minority girl who makes her dreams come true. It felt like being a step away from throwing on a Lakers' Jersey, heading to the Bronx blaring R&B, and trying to start an outreach program at a KFC. "Hey, guys! I'm just like you!" What would be next? Someone would walk in and hand me a stack of cliché, inspirational teacher posters of MLK Jr. and Gandhi, toss an apple in my direction, slap me on the ass, and tell me to "go change lives?!"

At least then I'd have some shit to put up on the walls.

On the way back into my room, I dragged a hard plastic chair that was abandoned in the hall to my desk and looked through the folder.

I grew furious.

Inside the purple folder was an absurd, minute collection of busywork that looked more like various punishments for students than actual lessons. Unconnected worksheets. A few examples. Old proofreading charts. *How?* I wondered. *How's it possible that this school doesn't even have the basic resources I need? It's not exactly new. It isn't like this is the first ninth grade English class that they've ever had here.*

I wondered how I could even do my job. I knew that I would have to spend countless extra hours putting something together, mining the internet, stealing and copying what I could, just to make it through the year.

I closed the folder with clenched teeth and pressed my temples. Then I reopened it, hoping to find something I missed the first time, the way you search your pockets for keys already knowing there's nothing there.

Useless busy work.

That's it? This is all you have? After years of teaching… a stupid purple folder? I thought.

My previous school had binders of shit, a book room full of resources, and teachers who had already taught the lessons I would teach. If I had a question, I could have just walked across the hall. Not anymore. A stupid purple folder with maybe seven different worksheets in it was all she had to show for years of teaching.

I was livid because I knew I'd have to start from scratch.

To be honest, knowing what I know now about education and how little time and money teachers have to plan, I don't blame her. I was angry then, but I hid it. I liked her. And I didn't want to ruin a budding professional relationship and find myself repeating the events from the previous year. So, I sucked it up.

After a brief search on my rather old and shitty (but very free) laptop provided by the district, I discovered the novel she recommended was for fifth graders. It would have probably been faster to walk to a Barnes & Fucking Noble and ask someone who worked there about it rather than wait for that archaic piece of shit to download a synopsis, but it wasn't like I needed a lot of time to set up my room.

I kept thinking that there was no way I could teach a book at a grade level that low to my freshmen. I couldn't even teach it to the one eighth grade class that I had that year. Knowing what I know now, it probably would have saved me a lot of stress to have done as Veal suggested, but I still had standards at that point.

I may have tiptoed the line to surrendering my dream of being a teacher, but if I was going to go out, it was going to be on my terms.

It was *my* dream after all.

I had no curriculum. No books. No lesson plans. Not even a fucking poster of some vague nature scene with an inspirational quote to motivate the teacher, let alone the students, to put up on my wall.

Wilson suddenly burst into my room unannounced and startled me. He held two large boxes in his arms. "Veal wanted me to give these to you. There's a couple more. I'll be right back!" He quickly set them down before bolting out of my room. My excitement that she may have uncovered some extra resources I could use was very short-lived. I opened the boxes to discover the novel she had suggested and a ton of dictionaries. *Dictionaries.*

Who the fuck uses dictionaries? I thought.

I slumped down in my chair and massaged my temples.

A few minutes later, Wilson returned with another box of dictionaries. "Don't forget, we have to meet up and practice our song before we head home. I think that's going to happen in about twenty minutes or so."

The song.

Now that's another story.

CHAPTER THREE

Districtwide Circle Jerk

Each year, the Wednesday before school started, the school board led a "District Extravaganza" at the main campus, the flagship school. That was where I had taught my first year. We would crowd the auditorium and listen to nearly four hours of inspirational porn and professional guilt, held hostage by our desire to make a difference and shamed with poor test scores. Then, they showed us a collection of graphs and data none of us really understood. And finally, we were finished on with an inspirational money shot before being jettisoned into the new school year without so much as a cuddle or a tissue to make ourselves moderately presentable for our Uber drivers.

None of that bothered me. That's teaching. What bothered me was the periodic "breaks."

Each school was required to pick a song and change the lyrics to reflect their mission for the year. Then you had to practice. A lot. Then you had to sing it in front of the whole district and school board. And then the school board ranked you. There was even choreography and props.

The best one earned a trophy.

That was their idea of a break.

I didn't want to learn a song. I didn't want to hold props. I didn't want to dance. I just wanted to sit in my room and figure out what the fuck I was supposed to teach. I get that teachers make students do embarrassing shit all the time: read out loud, present, work in groups. And maybe in a way the song bullshit was supposed to humble us, remind us of our place, and what we were asking of our students. Still, I think everyone had bigger issues to worry about rather than singing about improving test scores to the tune of "Don't Stop Believing."

I just wanted to teach and not get fired.

After far too many practice sessions over two days, we piled onto the bus and went to the District Extravaganza. Luckily, there was a barbecue afterwards with burgers, hot dogs, and plenty of condiments. Oh! And fun-size bags of chips. You can't hate on fun-sized bags of chips. You know the moment that you saw a tiny bag of Doritos with your PB&J you felt like royalty. *Good times.*

The bus dropped us off near the front, and everyone filed out towards the auditorium in a herd. I hadn't appreciated the beauty of the campus while I had worked there. But it was gorgeous. The modern architecture had fresh landscaping like a new housing development that hadn't been wilted by time or broken by crime.

We trailed down the neatly edged path, and up the stairs to the auditorium. On the way there, people kept pointing out how pretty everything was, "Oh, look over there," and, "Oh my, would you look at that." I got it. It was gorgeous. Whatever.

Even the concrete was stainless.

Once inside, our school formed a blob in a corner of the expansive cafeteria while waiting for the auditorium doors to open. Other schools had congealed into little cliques of coworkers as well. A few vagrants moved between these groups, and that was when the over-the-top greetings bellowed over the cacophony of various conversations. They would screech, "I'm so glad to see you!" ten decibels too high. It made me cringe because I knew that it was either fake or the result of an excessive dependency on pharmaceutical grade antidepressants.

When my previous team members noticed me, they turned away in whispers.

Meanwhile, our elementary teachers began enthusiastically pulling out props (judging by the fact that most of them were married with kids, props were about the only thing they pulled out). They were really getting into what was about to happen.

That annoyed me.

Fact: elementary teachers tend to do way more drugs than secondary teachers.

Fact: their sense of ego and self-preservation is vastly different.

Fact: elementary teachers will literally dance with students singing shit like "Fruit Salad" or the "PB&J Song."

Not secondary teachers.

We're cautious, cynical, and judgmental. In middle school, we were the ones who stood off to the side during the school dance calling everyone stupid. We'd comment on the social-political power structures at play in the typical festive school function while explaining how the act of dancing was conformity and the complete subjection of one's will to the masses or some bullshit like that. We'd mumble this to anyone who'd listen because we were a cigarette, a beret, and a copy of *La Peste* away from a full-blown existential crisis by the age of twelve.

The doors to the auditorium opened, signaling that it was time. Suddenly, I grew very nervous and turned to Wilson. "I didn't spend five years in college to sing and dance like some kinda cabana boy."

"You and me both," he said. I was actually happy to see something upset him.

Veal and Paige's similar dire looks also brought comfort.

People continued to trickle towards their seats as the lights dimmed and the room quieted. After a moment, a woman who looked entirely too happy took to the podium. "Welcome, educators, to the new school year! I know you are all excited to be back and doing what you love!"

I needed her to tone it down. Teachers treat the summer months as a holy pilgrimage towards sanity. The eclipsing final days of freedom brought about a certain sense of dread, no matter how much you enjoyed teaching. Her exploding on stage with the radiance found only in a Prozac commercial, offering an unsettling smile and an inhuman level of positivity, made my bowels water.

"I know you're probably thinking another week of summer would be nice," she said. A cheer went up through the crowd, some laughter. "But what we do is important and vital to our community." Just like that, the laughter whimpered away into muffled side conversations.

The presentation started by shaming us with test scores (not surprisingly). We were below average. There were plenty of reasons for this, and I'll spare you all of them. I will say that those graphs don't take into account anything other than test performance. Our district, a small, eclectic group of kids just on the edge of an urban population, had its share of difficulties. Unfortunately, none of that matters. Only the numbers do.

The lights went up.

"It's time for our first performance," she said. They began calling up schools to perform. The songs varied: classics, pop, old rap. Some used props, others danced. Some did both, and one school was brave enough to stand up and mumble some rendition of "Call Me Maybe" with no other goal than to remind us that the song still existed. There was a fine arts school that actually brought out instruments and sang surprisingly well. But for the most part, they were all uncomfortably bad.

Those who can't...

I can't remember the song we sang that year. I've searched my brain for it without success. When I think back to that moment, when we stood up, the assistant principal counting down "three, two, one" and then the explosion of air pressed out in the form of a song, all I can remember is finding my happy place, biting down hard, and letting it happen. I don't even think I sang. It was more like the screeching sound that penguins make when seals rape them.

Three out of five stars.

Average.

My previous school went next. They stood up and pulled out inflatable instruments, put on wigs, and proceeded to sing and dance to "Grease Lightning." When they finished, an explosion of applause erupted around me.

They walked away with the trophy.

But really we had all won because it was over. At least, until the next year.

They finished us off with a TED Talk about success. And look, I get it, inspire, inspire, inspire. But I wanted something useful. I thought back to how empty my classroom was. I would have to start the year with mostly nothing. I could inspire and motivate myself. I didn't need the support group, the therapy session. I didn't need the guilt. I needed time to put something together. But no. The people in charge felt those things worked.

They don't.

They never do.

The warm feelings fade to frustration well before the year

ends. The kids push you there. It's their job. But what doesn't disappear is structure, resources, things to teach so teachers can spend time helping kids, working on ways to reach the challenging ones. Instead, they gave us a few minutes of shame-soaked inspiration and left us to hunt for what bits and pieces of curriculum we could find on our own, pieces we would have to stitch together by night, as if we were creating some horrible creature-like curriculum.

In that room, sitting there, watching some guy talk about how he achieved his goals in business by directing his focus or whatever, I couldn't help but reflect on education as a whole. We were sitting there being told how to do our jobs by people who had probably never taught a day in their lives. Those people had other people telling them how teachers should teach. And so on. So much of education is people standing outside screaming at you to do it differently without any of them knowing what the fuck they're talking about.

As the video ended, I felt the satisfaction seething from those around me. Motivation is like catnip to teachers. They get off on it. Hell, even a few people stepped outside for a smoke afterwards.

The lights went up, and the school board took the stage again and asked if the winners could perform one last time before collecting their trophy.

We suffered through that experience, knowing that freedom was a few more off-key notes away. When they finished, we stood up slowly and began to leave, the promise to improve test scores floating in the back of our minds with about as much commitment as a New Years resolution.

In there, in that room, surrounded by teachers, away from the reality of the classroom and the kids, before the year even started, with the year's potential appearing as a distant visage on the horizon, it was easy to be optimistic. I felt inspired. I won't lie. I'd have been in the wrong profession if I weren't eager to get back into my classroom and make a difference. There was a whole year in front of me and with it, the opportunity to once again fall in love with teaching, to be proud of what I did, to feel like I was making a difference.

I just didn't know how to make it happen.

It hit me on the bus ride home.

There was this sudden, epiphanic moment that came when I was gazing out the window trying to avoid talking to the Chinese teacher that I could barely understand. I realized that if I had total freedom to teach whatever I wanted, then I should choose a novel that I enjoyed. And if I could teach my favorite novel, then certainly, I thought, it wouldn't matter if I had to put in extra work. And if I was still frustrated in the end, still at odds with teaching like I was at the end of my first year, then I'd quit.

It was an older book, and older meant cheaper (for both hookers and literature, apparently). There would also be plenty of resources I could use online. Beg, borrow, and steal, it's the teacherly way. That would leave me with more time for other stuff and some money left over to buy a few supplies.

Suddenly, I was excited. The thought of teaching my favorite novel, of standing in front of my classes, showing them how it was possible to be passionate about literature, rolled around in my brain like a catchy tune.

I was having the "Call Me Maybe" of ideas, and I went with it.

Frankenstein.

I would teach *Frankenstein*.

It made sense at the time.

CHAPTER FOUR

Teaching Frankenstein

It was the end of October.

The inspiration and zeal that I hit the year with had eroded fast. Saying the school was challenging was an understatement. I was in the trenches, living day to day, hoping only for survival. I wanted to be guiding students toward new, brighter futures, but that was a fucking pipe dream.

I struggled with teaching the basics: reading, writing, note-taking (things freshmen should already know). Two of my freshmen classes had barely finished a short story during the first quarter. Then there was Period Nine. They seemed to channel evil straight from the darkest, most forgotten depths of hell.

Throughout my experience in education, I had always finished whatever I had started: book, short story, an insanely complicated essay project. Not finishing was a first.

With all the interruptions and behavioral bullshit, Period Nine had made it halfway through a short story by the time the quarter had ended. I had to give up and move on to something else.

It had been a disaster.

On top of that, I had other classes to plan for and teach, an eighth grade English class and a World Literature elective. At my previous school, I had only taught one class four times a day. And let me tell you, by the time you hit your final class of the day, you're a goddamn expert, having repeated the same thing three times in a row. Your brain shuts off, and you start thinking about crossing the parking lot on your way home to freedom while you go about your lesson. It's great.

That was no longer the case.

I wanted to be fun and friendly, but that school was different. I knew if I betrayed any sign of weakness that they'd take advantage. Instead, I stuck to my teacher training and kept my distance. I was cold, professional to a fault, nearly robotic, but it was better than losing control of my classroom.

And the observations never stopped. The principal or assistant principal would show up unannounced to see how I was doing (luckily, they never stopped by at the end of the day during Period Nine).

I couldn't risk looking incompetent. I turned off emotions and stuck to the lessons. I was an asshole in a suit, hiding a hole in the bottom of my shoe, subjecting them to the continuous torture of reading and writing. And if you're thinking: why still teach *Frankenstein* if it was already that bad? It's because that by the time I realized how low they all were, it was too late. The books had arrived. I had already planned out my whole year. I had even bragged about it to my bosses. Backtracking would only show them that I didn't think out my actions, possibly betray incompetence, and give them a reason to doubt me.

I also didn't want to let them down. Nimitz had taken a risk in hiring me. The last thing I wanted to do was prove my previous principal right.

We were two days into the novel, and someone had

decided to draw a cock on one of the new books. It was a theme of those freshmen.

I was not handling it well.

"Are you serious?" I was nearly shaking.

Anita said, "It wasn't me, Mister."

"I figured that. This is something an immature boy does." I may have been gnashing my teeth. Let's go with that. "Hopefully, whoever drew this is a better student than an artist."

"Oh shit," Charles said. "Savage."

"I don't even know what I'm looking at here. I mean, I'm guessing those are the balls, but what the hell is that?" I said, to no one in particular. "Is that a bowling pin?"

"It's the shaft," giggled Bob.

"I hope it's not drawn to scale," I said, glaring at him.

"Fuck. Savage," Charles said.

"Stop saying savage. It's so annoying," Anita said.

"It's the only word he knows," said Joaquín.

"Ohhhh…savage," Charles and Bob said.

I wondered if they were high or if that was just how they acted. *Did I behave like that at their age? If I did, I definitely hid it better.*

"You okay, Mister?" Anita asked.

"No. I'm not okay," I said, taking a deep breath.

To be honest, looking back, it was just a poorly drawn dick, not some veiny monolith that soaked through the pages of the novel and into the very soul of my English classroom. I should have scribbled it out and moved on, but I was not able to let the anger go.

Teachers are human.

I was stressed. The school had been a constant struggle. The lesson I had planned for my observation had taken three classes to finish instead of one. I had personal issues I was trying to handle. And on top of all that, penis graffiti kept popping up throughout the school: in the bathrooms, on the whiteboard, on assignments and projects people turned in for grades, and now in the novel that would decide my fate as a teacher.

A big dick Sharpied onto my future.

I was exhausted. So, I took it out on them. "I get it. A lot of you think this is a joke because everything about your educational experience has been a joke. Your lives are probably jokes. You spend your whole life giggling at the train wreck of your existence, and you don't even try to take control and change it."

I held up the book. "This isn't funny. This, like your writing ability, like your work ethic, like your sense of ambition…" I paused, "is pathetic."

The laughter stopped.

I wasn't sure if they cared or if a life of hardship had taught them to act like wounded puppies when someone yelled at them, to bow their heads and tuck in their tails, but I knew I hit a nerve. I knew it hurt.

The room was quiet.

"Think back to the first quarter. We read a short story that I had to make photocopies of so that you could read it. You all complained about it. Now, we finally have books, and this happens. Look at my classroom. Everyone. Look. At. It. What's missing?"

"Art?" Anita suggested.

"Desks that match," someone said.

"Ceiling tiles that aren't falling apart?" another chimed.

"Decorations?"

"A better building?"

"Carpet that doesn't look like someone dropped a fat deuce on it?"

Okay. That was all very accurate, but it wasn't the answer I was looking for. "Look at my bookcases. What do you see?"

"Dictionaries," Charles said.

"Holy shit, Charles knows something," Joaquín teased.

Charles said something back that I couldn't hear, and Joaquín sneered.

"At every single school that I have ever stepped inside of, whether I was the teacher or a student, in every single one there were books. Classroom libraries with stacks of novels, shelves full of books. We have dictionaries. And as exciting as those are, you always know how it's going to end. Zebra. It ends with Zebra, so no one cares. We don't have books because you all do dumb stuff like this." I slammed the book on the desk.

"Does it really?" Joaquín said, picking up a dictionary from beneath his desk.

"I walk down the halls at this school and see a building falling apart. Broken-down classrooms, a library with no books in it, garbage everywhere, a bathroom with no dividers in the urinals because people keep ripping them out of the wall, I see all this, and I wonder, why? Why is it like this? Does anyone care? Do you know what the other schools think of you? I'll tell you. They think you're a joke. They think this school is a joke. No one wants to come here. And if you don't believe me, remember that I worked at another school in this same district."

"Savage," Charles said.

"Shut the fuck up," Anita said.

I waited. "But over these last months, I've noticed something I didn't see when I started here: potential."

Okay. At that point, I started lying. I was pissed, and I knew I had laid into them pretty hard. I needed to turn it back into something remotely positive otherwise they'd just write me off as another asshole.

I paused and let that soak in. "You all have potential. This school could be the best in the district. It could be the one school everyone fights to get into." I was stretching it pretty thin. This school would make the staff of a triage clinic on some remote jungle island shiver in apprehension. And I was beginning to hate it, but still, they weren't my punching bags. My personal problems weren't their fault. The system wasn't their fault. I was overreacting because someone drew a dick on a book that cost less than $3.

I get that now, but at that moment, I wanted to make a point. I knew that if I didn't, someone would draw on another book, and another, and then books would have torn pages and broken spines. I knew that if I didn't act, I'd show up to school one day and turn the corner to see dingoes devouring a calf freshly torn from the twitching body of its half-eviscerated, still "moo-ing" mother.

Extreme? Maybe. But you get the point.

I could work at a shit school and hope it'd get better. But what I couldn't do was work at a shit school and do nothing while it continued to worsen.

"I see this crap, and it makes me wonder if I'm mistaken. You guys don't believe you deserve good things." I laughed like a crazy person. "It's a penis. It's funny." Then I yelled, "No! It's not. What do you think is going to happen when people come here to see this school? You think people want to be a part of a community where students draw dicks all over everything? A school with no books on the shelves? Do you want to be associated with a school like that? How many of you are embarrassed that you go to school here? Stuff like *this* makes people stay away. And it makes teachers give up. You might think it's funny, just a little bit of graffiti. No big deal, right? It *is* a big deal. It shows me that you don't care. And if you don't care, why should I?"

The silence continued.

"Think about that. Because when I look around, I see potential..."

I'm going to stop right here and tell you that this isn't some Hollywood novel on teaching. If you're expecting that, you should put this book down and walk away. Teaching isn't like that. Get that idea out of your head. All those inspirational movies about teaching are bullshit. It's a grind. My goals then and there were selfish: I wanted to enjoy teaching again. And I wanted the immature, middle school antics to stop. I didn't have the patience for it.

I waited and let my words soak in.

"I know I can help this school grow. But you all keep pushing away the people who care about you. If you keep that up, you'll wake up one day experiencing a very different kind of cold. The kind of cold that sinks in when you realize that all the people who've ever cared about you gave up and moved on. The kind of cold that sinks into your soul. And when you feel that chill, there isn't a blanket big enough out there to warm you back up. Remember that."

People say, "Teaching isn't a job. It's a passion." There's a danger in that way of thinking. You can find yourself caring too much and overreacting when you should just let things go.

I was genuinely upset. I was trying and failing to care about teaching. And so I found myself angry almost all of the time.

"Yo, Mister! It actually doesn't end with 'Zebra.' It ends with—"

CHAPTER FIVE

TMI

I had broken up with my girlfriend the night before. I shouldn't have been surprised. Shit happens. But, I could've handled it a lot better. And after a sleepless, sobbing night, I managed to drag myself into work.

Not much time had passed since I started the novel, a week maybe, but it was the last thing on my mind that day. Instead, I would be trying not to weep into unconsciousness. My eyes and nostrils had become viscous tentacles of fluid that forced me to hydrate regularly for fear of shriveling up like the ball sack of an eighty-year-old man.

It was seriously pathetic. She was my first real relationship. I guess that made it a bit more understandable, and it had caught me by surprise. Looking back now, it should've happened much sooner. Hindsight is a hooker knocking on your door at three in the morning after you've already deleted your browser history. Too little, too late.

I had managed to calm down enough to show up to work, my eyes bloodshot with tears. Dreams had offered no escape as the reality of the previous night's events had haunted me there, causing me to erupt suddenly into another conscious fit of tears. I felt empty, a dried-up husk from a freshly molted bug.

If you're asking why I didn't stay home, the answer is simple. The last thing I wanted was to be alone, surrounded by everything that reminded me of her and what she did, with only the perpetual gray of November to distract me.

Luckily, there was Xanax for when I was at work and booze for when I wasn't. Like any true-blooded American, I believed feelings functioned best when pushed down by any available substance.

I was sitting in my stupid plastic chair, staring at the tears collecting on my desk when the door opened.

I turned away.

"Same as before?" Wilson asked. "We'll leave right at the beginning of our plan and hide?"

A quick backtrack.

The district had moved my previous principal into a new position. This person was now in charge of developing how English teachers taught reading and writing in the classroom at the middle school level. Wilson was our middle school English teacher, but I also had one middle school class. So, we were both subjected to that waste of time.

We now had more meetings and more observations. The same former boss who had fired me, the same former boss who for some reason was no longer a principal at my previous school, would be stopping by to watch me teach. That same person was also supposed to help me improve. That hadn't exactly sat well with me.

School districts have a sick sense of humor.

The administration had given Wilson and I the news right after I had started teaching the novel. I had been annoyed, but Wilson had been a genius. He had explained that if we decided to "work together" we could go hide in the teacher's lounge or workroom for our entire plan. My former boss would just give up when we couldn't be found and leave.

And if we were found, well, we were working together. Or we had left a note on the door, and one of the kids must have torn it down. Or we had mixed up the days. Either way, we had our bases covered.

It had worked perfectly before, and so my ex-boss had rescheduled. And there was Wilson, right before class started, ready to reaffirm that we would take off right at the beginning of our planning period.

Except, instead of me laughing and easily signing up for another round, he opened the door to see me fighting back tears like someone had just put my dog down.

I quickly wiped them away and muttered, "Sounds good."

"Are you okay?"

"I'm fine," my voice cracked.

The door clicked shut. I heard footsteps and turned to see Wilson sitting on a desk next to mine, "What's wrong?"

I didn't want to be that guy. You know the one. The guy at the bar, readily sharing all his deep dark secrets with total strangers over a beer. Wilson and I were coworkers, colleagues, but not friends. Still, I couldn't sit there and keep it all inside. I needed to tell someone.

"We broke up," I mumbled.

"Fuck," he said after a pause. "I'm sorry."

"It's okay. Don't worry about it." I grabbed a tissue and dabbed my eyes.

"Why are you here?"

"I'm not about to stay home crying like a bitch all day," I said, forcing a smile. "Although coming here to cry like a bitch doesn't seem any better."

"What happened?"

It was such a boring cliché. When I finished, he said the best thing any friend could say: "What a cunt."

I laughed as more tears fell. "I don't know what do to about this."

44

"About what?"

"I don't want to be here. I don't want to be at home. I don't want to be alone. I...what am I supposed to do? Cry in front of my students all day? I don't think I can make it through the day without crying. Maybe I should just go home."

"That depends on how you feel." He leaned forward and clasped his hands between his legs. "Work is a good distraction. If you don't want to stew in your thoughts, this is the place to be."

"How do I keep from crying?"

"Try not to think about it, but be prepared that it could happen."

"What if I cry in front of them? What do I do?"

"Are you asking me what *I* would do? Because what I would do is probably different than what most teachers would do."

I looked at him, my eyes throbbing. He had been in the game a lot longer than me. I hadn't known him long, but I trusted him for some reason. "What would *you* do?"

"You're a great teacher..." He hesitated. "But you're cold and distant. These kids fear you."

"They should fear me."

"No. They should trust you. Fear may keep them in line, but trust gets them to grow. If you want to be successful at this school, you need them to trust you. I think letting them know what you're going through shows them that you trust them. If you trust them, then they'll start trusting you. And if they trust you, they'll start to succeed. Our kids don't do well because they want to go to college; our kids do well because they don't want to let us down. Open up to them. Let them know what you're going through. You'll see a difference. If it were me, I'd tell them."

"Tell them? No fucking way. The last thing I want to do is to share my personal problems with a bunch of teenagers like

I'm on the most pathetic kind of daytime talk show. No. That's not happening."

"You don't have to give them any details. Tell them you're going through a breakup. Tell them it hurts. And let them know that you're telling them this because you aren't going to be yourself for a while, and you don't want them to think it's because of anything they did. They'll understand."

"You think that's the best idea?"

"Trust me. I know these kids."

"Everything I've ever learned about teaching tells me to do the exact opposite of what you just said."

"Stop treating this school like it's a college course. It's not. You think everything they taught you in your program is accurate? Ideas about education change more than the emotions of an eighth-grader. Being a good teacher isn't about being a living, breathing graduate textbook. It's about showing students how to find success in their lives. For them to see that these moments happen to everyone and that even teachers have to navigate through them is a lesson that will prepare them for the future."

"You think this will *help* them?"

"You can try to keep it inside, but you'll be sad and angry. They'll think it's because of them. They'll take it personally, and they'll start to hate you for it. Why not turn it into a teachable moment? They'll respect you more for sharing your struggle. Keep it professional. But let them know you're going through a rough time."

"What if they make fun of me?"

"Not our kids. They may act like jackasses, but they respect suffering and pain. They've been through a lot. This isn't suburbia. They don't give a shit if you can quote Whitman or differentiate between a Petrarchan and a Shakespearean sonnet. They want to know you care about them as people."

"And professional distance?"

"You're not grabbing beers with them after work. You're showing them that you have a heart."

"Maybe," I said, feeling the effects of the Xanax.

"If you don't feel comfortable doing it, don't. Maybe sharing isn't the best answer. I'm just telling you that if I were in your position, and I have been, I'd share."

"You've been here before?" I said.

"Stay in this profession long enough and you'll have to work through all of life's problems at some point. It happens. You'll be fine, my good man," he said, clasping me on the shoulder. "I'll give you some time. If you need me, let me know." He walked to the door and closed it behind him, leaving me once again to the quiet of my classroom.

Time passed, and the bell rang.

When my first class came in, I wasn't ready to talk about it. I gave my eighth-graders some work and tried to ignore my buzzing phone, undoubtedly texts from concerned friends, or worse, her apologizing.

I didn't bother looking.

"Hey, Mister?"

I looked up from pretending to work to see one of my tiny eighth-graders standing by my desk. "Yes, Sofía?"

"Are you okay?" she asked.

I noticed several students behind her looking over at me. When our eyes met, they shot back down to their reading. I forced a smile. "No. Not really."

"I hope you feel better," she said and turned around.

"Thanks."

The bell rang. Class emptied. My ex-boss failed to show up even though I didn't go with Wilson to hide.

For the next forty minutes of my planning period, I replayed three years' worth of memories, trying to understand how I ended up where I was. I managed to hold back the tears. I couldn't start my next class looking like I had spent my planning period hot-boxing in the janitor's closet.

When Period Four started, I sat on the end of a desk and waited. The noise died down. A tear fell unimpeded onto the ugly brown carpet that had spent an existence hiding other people's accidents and mistakes.

Wrenching a copy of *Frankenstein* in my hands, last night's events began to replay…

"What's wrong," Anita interrupted the unwanted flashback.

I stopped thinking and looked up. "Something…" A harsh, awkward voice. I cleared my throat, dabbed a tear with my palm. "Something happened last night that I have to deal with, so I apologize if I'm a little…off."

I sat there on a desk with my legs dangling, a tissue in my hand.

"What happened?" someone asked.

"Shut up, stupid," Anita said. "Maybe he doesn't want to tell us, you nosey fuck."

"It's okay," I said. "I…broke up with my girlfriend."

"Shit," someone said.

"Ah fuck, that sucks," another said.

"Was she with another man?" someone asked.

"Dude. Shut the fuck up. It's none of your business," someone said.

"Yeah, man, don't be a dick," someone else.

"Sorry," another.

"Cheer up, Mister. It's cool. There's plenty of hoes out there."

I forced a laugh. I don't remember who said what. I was too busy staring into that static brown pattern on the floor watching little drops hit the carpet, watching the color remain unchanged.

"Does this mean we don't have homework?" a voice that was clearly Charles asked, his freckled skin glowed underneath the fluorescence.

"Dude. Shut the fuck up," Anita said. "This is why they say gingers don't have souls."

"What? I just asked," Charles said. "Besides, you have red hair."

"It's fucking dyed, dude. You're being a dick. Just sit there and shut the fuck up. You've obviously never been through a breakup cuz you've never had a girlfriend. And that's because no one will ever love you."

"Savage," Joaquín said, despite being Charles's friend.

"Whatever. I was joking." He leaned back and fiddled with his pen before he popped the cap off and scribbled on his notebook, mumbling to himself.

There were other whispers in the class.

"Why are you here?" Joaquín asked. I looked at him sitting there in an ironed Polo, his dark brown skin contrasting his translucent friend.

"That's a good question," I said. "Because you need me here. I could sit at home and cry into a pillow all day and hate my life, listening to sad songs on repeat, but that won't do anything."

My eyes were raw as I dabbed them with the tissue and continued. "I'm here because I need to be. And because if this happened to you, I would expect you to be here, too. But I think it's good, you know? It's a reminder that there's more to school than tests and reading. We all have personal problems. I'm guilty of forgetting that when I stand up here. I'm here because life goes on. When bad things happen, you have to keep moving forward, no matter how much it sucks. I guess."

"Preach," someone said.

"I can't demand the best from you and then retreat into my shell and give up because something doesn't work out the way I want it to. I have a responsibly."

"You want me to cut the bitch?" someone asked.

"That's thoughtful, but I think I'll be okay." I smiled. I wasn't really sure why they all seemed to care. It didn't make sense.

"I'm sorry, Mister," someone said.

"That sucks," someone else added.

"But that's life," I said, pausing. "And sometimes life fucking sucks."

Silence.

"Truth," someone eventually offered.

"I'm no longer a part of her life, but I'm still a part of yours. And we got a lot of work to do to get you to where you need to be." I pushed off my desk a little too enthusiastically. "Let's read some *Frankenstein*."

"You don't have to if you don't want to. We can just chill," Charles said, still scribbling.

"I think I'll manage. We gotta get through this book. I know it starts off slow, but it gets better. I promise. Where were we last time?"

I waited.

"That old guy was on a boat heading to the North Pole," Anita said.

"Right. Our narrator heads north," I said, dabbing the last trailing tear.

"I think he's the monster," Bob said.

"What?" Anita stared out over her book at him. "Have you smoked yourself retarded?"

"What? Why are you always coming after me?"

"Because you're a dumbass. Did you even read the book? How's a monster going to get a ship and pay a bunch of sailors to travel north AND write to his...what? His monster-sister who lives back in London or wherever?"

"Oh..." he said with a faint smile.

"Smoke less, think more," she said.

"Savage," Charles said.

I ended up telling the rest of my classes what had happened, except Period Nine. With them, I went straight into the novel. Most of them spaced off. Some of them were too stoned to function. The others spoke so little English that they barely understood anything I said most days. There were a couple of interesting kids in that class, but the rest were catatonic, sitting at their desks, waiting for the bell to ring so they could leave.

And I felt the same about them.

On the way out the door, after the final bell rang, a quiet, rather small student came up to me and said in a barely audible voice, "I'm sorry about what happened, Mister."

CHAPTER SIX

Motherfucker

I was willing to let the kid sleep until he started snoring.

"Jeff," I said louder, hoping he would hear me and jolt awake. Nothing.

If a kid falls asleep in class, you're supposed to wake them up gently. I knew that. I think every teacher *knows* that. It's because we all realize that there are a·*lot* of reasons behind a kid falling asleep. Teenagers deal with a lot of shit. Their bodies are growing. Their emotions are all over the place. Their minds are a clusterfuck of anxiety because they overanalyze the shit out of everything. And that's not even taking into account their home status. Maybe they don't have food or electricity, or perhaps it's not safe.

Every student has a story.

I get that.

Being a teenager is exhausting. But not every sleeping teenager is a whimpering cry for help. A lot of them just make stupid choices, like not going to bed until three or four in the morning.

Jeff was one such kid.

When the class had started, he had told me, "Mister, I played *Call of Duty* until four in the morning, so just let me sleep."

His head was half-buried into his sweater, eyes completely closed, breathing slow and rhythmic. Then came the snoring. I called his name again. Nothing. He was out.

I walked over to him and saw the slow rise and fall of his back as he drifted off into the sublime abyss that napping brings. My class was waiting, curious about what I would do. I thought of the proper techniques for waking sleeping students, revisited my training and my readings, and pondered my approach. Then I shrugged, grabbed a dictionary and slammed it down hard on the desk.

The sound reverberated throughout the room.

His entire body jolted back. Confused, he gazed about the class.

I stood back and smiled at him.

There was an imprint of his sweater on his face. "Uh… Mister…I was sleeping." He used a palm to wipe a bit of drool from his lip.

"Looks like you woke up. Take notes."

"Ugh. Your class is so boring, Mister. Can we just watch the movie?" he whined.

"How would you even know if it was boring? You've been asleep since you sat down."

"Because it's *always* boring."

I don't care how thick your skin is. No teacher wants to hear that. Most of us bust our asses, rack our brains, and run around putting things together to try and make what we teach enjoyable for our students. No teacher wants anyone to think the subject they enjoy so much they majored in it is boring.

"I don't care if you're bored. You need to do the work."

I didn't want to be boring. I wanted my students to like my class. But they wouldn't do homework, and they couldn't read the book without guidance, so I was forced to have them read in class.

It sucked.

While they sat daydreaming, I was running around trying to inspire and stoke interest. And not just once, but for all three of my freshmen classes.

Jeff was still dazed.

"Do you think he just shit himself?" Anita asked Joaquín.

"I don't know. Jeff! Hey, Jeff! JEFF!" shouted Joaquín.

"What!?"

"Did you shit yourself?"

"No." He shook his head, wiping the sleep from his eyes. "Your mom shit herself."

"I don't think that works in this situation," I said. I looked around the room and saw tired faces. "I get the feeling that a few of you think this book is boring. Give me till the end of chapter four. If it doesn't hook you in by then, we can talk. Keep in mind though that everything happening in these pages sets the stage for the action later. It's like eating the crusts off your sandwich. Once you do that, you can sit back and enjoy the rest."

"My mom cuts the crusts off," Jeff said, still not fully awake.

"Go back to sleep," I said.

"Okay," he put his head back down.

"Jeff. I wasn't serious. Jeff. Jeff, pick up your head."

"You told me to go back to sleep. I'm listening," he said, his head on the desk.

I rolled my eyes. "You're in high school. Act like it. This isn't story time. I don't need you to like the novel. I need you to read it and pay attention. I want you like it. I want you to enjoy it. But that isn't a requirement. You still have to read it. I need all of you engaged with the book, asking questions, making predictions, noting important events. For the first time in your lives, you're learning how to read."

"Wow. He thinks we're too stupid to know how to read," Charles said. "Savage."

"Don't twist my words. If you knew how to read properly, you'd be testing at or above grade level. Most of you aren't. But we can fix that. How many of you actually imagine the scenes we read? What did you picture just now? What did you imagine?"

"Jeff shitting himself," someone said.

I rolled my eyes and waited.

Quiet.

"Jeff, what did you picture?"

"I dunno." Another common response that I hated.

"Jeff. Pick up your head. Pick it up!"

"You said you wanted me to sleep."

"Jeff." I waited. He hesitated. I repeated, "Jeff!"

"Ugh," he said and sat up. "I said I don't know."

"Try again," I said.

"I dunno," he said again.

"I'll wait until you come up with something."

Anita helped him along. "Answer the fucking question, dumbass."

"Jesus. Calm down," he said.

"Jeff, I'm waiting for an answer," I said.

"Fine," he opened his book. "What page?"

I told him.

Reluctantly, he flipped open his book to the page. "Okay, what?"

I took a deep breath, reread the paragraph, and then paused. "Okay. Jeff, what did you picture?"

"I dunno, like lightning or something," he said.

"Brilliant. Thank you," I said. "Someone else. What do you picture?"

"Like a storm or something."

"Great. Anyone else?"

"Like a big storm destroying a tree by a house," Anita said.

"Getting there, getting there. This is good. This is good. Look. So many of you are used to images rushing past you in this intense storm of explosions and flashing lights and fast-paced music and—"

"Michael Bay!" some shouted.

"Yeah," I said, looking over. "Like a Michael Bay film with all the explosions and epic music. But reading isn't like that. And reading a book from the nineteenth century is definitely not like that. The action is there, but you have to slow down and imagine it. You have to let go and put yourself in the story. You have to live it."

"Michael Bay," Bob muttered and started laughing.

I looked at him and shook my head. "Yeah...well, when you read, it's different. You have to imagine it. You have to feel it. It's slower, sure, but the image belongs to you. When you read these words, the experience becomes yours. No one else can change that or take it away from you."

As they gazed back at me, I got an idea. "Let's try something. Close your eyes."

They looked around at each other.

"Seriously. Close them," I went over and turned off the lights. "Trust me."

The room darkened, lit only by the dull, wintered gray that trickled through the shaded windows.

"All of you, close your eyes," I repeated.

"Close your fucking eyes," Anita said. "Or I'll gouge them out of your fucking skull. Jesus."

Once most of their eyes were closed, I began. "I want you to imagine standing on a hill. Below you stretches a green valley, gently rolling hills, not too many trees. And to your sides stand the sharp climb of gray mountains: these big, jagged gray teeth jutting or erupting sharply from the peaceful plains below. You're in front of your cottage, feeling the cool breeze begin to gust from a distance. You can smell the rain. Not around you, but you can smell it on the wind. Your eyes turn to see heavy dark clouds cresting the peaks. A storm approaches. You wait.

"The coming night darkens the grays and brings the nervous trickle of a few drops that tease a sudden downpour. The sky darkens still, with momentary glowing trails of lightning spreading across the clouded ceiling, too close. These flashes highlight the shadows, and the following sudden boom reverberates through you. There's a prickle of goosebumps as the sound echoes through the distance. It's replaced by the quiet, constant hum of rain and the smell of wet grass and stone."

I paused and surveyed the room.

"Looking out at this landscape, you feel small, tiny, insignificant. You feel as though one false move and the valley will swallow you up. The last of the sunlight fades as the wind blows in blackness. The air cools. It's cold, now. You can feel the rain tickle your cheeks as the last of the light leaves the landscape. You stand there in total darkness, listening to the wind. The rain." I paused. "And then...BOOM!" I yelled, slamming my hand against the whiteboard. There were a couple of screams. "The air crackles and your bones shake. Everything is bright, and in an instant, it's gone. Your teeth chatter as you regain focus."

They were looking at me now.

"You scared me, Mister. Not cool," one of them said.

I smiled. "Imagine being out there, but there's a storm now, and you have to run inside. You're young. Terrified. And so you hide under the bed until morning."

"Pussy," someone murmured.

"You are what you eat," someone else said.

"AND," I said louder, "when you wake from under your bed in the morning and look out the window, you see the aftermath from the storm. The scene before you is mostly unchanged; except, there's a pile of smoldering bits and charred wood where a huge oak tree used to stand, a tree you had spent summer days under, stealing its shade. It has been blown apart by the blast. Nothing remains. And you're young. Impressionable. You don't know what to think of it, but you've never seen such power before. And as you stare out at that destruction—"

"Like me after a night with your mom," Charles said to Joaquín.

I ignored them. "Frankenstein was fifteen when he saw this. It changed his world."

"As was I," Charles said to Joaquín.

"Shut the hell up," Joaquín said.

It was a good one; I'd give him that.

I turned the lights on and let the room return to focus. "When you read, you have to imagine the story, put yourself in it, make it real. Only then can you begin to understand it. Write this down: Everything in a novel has a purpose and a place," I said.

I repeated it.

"Mister, are you still single?" Sasha asked me suddenly.

My stomach twisted.

"What the fuck?" Anita said. "Why would you ask that?"

"I'm curious," she said.

"Oh shit," Charles said. "It's about to get weird. Sasha got a thing for the teacher."

"Dude, that's a weird question to ask a teacher," Anita said.

"Chill out. It's for my mom," Sasha said. "She's single, right? You're single. I figure, you could bang her, and then I could just get an 'A.' It'd be easier than doing this work."

I shook my head as students laughed. "Write this down."

"That Sasha's mom is single?" Charles asked.

I looked at him until he picked up his pen.

"Is that a 'no,' Mister?" Sasha followed up.

"Make sure you're taking notes, Jeff," I said. "And pick up your head."

"I don't want to."

"This isn't a democracy. You don't get a say."

"Actually, America is a democracy," he said.

"This isn't America. This is my classroom. I'm the president, king, dictator, czar. The only way to pass is through me; so, you need to pick up your pen, and start taking notes."

"I don't have a pen."

I rolled my eyes. "Who comes to school without a pen?"

"Me," he replied.

I walked over to my desk, pulled something out, and handed it to him. "Here."

"This is a crayon."

"Brilliant observation," I said.

"Thanks."

"Take notes."

"Why? Why do I need to take notes? I'll remember it."

"Oh my god. Just shut up, and quit being stupid," Anita said.

"You shut up," he said to her. Then he repeated, "Mister, I got this."

"Really? You'll remember all this? You got this?"

"Yeah, Mister. Don't worry."

"What did we read yesterday?"

Nothing.

"What's the main character's name?"

Nothing.

"Who wrote the book?"

Nothing.

"Dude, the book is right in front of you," Anita said.

"Oh...um, Mary. It's Mary," he said.

"Take notes," I said.

"I'll be fine," he persisted.

"Not judging by your current grade," I said without thinking.

"Oh shit," Charles said. "Shots fired."

"Shut up, ginger," Jeff said.

"'Bout to shut you momma up when I fuck her and give you a little ginger brother," he fired back.

"No one is having sex with anyone's mother," I said, exasperated.

"Damn," Sasha said, leaning back in her seat and picking up her novel.

CHAPTER SEVEN

Snitches Get Stitches

I was in the middle of dragging my garbage laptop through an extensive internet search, trying to steal everything I could find on *Frankenstein* to make my life easier, when the assistant principal opened my door.

"Do you have a minute to talk?" Ritz asked. I gazed into her eyes a little longer than was necessary. She had an attractive playfulness that flowed from her.

Too soon, I thought.

She also had a ring on her finger.

"What's up?" I glanced down at the laptop's screen to see a wheel spinning as the website loaded.

"There was a parent complaint about you. Two, actually."

My stomach twisted. I hated how quickly I grew anxious. "What was the problem?" I asked.

"Apparently there was an issue with a cell phone?" She said.

I had lost a student's cell phone earlier in the week.

It hadn't been my fault.

I had taken it from this kid because he was texting in class. There had been this massive eighth-grade drama-fest. And he had been sending texts to people, stirring shit up, escalating it even further. The whole class had been doing a shit job of keeping it on the down-low. And I had wanted it to stop, so when I caught him texting I asked him to hand it to me.

Let me take a step back.

I had never wanted to teach middle schoolers. Listening to thirteen-year-olds was about as exciting as taking notes on an infomercial. You can't really have an intellectual conversation with one. They have the attention spans of small puppies. They have the absolute worst sense of humor. And they have no emotional stability. I mean like none whatsoever. One minute they're having the time of their lives, the next minute they're slinging strings of snot out of their noses, calling their best friends cunts, and hoping for their deaths. I've heard that when Satan runs out of space in hell, he rents out a middle school classroom.

And yet, that was part of my gig. I had to deal with eighth-graders three times a day (teaching schedules can be painful). By the end of the day, I couldn't and didn't care to keep track of their bullshit. I was just there to teach them and then kick them out before they grew too comfortable in my classroom.

Where were we?

So, I had taken his phone because he was on it in class and stirring up shit, and had placed it in the top drawer of my desk, and then I had gone about teaching. Nothing too extraordinary. But when the bell rang, the crying and fighting had erupted again, and I had been distracted. By the time I had gone to grab this kid's cell phone, someone had stolen it.

He had been furious, and I had told him that he was shit out of luck. It hadn't been the best response, obviously. And now the parents were pissed.

"They want you to pay for the phone," she said.

I went cold. "That's not going to happen."

I knew who had stolen his phone, but I couldn't prove it. It was a kid named Brutus. He had grinned while protesting his innocence. Eighth-graders are bad at everything, especially lying. Maybe teaching makes you paranoid. And maybe he was just an asshole. Either way, he was coy, and I didn't trust him.

Even if I was wrong about the theft, cell phones aren't exactly cheap, and there was no way I was forking over cash for one. I was living with my friends in their spare bedroom, working more hours at my other job to save up money to move into a new place. I had no money, no time, and no patience. *Fuck the mother, and fuck the phone*, I thought.

"Agreed. I already talked to the mother. The district will cover it."

"I mean, I don't want to sound out of line here, but what am I supposed to do if I catch students using their phones? Am I not supposed to take it? I don't want to piss off more parents, but I also don't want to create more work for you," I said.

I was nervous. Asshole clinched. I had until Thanksgiving to find a place to live. I couldn't afford write-ups, stress, a lost job, any of that. And, as I said, I'd never been great with anxiety or confrontation. So yeah, I kissed ass a little bit. It wasn't exactly a bad ass to kiss.

"That's sweet of you." She smiled. "The policy is to take cell phones. Just make sure you send them straight to the office or keep them on you until the end of class."

"I'll send them straight to the office. I usually hold off on that because it creates problems." This was because the secretary would only release the phone to a parent. If you want to see teenagers go apeshit, take their phones and make their parents come and get them. They'll have a fucking meltdown. "I don't want to deal with any more complaints. It's a waste of our time. I'll just send the phones to the office. Plus, it's not like I have any more room in my pants."

Her eyes widened a bit.

"For another phone. My slacks are pretty fitting."

"Noted," she said with a slight smile.

There was an awkward pause.

"So much for leniency," I said finally.

"They lost that privilege the moment someone went into your desk. Parents can show up to collect the phones. We'll stand behind you on that one-hundred percent."

It felt good to have that kind of support. "Thanks. Anything else?" I asked.

"There's one more parent complaint I want to speak to you about."

"Oh yeah, I forgot there had been two. I'm on a roll this week."

"I know you're in a rough patch, and I hate to add any extra stress," she said.

"What else did I do?"

"Walter, one of your freshmen, told his mother that you said the 'F-word' in class. His mother called to complain. She asked to speak to Nimitz. But I was in the office, so I talked to her. I told her that you would never say anything like that. Usually, parents take their concerns up with the teacher directly, and if they aren't resolved, then they come to us. But I figured I could help you out on this one. I told her that you would never say anything like that, that you were a professional, and that she had nothing to worry about."

"Absolutely," I said. *Sounded like me…a professional.*

"I wanted to talk to you about Walter before I spoke to him. Something tells me there's more to this story. The mother seemed rather bent out of shape."

It was true. "He's refusing to complete an assignment."

"Uh-huh," she said. "What exactly happened?"

"The cursing incident happened the day after my break-up. They were asking me why I was at school instead of staying home. I told them that," I paused, "I told them that life gets shitty sometimes. I didn't say 'fuck.'"

It was a small lie. Did it really matter whether I said "shit" or "fuck"?

"That sounds more believable," she nodded.

"I told them that life throws challenges your way, and you have to deal with them and move forward. I was opening up to them, sharing a life moment as a teachable moment." I thought about Wilson's words. "I was trying to show them how to overcome adversity. I didn't realize it would come back to bite me in the ass."

"This makes way more sense. I knew there had been some confusion."

"The real problem is that Walter doesn't want to do a creative writing assignment."

"She mentioned something about that."

"I asked my students to write a short story using a narrator of the opposite sex. Girls have to use a first-person male narrator; guys have to use a first-person female narrator. It forces them to try and see the world from a different perspective."

"Sounds reasonable," she said. She put her coffee down and leaned back. Clasping the back of the desk, she looked at me reassuringly. Despite being tall, she was able to pedal her feet out in front of her like she was hanging from a tree swing.

I realized I was gazing too long and looked away. "A young woman wrote the novel we're reading. She was eighteen at the time, but the main character is male. I wanted them to try and put themselves in the head of the author. I wanted them to understand the difficulties of trying to see things from a different perspective. They're supposed to share their stories with the class."

"I like it," she said. "You're challenging their perception using creativity."

"Except, he says it's offensive. He said his mom thinks that it's 'inappropriate to ask my son to pretend to be a woman.'" I quoted in the air for emphasis.

"Oh wow. And you've explained the goal of the assignment to them both?"

"I already emailed her on it." I hated, absolutely hated talking on the phone. "And I've talked to him several times. He seems to get it, then the next day, it's like a blank slate. It's challenging. He doesn't seem to grasp that I'm not asking him to pretend to be a woman."

"It sounds like he's trying to exaggerate these ideas to avoid the assignment. My guess is that he also embellished your cursing to move his mother against you. It sounds like he's playing his parents. I'll pull him during lunch and have a little chat," she said, smiling and standing up.

"I appreciate that." I was slightly sad she was leaving.

"No problem. You don't have to fight these battles on your own, you know? I'm here for you."

"I didn't want to bother you with something this trivial," I said. "But thank you."

"That's why we're here." She stopped on her way to the door. "Is everything else okay?"

"I think so. *Frankenstein*'s had a slow start, but I'm hoping interest picks up once they see how cool it is."

"And the other situation? Your breakup? Are you okay?"

"Oh," I said, a pang twisted inside me.

"You don't have to talk about it if you don't want to."

"It's...um...it's a process, but I'll survive."

"You better. You're doing good work. We keep hearing great stories about you," she said.

I didn't believe that.

"And we like having you around here. Well, some of us do." She smiled with a hand on the door, the heavy rock glistening in the fluorescence. "I'll talk to Walter at lunch and clear this up."

I watched her walk away.

I was grateful she would talk to him, but I would need to say something myself. I couldn't quite understand why it was so difficult for him to grasp the assignment. I also didn't want him to think I was a pushover.

As for my language, she had given me a pass.

I turned back to my computer to see that it had frozen.

CHAPTER EIGHT

Technical Difficulties

I inhaled and shivered. It didn't even smell like coffee.

Nimitz would drink a pot of that shit a day. Black.

That's what I got for leaving my coffee at home. I took mine like the most basic of bitches: lots of cream, lots of sugar. The less coffee I tasted, the better.

While my typical syrupy sweet, toffee-colored morning brew had enough chemical preserve to give me some form of cancer, the shit I was about to imbibe from the coffee pot in the teacher's lounge *was* actual cancer. I mean, it had managed to stain glass. And when I swirled it around the pot, it clung to the sides like a Tawny Port.

It was the cheap, industrial-grade stuff you expected to find during a 3 a.m. run to 7-Eleven.

I poured it into a small styrofoam cup, took another sniff, and cringed. I set it down and began tearing packets of powdered creamer and sugar, pouring one after another into the black abyss, watching it remain unchanged.

I began to stir it with a thin, mostly useless plastic straw (the kind that sea turtles love to play with) and blew on it as I surveyed the "lounge".

There was nowhere to *lounge*, just a bunch of mismatched

metal chairs surrounding two wooden tables pushed together in the middle of the room.

My copies were hopefully still printing off in the workroom down the hall, and I was killing time.

I took a sip and burned my tongue.

Time and neglect had dulled the linoleum floor and covered it in scuffs and scrapes. On my left were two microwaves. One didn't work. The other was larger than most TVs. Behind me, built into the cabinets during the '80s or '90s, was an old stereo. It had a cassette player and everything. There were also two refrigerators, presumably packed full of food. I didn't look. Instead, I walked up to the window to peer through the blinds.

It was still mostly gray outside. I could see the basketball courts, hoops without nets, a volleyball court, a parking lot that ran toward the main street where two kids were taking off, backpacks bouncing as they ran. I let the blinds snap back and took another cringing sip.

Not all was bleak. Two fake trees standing in the corner and a semi-abandoned plant on the table added a mild green accent to an otherwise brown, bland scene.

I tapped an impatient foot, felt the cold air slip in through the hole that was about the size of a quarter, maybe more, in the bottom of my shoe.

A putrid stench emanated from the sink, and I moved towards the door to escape it. Someone had written an inspirational quote on the board a while ago. Walking by, I erased it with my hand.

I don't know why. I just did.

The coffee continued to cool, and I set it down and reached for the container of generic, store-bought cake resting on the table. A "SALE" sticker covered the label. Resting beside the cake, two containers of sugar cookies topped in pink frosting and sprinkles sat splayed open with less than half of their contents remaining.

Diabetes, the gift of gifts, I thought.

Xanax takes away your appetite, so I opted for another cringe of coffee, more out of boredom than a need for caffeine.

A piece of paper with a pen on it was pushed out in front of the cookies, its placement intentional. There were spaces for names. Someone was asking for donations for a kid or something. Three had signed up. I rolled my eyes and set it back down. The teachers were the ones who needed the donations.

Sufficiently depressed, I paused, took another sip, felt that it had cooled enough, and chugged the rest of my coffee. Once I finished, the *flavor* hit me like a chalkboard to the face, forcing me to stomp my foot a few times before the twisting subsided. Then I was off to see if my copies were ready.

I walked by the faculty bathrooms on the way out and heard someone shitting something fierce. I tried not to laugh.

It was the worst setup. Two toilets in rooms barely large enough for your knees not to skid against the wall sat back to back. There was no fan, only vents that poured the steamy contents directly out into the hall by the teachers' lounge. This meant that everyone who walked by had to smell and literally taste shit. Whether you were having lunch, grabbing a cup of coffee, checking your mail, or entering the office from the back, you had to walk through an invisible cloud betraying the sad state of teachers' digestive tracts that floated back there in perpetuity.

Some days there would be a line.

Nothing was more awkward than to be in there, blowing out the bottom of the bowl only to open the door to an audience you'd presumably have to work with for the next ten years. And yes, I get it, girls poop, but when you see a tea-cup-sized third-grade teacher walk out after going thirteen rounds with last night's quesadillas in a way that would have trivialized the entire *Rocky* series, it changed you.

We called them, "The Shame Cubicles".

A gregarious fart echoed a loud goodbye as the door to the main hall closed behind me. I laughed again.

I've never done meth, but the twitching I felt from the coffee I had just downed had to be similar.

When I entered the workroom, I heard only silence. That was not a good sign. I moved over to the copier and looked down at a machine more massive than a deep freezer and saw "Call for Repair Services" flashing on its tiny display.

I'm not making this up. These *little adventures* happened so often that you eventually accepted it as a regular part of your day. But at that point, I was still acclimating to the persistent string of readied failures.

I opened up the machine and tried fucking around with the insides, but that was pointless, and I was running out of time for my plan.

I fought the urge to kick it and took off before anyone could blame it on me.

My last hope was the Printer of the Ancient Ones. A printer probably used in NAM that had since been retired to the hall outside of Veal's classroom. No one knew how it got there or when. And while everyone knew it was a piece of shit, they respected it too much to move it. That and it weighed a few hundred pounds. The thing belonged in a museum of some kind.

But it was my only option. Otherwise, I would have to change my lessons for the day. So, I bounded down the hall, knowing that I would probably run out of time before I finished what I needed to do anyway.

The air was cold outside when I plowed into the metal door using my ass to hit the lever. It flung open, slamming into the wall. I quickened my pace over the asphalt and down the stairs to Veal's annex, feeling the cold slipping into my shoe.

I threw open the door to her annex a little harder than I wanted. It too slammed against the wall with an audible "boom." The one student in the room studying jumped at the sound. I banged it shut again trying to close it behind me.

I shrugged an apology to the kid. He simply glanced back down at his book.

Over by the old copying machine, I put in the papers, and pressed "start." It began making copies and a sound I can only describe as a robot in need of a thorough oiling trying to assault another robot sexually.

I turned away and leaned against the copier, thought better, and stood instead, staring out at the barren, decrepit, makeshift computer-lab-thing in front of me. Murmured teaching sounds emanated from the surrounding classrooms.

The sound of paper shredding slipped out suddenly from behind me, followed by a loud crinkling and several "beep-beep" sounds.

I cursed and turned around, opening the machine to reveal its intricate plastic insides. I began removing the excess papers through short, vigorous pulls, turning knobs, and bending my fingers into places I wasn't entirely sure I should put them. Hard plastic resisted against my delicate finger flesh as I magically hoped my fuckery would fix the issues happening there.

After I closed all the flippy-things, I went back to the screen. Something was still off. I opened the inside again, checking everything that looked like it moved, forcefully pushing pieces around until I heard an unusual "crack." I cringed and stood back.

I closed it precariously with the hope that that sound had been...natural.

I pressed "start" again.

The printing continued.

I looked down at my hands and noticed a fine dust of toner covering them. I looked at my shirt. More toner.

Great.

Again the sudden jarring sound of shredding paper and a cacophony of irritable "beep-beeps" halted the machine.

I opened it up yet again and began pulling out pieces of paper vigorously. My fingers hit on a hard plastic something inside and scraped painfully. I pulled out my ink-dusted hands, cursing under my breath. Once again, I cleared all remaining papers and put everything back in its perspective place.

This is why teachers only wear black, I thought as my face twitched.

I pressed "print," determined I would have my copies.

Thirty seconds later, a sudden tearing and screeching ripped into the silence, followed by that damn "beep-beep."

Grabbing the originals, I turned to the student who sat there watching me, pencil dangling from his hand.

I looked directly at him. "I was never here," I said and left.

As the door closed behind me, I could hear it repeating its chorus of beeps.

CHAPTER NINE

Lunchtime Confessioins

I started convincing Wilson to grab lunch even though he wasn't big on eating.

Between tutoring, planning and having meetings, having lunch as a teacher was a luxury. But what started as the occasional pause in our day became a semi-regular rendezvous.

We'd grab a sandwich from a deli down the road to eat in my classroom. I'd pick a four-cheese, grilled cheese with mayo and bacon: manna from heaven. And I would dip that greasy little bitch into a side of ranch.

"You're going to make me fat," Wilson said.

"Pick up running?" I suggested.

"How about fuck off," he said as we pulled a couple of desks together and sat down. He watched me open the clear container and saw the cheese ooze and trail out as I picked it up. "Is that greasy enough for you?"

"I can't gain weight," I said.

"That's probably the least teacherly thing you've ever said to me," he said. "Don't go advertising that around here. The other teachers will go running for their pitchforks."

I laughed. "I usually just eat half anyways and give the rest to an eighth-grader."

"That's why they're starting to like you. If you feed them, they'll keep coming back," he warned. "How are your presentations going?"

"A disaster," I said, biting into my sandwich. Miniature mouth-gasms escaped as I tasted the melted cheese and bacon combination. "I keep having to reteach them stuff. It's like having a pub quiz about current events with a team composed only of Alzheimer's patients."

"It's been way worse," he said. He began sharing some of the stories from the long, fucked-up history of the school.

It had been bad.

Really bad.

I won't repeat what he told me; it's not important. Every district has skeletons in their closets. And while the school may look bad in the end, it's the kids that have to grow up dealing with the consequences. It made my chest feel like it was caving in, to know the kind of stuff some of those kids had experienced.

I crunched on some chips as I listened, occasionally dipping them in the ranch.

"It got so bad that they had to come in and close down the school for a week. Admin brought in several parents and talked to them. There were even cops."

"They closed the school down?"

"They didn't have any other choice. Then Nimitz showed up. He fought for this place. He went to this school back in the day. He's from the neighborhood, grew up down the street. They respect him. And over the years, he's turned this place around. This place *is* him. Without him, they would've probably turned the school into office spaces or left it to squatters."

"How long has he been a principal here?"

"Seven years," Wilson said without pause.

"He cares that much about this place?"

I didn't get it. I found problems every day I walked into that building. Broken printers. Shitty facilities. Destroyed classrooms. Had you told me that gasoline covered the building, I'd have been the one to light the match. To me, it was beyond saving. But hearing that this man, Nimitz, fought for this place when it was in worse condition, didn't make sense to me.

"He loves this school. He built the staff, fought for funding, pushed for a lot of improvements. Every year I've been here, it's gotten better and better. There are exceptions, of course. Your freshmen class would be one. They are, hands down, the worst class I've ever taught."

"I keep hearing that from people. Are they really that bad? I mean, they're bad, don't get me wrong, but this is only my second year. They're slow and teaching them feels like talking to rocks, except even rocks do something over time. They erode. These kids won't even read the book."

"The fact that they read anything for you is an improvement," he said, taking another bite of his sandwich.

"We're a month in and only on the third chapter. A month in, and we've read like thirty pages, maybe. I hardly call that progress. At this rate, we won't finish on time. I didn't think it would be this hard, but every single day is a struggle."

"The class you have now is the worst class I have ever taught," he repeated.

"You've mentioned that," I said.

"But they used to be way worse. A lot of the psychotic kids in that class left. You have the diet version of what I had to teach last year."

"Is this one of those 'back in my day, we had to walk to school with our own alcoholic fathers strapped to our backs, beating our buck naked bodies with belt buckles each way as we trudged through the snow while our neighborhood priest

76

leered at us from a window' kind of stories?" I asked, inhaling.

He stared at me for a second.

"They were really that bad?"

"Ah." He forced a smile. "I'm being serious with you. They were the worst. I used to count down the minutes until they'd leave my class, no lie. The minutes. My first two years here were incredible. I had the highest reviews. I loved coming to work. I enjoyed being here. And then I had them, and everything changed. They pushed me to a dark place. It affected my health and my career. My observations tanked. Before I taught them, the administration used to rave about me. During that year, I received my first write-up."

"That's what you meant at the beginning of the year when Nimitz asked you in front of everyone how you improved your classes' test scores. Your response was pretty ballzy."

"You remember that?" He laughed.

"You straight up told Nimitz the only reason you succeeded was because you got rid of the previous class. Yeah. I remember that."

"It's true. We don't fail middle schoolers, so they either moved on to you or moved to different schools. Either way, they aren't my problem anymore."

"That pissed him off. I can't believe you argued with him."

"I respect Nimitz. Sometimes I get a little passionate, but he handles it. I can explode in a fury of rage, and he'll sit there and let me vent and then give me a calm answer. I think it's because he's a passionate man himself."

"And you lost it because of those kids?"

"On more than one occasion. Granted, it's not entirely their fault. They had a rough experience with the education system. Their fifth-grade teacher was fired halfway through the year, and then they had a series of subs. Then there was a bunch of other weird changes, stuff administration wanted to try, classroom experiments, new ideas, that kind of thing. So, they haven't had any real stability. Still, that can only excuse so much. They were out of control."

"Were they all like that? I mean, there's some shit heads, sure. But there are a couple of cool ones."

"You got some new kids over the summer. And like I said before, a lot of the crazy ones left."

"They're no walk in the park, though," I said, feeling slighted because they were still challenging for me.

"I don't doubt that at all. But like I said, most of the crazy ones are gone," he repeated again, like a mantra. "The thing is, that's what I was trying to push for last year, to expel a couple of students who were a constant problem. And that's when I got into trouble. This is where Nimitz and I completely disagree. He thinks there are no bad students, that we can save them all. I think you need to cut the dead weight, or it hurts the group."

"You make them sound like gangrene."

"In a lot of ways, a few rough kids can destroy a class."

"Luckily, most of mine are in Period Nine."

"Imagine having Period Nine for half the day, but worse. Plus, most middle schoolers, no matter how tough they act, don't skip school. They were there all day. How many of your freshmen come to Period Nine regularly?"

"How many of them come back after lunch?" I scoffed.

"Exactly. One time, I had this large girl, Camille." He leaned forward in the chair. "She stood up with a pair of scissors and yelled at me, 'You wanna bleed, Mister? You wanna see your own blood? I'll fucking cut you.' I sent her to the office. After twenty minutes, they sent her back. Imagine that. She threatened me with scissors, pulled them out and stood up at her desk, ready to cut me. I was furious when she reappeared in my classroom. I refused to teach."

"What happened?"

"Nothing. I called up the office, and they told me there had been no mistake. I sent her out again. This time Nimitz walked her back and spoke to me in the hall. We exchanged words. I ended up looking weak in front of my students, and I didn't feel supported. So, I took the next day off, called in at 4 a.m. for a sub, last minute. They couldn't find one and struggled with finding coverage. The next day, I came back and had words with Nimitz."

"That's frustrating. I would've dropped that little bitch," I said with a mouth full of cheese.

"No, you wouldn't have. Middle schoolers love their little cliques. Back then they tried all boys and all girls classes. It was a nightmare. The girls would team up against me. It was a constant power struggle. If I singled one out, the others would come to her aid."

"The kids teamed up against you?"

"Yes." He sipped his soda. "The class full of boys had their jackasses too, like that little bitch who drew dicks all over my books. I won't ever forget that asshole. But still, the girls were ruthless."

"You're still upset by that, aren't you?"

"He ruined probably two thousand dollars' worth of books. When you try to help someone out, and they do that —"

"Yeah, but I mean, it was just a few books. It's annoying, but not enough to make you hate a kid."

"No. It wasn't *just* the books," he said. And then he began to tell me the story.

I saw a side of him that had been hiding underneath the calm surface. In the comfort of our friendship and the safety of my classroom, he let loose the hot liquid magma of disdain that bubbled beneath, his words viscerally melting with poignant precision.

I won't say what he said. It was dark. It would paint the

wrong image of him. He, like most teachers, was far more patient and caring than he needed to be. And after enough experiences fighting to make the world a better place, fighting with society at your back, you begin to wonder if anyone even cares.

Darkness bubbles in the heart from time to time, betraying the inky blackness that lurks below, and when it boils, its lapping splotches stain everything it touches.

When you teach, you experience events you couldn't imagine. Some of them are great, life changing. Others are dark, terrifying, and also life changing.

You become a kind of tightrope walker, balancing on your sanity, trying not to fall into the abyss below. You make it to the other side, and everyone admires you, but if you fall, while tragic, people will ask why you were doing it in the first place.

"I've taught three students that I hate, actually hate. One killed someone as part of a gang initiation. They found the body in the trunk of his car in the school parking lot. One raped a seven-year-old child and is now in prison for life. And the one I just told you about."

"I don't have any words." I leaned back, setting my half-eaten grilled cheese down, feeling my appetite leave as I listened.

"If you teach long enough, you'll see it all. I've taught—" he counted up the years "—probably over three thousand students. I lost a student in Iraq. One to a heroin overdose. A couple to suicide."

"Shit. I don't know if I could handle that."

"You do what you need to do when it's time. That's what teaching is."

"They don't ever tell you this in college. The crazy shit you see and hear," I said, staring at my food. "I'm still trying to process what you told me last week about…"

And this is where I pause. I cut out that part of the conversation, the part where we talked about some of the really crazy, stupid shit the kids did. Look. I get that you may want to read it, but I don't want to immortalize every ill deed those kids did when they were growing up.

Every student has a story.

Instead, let me tell it to you like this. Take any deranged action of a forty-year-old drug-addicted alcoholic homeless person and ascribe it to a fourteen-year-old. Fucked-up shit happens in these kids' lives, and they do dumb shit. As a teacher, you have to wade through that garbage and try to help if you can. But you don't walk through filth and come out smelling fresh.

We continued talking about everything from the "Great Cell Phone Drama" to my breakup when I paused and awkwardly snuck in a Xanax after growing quiet.

Wilson asked, "So what's the problem with the reading? Why's it going so slow?"

I appreciated the change in subject. "I'm having a difficult time getting them interested."

"Why?"

"There's so much high-level vocabulary that's out of their range," I said.

"Wait a minute. I can't believe I didn't think about this." He turned and left the room.

He came back in and handed me another book.

Why does every English teacher's solution involve another book?

"Another book? They won't read the first one," I said.

"Check it out," he said.

It was a different copy of *Frankenstein*. Thicker. I flipped through the pages. It was mostly the same, but with one difference. It had all the hard words defined on one side of the book. "This might work. Do you have any more?"

"Unfortunately not," he said.

"I'll just make copies, I guess."

He smiled. "Spoken like a true teacher."

Wilson shared a few more ideas, and I eagerly listened. He knew how to teach, I'd give him that. By the end of the conversation, I was a little excited to try some of his ideas, small tweaks, but maybe just enough to help improve my class.

There are many beautiful moments in education that give you hope, temporary pauses in the storm. You can spend weeks trying to figure out how to reach your students. Then you have a moment. Whether you're planning in the shower staring at the water flowing towards the drain, driving down the highway reflecting on a lesson, or having a conversation with a friend who simply places a book in your hands, there are these moments where everything pauses, and a fizz of excitement washes over the frustration.

In those moments, it felt like I could keep trying.

CHAPTER TEN

The Red Curse

"Mister, I heard you had to buy Ezekiel a new phone." Brutus grinned.

"Where'd you hear that from?" I said, looking at the smug eighth-grader.

"A little birdie told me," Brutus said. "I hope you didn't go broke buying it."

Students flowed out into the hall. Ezekiel stood behind him, giggling. He turned away when our eyes met.

"You should probably head to class before you're late." I looked at the scrawny thirteen-year-old, wanting to bitchslap the little bastard.

"You should probably save your money, so you can afford rent." More giggling.

"Goodbye, Brutus," I said. He started to walk away. "Oh, and Brutus."

He stopped, and turned back around, his little hands tight on the straps of his backpack.

"I didn't have to buy the phone. The district paid for it."

"Sure. Sure," he said.

"You know," I said, looking at his friends, "if I was in your class, I'd be careful who I trusted. Seems like there's a thief out there."

"Thank you, Mister," he said. I couldn't quite make out what he muttered under his breath as he walked away.

I was supposed to be in the halls during passing periods, but I couldn't be bothered, so I stayed in my classroom.

As I was pulling up the journal for the day, Walter came in and handed me a piece of paper. "It's from my parents," he said.

"Thanks," I said and read the note: *Due to religious reasons, we respectfully request our child receive another assignment. If you do not honor this request, we will speak with the principal.*

I rolled my eyes and put the note on my desk. Without thinking, I shot the kid a glance that caused him to look away immediately.

After a time, kids flooded in, and the bell rang. I took a seat at a desk at the back of the class. "We're continuing with presentations. Make sure you speak loud enough so I can hear you. They've been good so far," I lied. "But remember to stay still. Don't sway. You're giving a speech, not having a seizure. Any volunteers?"

No one said anything.

"David?" He looked up at me with wide eyes. "Thanks for volunteering."

"I didn't volunteer," he said.

"Everyone be so kind as to thank David for volunteering."

"Way to go, David," Sean said.

"But I didn't volunteer," he repeated, dumbfounded.

"Thank you, David," I said sternly.

Sulking, David slowly opened his backpack, took out his notebook, and then slumped to the front of the class. Standing there holding a loose-leaf spiral notebook out in front of him like a shield, he looked like a little kid wearing his father's oversized clothes. His hair, a styled mess, bounded around as he stifled giggles.

"David. We're waiting," I said.

He giggled. "Shut up, Sean."

"I believe in you," Sean fired back.

"Shrek." Still giggling.

"David," I said.

"Sorry, Mister." He was looking at his notebook. "Shrek-looking ass nigga."

"David," I said. "This is for a grade."

When I started teaching, I used to hand out a dictionary to students who cursed in class. I would ask them to define a word and teach it to the class. It was either that or go to the office. That didn't last very long. Then I would write people up. That didn't last very long either. My second year as a teacher, I realized that those kids basically used profanity as commas. And by November, I was all out of fucks to give.

"Sorry, Mister." He looked down again.

I heard Sean mutter, "Your mom looks like Shrek."

"I'm going to stab you in the throat," David said, still laughing.

"Sean! Sit next to me. Now."

"Why me, Mister?"

"Now." I waited until he was next to me, then asked David to begin.

"So, uhhh, here it goes." A stifled giggle.

What had started off as a simple creative writing assignment was fast turning into a pain in the ass. I wanted it to be fun and expressive, but as you will shortly see, it was anything but that.

He cleared his throat a little too loud…

My name is Cassandra and Im walkin down the hall to meet my friends for lunch. Im so hungry, I cant wait to eat food. I enter the cafeteria. I see all these girls lookin at me. Guys are lookin at me. Im so hot. I know they all want to talk to me. But I need to get lunch first. Dont know why cuz Ill just puke it up later. But whatever. I stand in line. And Im waitin so my friends come and join me and they all fight to stand next to me cuz Im so popular and my makeup is on-fleek. Im the baddest bitch in this school. But I start to feel a pain happening inside me. And I realize that the red devil has come for his tribute. The red tide washes forward and I know what is gonna happen so I tell my basic bitch friends to hold my place in line and I run to the bathroom like oh fuck Im gonna to die before I get there. It feels like Im bleedin out all over the place. I dont think Im gonna make it. But I turn the corner to the bathroom and rush into one of the stalls and lock the door behind me. The pain is like so bad, I think Im gonna die. But at least I aint pregnant. So like my parents wont kill me for bein a teen mom. But then I look down as Im sittin on the toilet and Im like, oh my god. What the fuck is this? Im bleedin. Gushin out blood from my ax wound. Im like gonna die. So I start cryin and yellin. Fuck. And I know Im like dyin and it sucks that Im gonna die on the shitter like some basic bitch, but at least my makeup in on fleek and my sweater is really cute, so I guess its not that bad. So Im trying to stop the bleeding, but Im not like a field surgeon. So it just gets messy and keeps pourin out of me. Like theres fuckin blood everywhere, and I start crampin like a sonofabitch, and it feels like Satans tryin to drag me to hell by my uterus but Im not ready to go to English. Its horrible and Im trapped in here and Im burning up and Im a little dizzy from all the blood loss and I wonder if I like need a blood transfusion. I reach into my cute purse and look for a tampon but theres none in there and Im like fuuuuck. So I keep crampin and its horrible and like I dont know what to do cuz Im trapped in the bathroom and it smells like someone just took a fat shit and Im afraid that if someone comes in here theyll think it was me. I just need a fuckin tampon so I text Betty, but shes being a ho right now and not answering my texts. I think shes trying to move on my man. And that pisses me off. Im gonna to have to fight that bitch if I survive this. But my head feels dizzy cuz all the blood loss, but then I start thinkin about who else might be able to help me cuz no one is textin me back and this pisses me off cuz those sluts know that I am way hotter than they are and they want people to laugh at me. I want to start screamin and call 911 cuz this is a fuckin emergency cuz my street cred is on the line here. And then like this girl comes in the bathroom cuz she hears me cryin and like sees the blood and tosses me a tampon and I thank her a lot cuz she saved my life and now Im ready to fuck shit up cuz Im like totally healed. And so I go back to the cafeteria and I see that Betty is with my man and so I go up to her and am like, "Bitch, why you tryin to take my man?" And she says that she aint and I aint got time for this trick ass ho, so I go for her hair and start yankin that shit out because shes a two-timing slut. And Cameron tries to break it up like hes Moses trying to part the seas, but I come at his bitch ass like the Pharaoh and knock him back to the promised land and he has no idea whats goin on and so he cries like a little bitch and Im still a little light headed because I lost all my blood. And I need some chocolate. But the principal comes over and wont let me get a Snickers. And I kiss Kevin just to piss off Cameron so he knows we done, but the principal is pullin me away and Im screamin for a candy bar and...

He paused and looked up. "That's how far I got, Mister."

A few of the boys who were snickering clapped. They stopped when they noticed I wasn't amused.

I looked around. Several of the girls were rolling their eyes or shaking their heads. He sat back down.

"Not really even sure what to say," I said.

"You said you wouldn't get mad if I cursed," he said.

"I should have put a limit on it," I said. "You do know a period isn't some kind of visceral, macabre blood geyser, right? Like, that's not a real thing."

"I don't know, Mister. I've never had one." He stifled a giggle.

"Dumbass," someone said.

"I'm next," Alphonso said.

His story was similar, though not as graphic. Someone else

went after, another boy with another period story, although with much less profanity. Then another.

"You know there's more to girls than periods? You guys are stupid," Helen said when he finished.

Then another one. It was like they were channeling Saint Flo as an intellectual muse when they wrote their assignments. When the next student finished his rather shitty, obviously rushed attempt, I exhaled sharply and said, "Listen up. Everyone. Eyes on me."

I waited.

When they were all uncomfortably turned towards me, I spoke. "This is absurd. I'm disappointed. First of all, there's more to girls than periods. You're supposed to write a story with a girl as the narrator. Not pretend to be a girl," I said unnecessarily as I looked at Walter. He hid his eyes as I continued. "I didn't ask you to write base, disgusting bathroom humor. I asked for a story. A simple story. But yet again, you show me that you can't even do that. It isn't funny. It's pathetic. If I was a girl in this class, I would be angry. I would be asking myself why I'm surrounded by a bunch of grungy, immature boys too busy pulling on each other's fingers to fart rather than learning to grow and change as a person. You should have left your sense of humor in the seventh grade."

"Amen!" Helen said. "You tell them, Mister!"

"How about you go, Helen?" David asked.

"There you go," I said. "Helen, show them how to do it right."

She looked down. "I'm not ready."

"You really suck at school," David said.

"Fuck you," she replied.

"David. Talk to me after class," I said. "Helen. Tomorrow. Be ready."

"What did I do, Mister?" David said.

"Who's next?" I asked.

"I'll go," Paris volunteered.

"Thank you," I said.

She walked to the front of the classroom with her notebook in her hand and stood there, shaking in her hoodie. Her dark brown hair fell evenly around her like a curtain, partially covering her face.

"You got this," I said.

She began…

"I walk into the classroom and see Brenda sitting across from me. Does she always have to look so pretty? I don't know what it is about her, but I long to see her all day, and when the moment comes, when she walks in front of me, my words jumble, and my body shakes.

Why is it so hard for me to speak to her?

I decide that today is the day I talk to her. My friends tease me at lunch saying, "Why don't you just grow a pair, bro?" Today is the day I do it. I'm going to ask her out. I'm going to push aside being nervous and grow a pair. I've had a crush on her too long. I'm tired of only dreaming. I want to know. The thought sends shivers over my skin and makes me shrink inside. It's like standing on the edge of a cliff, looking down at my death. And wouldn't it be my death? Rejection is a kind of death. A death of dreams.

I have to do this. I can't go on not knowing.

We're in English class together. The teacher reads, and some people pay attention and take notes. I try to focus, but I can't. How can you imagine a story when your mind is tangled up in the endless epic her casual glance provides? Words mumble in the background as I steal away from the pages to gaze at her. Each look breathes life into a fantasy that seems to dance in my mind between bells. Her desk sits across from mine.

Did she steal her glow from heaven before she fell into this strange, dark place?

Am I being creepy? I wonder. But I cannot pull away. I see her smooth red lips and wonder what it would be like to place a kiss there. Maybe falling?

I sat there, only half-listening in class.

I had never kissed a girl. My friends all think I've done more. That's what you do when you're a guy, you lie. You have to impress everyone around you. But all I wanted to do was hold her hand, feel her soft palm in mine. I wanted to walk with her through the rain and lean in for a long-awaited kiss.

The teacher called on me to answer.

I stumbled back into reality. People laughed. I looked around. She was looking at me. I looked back into the book and waited for him to call on someone else. Was she annoyed? Was she laughing at me?

The spotlight moved away when someone else answered. I waited before looking up to steal another glance. She was writing heavy and fast.

What?

It didn't matter.

She was my only lesson, my only teacher. I sat in her classroom and listened. Her lectures were in her deep sighs, the way she pulled a strand of hair behind her ear, her each and every breath. Her assignments were to count her every heartbeat, to paint her eyes from memory, to inhale the essence that trailed in little eddies behind her.

Class ended. I packed up quickly. I wanted to see her in the hall. Maybe there I would find the strength to speak with her.

I began to push my way towards her through the crowd, but she slipped away like the surface of a lake slips away from someone drowning. I should have swum faster towards her, but the others splashed around me, submerging me in their eager waves.

And I let them.

I let myself drown in possibility rather than live knowing I was a failure.

If I kept dreaming, I would never have to wake up.

There was a pause.

She was looking down at her shoes, "Oh. That's it."

There was silence.

Someone started clapping. Then others.

I joined.

"You go, girl! She set all you little bitches straight," shouted Helen.

"Helen," I said again.

"Sorry, Mister," she said.

"Paris, that was awesome. I can tell you worked really hard on that," I said.

"Whatever. She just wrote a story as a guy instead of a girl," David said.

"That's what you were supposed to do!" I shouted.

"Dumbass," Helen said.

"You didn't even do it. You're the dumbass," David responded.

"I'm going to do it. Mister, I'm going to do it. And it's going to be that good. Well, not *that* good. That was really good, but it's going to be better than David's."

The presentations continued. Most were mediocre. And so many more didn't even bother. When I called their names, they just looked down with a sense of shame like a puppy caught shitting on the rug.

"We have time for one more," I said.

"I got this," said Sean.

"Way to go, Shrek!" David yelled.

The giggling wasn't a good sign. I was afraid it was going to be as bad as David's.

I was wrong.

It was much, much worse. I sat in disbelief as Sean told the tale of a streetwalker having sex for money to buy meth.

I stopped him when he got to the part about snorting a line of coke off her dealer's...use your imagination.

"Outside. Now," I said.

He didn't protest. He just left.

The door closed behind him.

I waited in silence, trying to process what had just happened. Finally, I said, "We will no longer have creative writing assignments in this class. From now on, you will only write essays." Then I walked to the door, ignoring their complaints.

Sean started to talk as soon as I walked outside. The door clicked shut. I spoke over him. "Do you have brain damage? Actual brain damage? I need to know if at any point in your life you experienced a trauma that resulted in you being this fucking stupid because then I would feel bad for what I'm about to say."

"I—" he started to speak.

"No. You shut up and listen. Do you realize what you've done? You stood up in front of the entire class and read, out-loud, out-fucking-loud, a highly sexual and graphic story that could have you sitting in the principal's office. How would you feel if I asked you to read that story to your mother?"

"I thought it—"

"No. You couldn't have possibly thought. Thinking would have led you to the realization that what you just did was a really, really bad idea. Writing it was a bad idea, but volunteering to read it, that was just plain stupid."

"I'm sorry," he mumbled. He was tall, even for his age, but I was still much taller. "It was stupid. I'll go to the office." He started to walk away. And I let him reach the end of the annex before I called him back.

He returned with his head down.

"This is what's going to happen. You're going to stay out here for a minute, and you're going to compose yourself. And when you're ready, you're going to make a formal apology to everyone in my class. You're going to make it very clear to everyone that you're really, truly sorry because if you don't, then you'll be in the office talking to both the principal and your parents."

"Yes, Mister," he said.

I grabbed the door handle.

"Why?" he mumbled.

"Why what?"

"Why aren't you sending me to the office?"

"Because…" I looked at the kid. There was a slight spouting mustache forming above his lip and tears in his eyes. He may have tried to act big in front of his friends, but out there in the hall, he was scared.

What he did was stupid. There's no doubt about that. But I was fast learning that the kids at this school weren't snowflakes. My students probably hadn't been offended. If anything, they'd respect him more if he was suspended.

No. The only way to change the culture would be to have him admit he was wrong. He wouldn't go down as the legend that was kicked out of class. Instead, he'd go down as the kid that had to apologize. And apologizing was always worse.

I also hoped that if he realized I had given him a chance, that maybe he would try a little harder next time.

"Because we all make mistakes."

CHAPTER ELEVEN

Parent-Teacher Conferences

It was the end of the day, and Wilson came into my class after the halls had cleared out. "Don't forget that we have parent-teacher conferences today," he said. He might as well have backhanded me across the face.

"What!?" I said. "Isn't that tomorrow?"

"You really should read your emails," he said.

"Not sure what's worse, parent-teacher conferences or emails."

"Really?" he laughed. "It's my favorite part of the job."

"Are you insane?" I led him out of my class and locked the door. "It's the same thing over and over again, 'Why is little Bobby failing?' 'What can stupid Candice do to bring her grade up?' 'Please let me know the minute he gets outta line, and I'll have a talking to Michael.' If I wanted to be lied to regularly, I'd go to church."

You ever sit through a Thanksgiving meal listening to your crazy, drunk aunt ramble on about the world ending and the Illuminati? The one that's fucking nuts and spends too much time watching YouTube conspiracy videos, half-wasted on psychedelics and reeking of incense like she's some kind of new-age grief counselor? You know the one I'm talking about. The one you and your whole family loathes sitting next to at the table every year, the one no one ever mentions directly by name, but you all give each other that same look when anyone mentions one of her "particular behaviors?" The one you and the rest of your family stare at, listening to, waiting for the combination of booze and pills to kick in so she stays sedated long enough for everyone to leave the house, even the people who own it? You know the one I'm talking about?

That sums up parent-teacher conferences.

The worse one I ever had happened the previous year.

I knew it was going to be a shit show the moment the mother arrived.

She was a heavy-set woman with a thick, brunette perm and a sneer permanently welded to her face. She pulled out her son's paper, wielding it like a barbarian holding a flaming sword about to charge into battle.

I stood up to greet her, and she responded with, "You're young."

"And highly qualified," I said staring back at her.

The mother pursed her lips. "The first order of business is to change my son's grade. I have his essay here that you failed." She held the essay out to me with a shaking hand.

"I have a copy," I said, having spent several planning periods preparing for that meeting. Her child had plagiarized, noticeably, and he would fail the quarter.

The mother stared wild-eyed at me.

It was always the same whines: You failed me. You gave me a bad grade. You got me in trouble. Rarely did people take responsibility for their actions. And with Mrs. Hochuli, the kid's support teacher, in the room with me, I had a feeling what would happen next.

The kid, like a few others, had a troubled past. He worked with Mrs. Hochuli once a day. I knew that when the mother couldn't find fault with me, she'd use that as the next excuse.

The mother raised her eyebrows and squinted at me. My face remained blank. The essay continued to hang in the air, stretched out toward me, shaking in her hand.

I took a seat and waited.

"Have a seat, please," Mrs. Hochuli said.

The mother waited, staring. I looked right back at her until she finally sat down. Her son followed.

"I looked over his essay," the mother said. "I can tell you that he worked very hard on this. I saw him on the computer for hours. He typed it. He reviewed it. He must have spent at least two hours on it. Maybe more. And then you—" she turned to me "—you said he cheated. That's ridiculous. I would like you to apologize to my child and me. I am offended. My son does *not* cheat. I didn't raise a cheater. He knows better."

A whole two hours on an essay, quite the expedition.

"I'm sorry you feel that way," Mrs. Hochuli said. "These are the sources your son copied from." She slid over the printed copies I had made.

I sat quietly as the mother examined the papers. I had highlighted everything he had copied.

After what felt like a few minutes, the mother pushed the papers across the table over to me. "I don't see what the problem is."

And that's when I questioned my sanity.

I looked at her son, who turned his gaze from me, staring blankly at some point on the table while he let his mother crusade for his innocence.

"The problem," I said, after another long silence, "is that you plagiarized your essay. You cheated. I knew there was a problem when I started reading it." I read from the first paragraph: "'A kaleidoscope of existential proclamation?' You don't talk like this."

"Are you saying my child is stupid?" the mother asked. "I've heard him talk like that before. He's a very intelligent child, despite what you may think of him." Her bizarre, gaping gaze offered a haunting glimpse into her mind.

"This is from a paper written three years ago," I said. "The truth is that unless you think there are several academics from prestigious universities stealing your son's writing, publishing it, and then posting it online...three years in the past, I'm afraid your son has plagiarized. And because he plagiarized, he fails."

"This is outrageous! No one told him he couldn't do this."

"No one told him he couldn't..." I paused trying to process what she was saying. "No one told him he couldn't plagiarize?"

"Yes. You never said my son couldn't do this."

"I explicitly told them they couldn't. Not only that, but I gave every class an entire lesson on plagiarism. We had an activity. They all signed agreements saying that they wouldn't plagiarize," I said, choosing my words carefully. "I spent a week teaching them how to cite sources. They all knew very well what would happen if they plagiarized."

At some point, I thought logic would step in, but logic had long left that room. Instead, we talked in circles for thirty minutes. Eventually, my ex-boss showed up, and we repeated the story.

The mother kept coming up with excuses.

I ran out of patience. The more she protested, the more irritated my responses became. Eventually, they sent me out of the room so the principal and the support teacher could talk to the mother and the kid alone.

I went back to my room and started packing up my belongings. Conferences were supposed to end over thirty minutes ago. I gazed out my windows at glowing bulbs of light scattered throughout the parking lot and watched as they illuminated the falling snow.

I couldn't understand how someone could be so disconnected from reality. Nothing about any of that meeting made any sense to me.

I needed a drink.

After about ten more minutes, Mrs. Hochuli came into my room with the essay. "He admitted he cheated on the condition that he'd be allowed to redo his essay. We gave him two weeks to get it to you."

"He cheated," I said.

"I know. You've been very patient through all this. We thought it would be best to give him another try and to make sure he didn't plagiarize this time."

"So, a student can cheat and get a second chance? And now I have to regrade an essay that I've already graded after I spent time hunting down proof that he cheated."

"We have to give each child the opportunity to succeed."

"I understand that, but we also have to show them that their actions have consequences."

She offered a shrug and left.

I grabbed my bag and followed. I needed a beer. Outside, a light snow continued to fall, and I hoped that a liquor store was still open. I needed something with some substance, an IPA. I was imagining something around 8 percent because I needed to kill off the brain cells that held the memories from that evening. I wasn't a drinker, so I hoped it wouldn't take much.

Two weeks later, the kid turned in another plagiarized essay. There was another conference (without me that time). They decided he would fail the semester.

With that memory fresh in mind, I walked into the gym and found a table marked by a white sheet of paper dangling from the front with my name on it. I took my seat in a foldable, metal chair and set my shitty laptop down, wondering if the battery and my soul would last the next three hours.

Lines formed with concerned or angry parents.

Once conferences started, I briefly talked about my classroom and the expectations for the year with all of the parents. Sometimes students would translate for their parents. And sometimes parents were genuinely curious. But most only cared to know if their child was failing.

That's the thing about parent-teacher conferences. You'd be pissed at some kid, and then he'd show up with his father, and you could tell that the kid was about to shit his pants kind of scared. So, even though you had this whole spiel about how garbage the kid was in class, he gave you this pleading look, and you folded.

At least, I did. I was often afraid that if I were too harsh on a kid at one of those things, he'd show up the next day with a black eye or something. And that wasn't something I could live with, not after my childhood.

The night was nearly at an end when a freshman came up with his mother. I put on a smile for one last time and introduced myself.

"Oh, I know who you are. My son's told me about you," she said, smiling. Her son, who was not smiling, stood behind her. "Not a lot of it pleasant, unfortunately. I'm Ralph's mom. It looks like he's failing your class."

"He has mostly zeroes."

"That's because your notes are bullshit," he said.

"Ralph!" she said to her son. "You and I are going to talk later," and then to me, "I am so sorry."

"I've heard worse. And I understand why he's pissed. My class is a little different than what he's used to." I went over the basics and when I was done, I looked at the kid. If he could, he probably would've kicked me in the throat. "Ralph, I know you hate me. That's understandable. You're mad because I'm challenging you and forcing you to grow. Everything I'm putting you through now will make sense when you start to see progress."

Really, I just wanted to get the fuck out of that room and go home. It had been a long day.

"He does *not* like reading," his mom added. "He tries so hard, but he doesn't get it."

"Look, Ralph." He turned towards me and glared as I spoke. "You don't take notes. I know you hate them, but it's hard to pass the tests without them."

She turned to her son. "You failed an open-note test? Oh, we are going to talk about this when we get home. That is *not* what you told me. What can he do to fix his grade?"

Oh, how I hated that. It always translated to, "What extra work can you do to fix my kid's failure?" I told her what he was missing, cringing at the idea of having to regrade something. There was a distant relief in knowing that most didn't even bother once they walked away.

"I guarantee you that Ralph will be here early every morning until his grade improves. And if it doesn't improve, he'll be visiting you at lunch for the rest of the year if that's what it takes."

Wonderful.

She looked at her kid. "Don't you dare roll your eyes." Then she leaned over and shook my hand, and I forced a smile as she thanked me again.

The parents dwindled as the conferences ended.

I watched Wilson relish in it. He leaned over the table with animated gestures emphasizing everything he said. All the other teachers were exhausted. They slumped in their chairs. Veal was on her phone. Paige was talking to the middle school social studies teacher. Throughout the rest of the gym, the other teachers waited at their tables.

The minute conferences ended, we packed up and left.

Strange, I thought as I walked towards my car. It had been exhausting, talking non-stop about the same shit for three hours. But not once during the whole time had any of the parents blamed me. Every single one of them had held their kids responsible. It seemed like most of them weren't around and just assumed their kids would do what was necessary at school, if they cared at all. Either way, they didn't seem too concerned with me.

As I moved towards the car I was borrowing from my friends (my ex and I had shared a car), I walked carefully over the thin layer of snow that had fallen, feeling an uncomfortable chill seep in through the sole of my shoe.

It was over, at least, for the moment.

CHAPTER TWELVE

Jaundice

Would you create a monster if you could?

It was a simple journal question to start class with and one many of their parents had answered years ago after they forgot to pull out. And yet, only a few people wrote down their answers.

"Journal's up. Your notebooks should be out. You should be writing. It's the same thing every day, people. Come in. Get out your stuff. Read the journal. Write the answer. It doesn't ever change. Let's go. If you don't finish, it's homework."

The door banged open with Bob bumbling in late. He didn't seem too bothered by it.

A few students surrendered with the rustling of opening backpacks followed by notebooks hitting the desks. We were minutes in already. It was supposed to be a short warm-up activity to get their brain juices flowing. "You have a couple of minutes left until we discuss."

My computer dinged with an email from my ex-boss. I read the first sentence, something about another observation, and deleted it.

After a month of *Frankenstein,* we were maybe a fifth of the way through the book. That was my concern, not more observations.

I refused to accept the idea that we wouldn't finish the novel. But at the rate we were going, it would be May before we turned the final page.

It was time to raise the bar.

Despite a reminder, people still talked. They hadn't even made an effort to pretend to work. Their notebooks remained closed, their pens down. A few others had their backpacks on their desks, using it as a pillow of sorts.

Despite my attempts to apply what I had learned from various journals, books, and college classrooms, they still needed constant reminders every single day. It irritated the shit out of me.

"The journal is up!" I yelled. "Write down the question because now it's homework. You'll turn it in tomorrow." I said that because I didn't know what else to do besides make things a grade if they didn't listen.

Didn't do the journal? Now, it's a grade.

Didn't answer the questions? That's a grade as well.

Didn't wash your hands after the bathroom? Well, you're disgusting, but guess what: *Boom!* Graded.

Go home, you fail.

A few students looked up at me as I stared over at Bob. He was smiling, his face glazed over. *High?* We hadn't even had lunch yet.

"I feel like a broken record. It's almost December. The bell rang five minutes ago. You still haven't started. I'm tired of repeating myself every day. You know what to do. I imagine you knew what to do last year when you were a freshman." A few of them understood what I was saying. I hoped Bob did. But if he did, he was too blitzed to be bothered. "Maybe if you try and focus you'll have it down when you're a freshman next year. I hear the third time is the best."

103

Again, like sad puppies, they looked down. And like an annoyed, asshole teacher, I kept on with the usual examples. "Why do you need to be reminded every day to do the same thing? Does someone stand outside the bathroom and remind you to wipe after you poop?" Etc. It was weak. I could have done better, but I was exhausted, so I stuck with the classics.

Standing in front of the class, I finally said, "Let's discuss the journal."

It was mediocre. Students said things like, "I wouldn't want to create a monster because he would do bad things." Or "I'd create a monster and have him bitchslap (insert kid's name here)."

It was an awkward conversation that they stumbled through until Bob ended the discussion by saying he would create a "monster drug dealer that would make that skrilla."

"Moving on," I said. "We're on chapter four. I'll read. We'll take notes. You'll write a summary."

Chapter four was my favorite.

And so with great ardor, despite being annoyed, I read the passages stretched out before them like a macabre creation immobilized on some surgical table by the oppressive weight of death.

There was quiet.

The walls fell away; the hum of the air conditioner pumping in cool, November air into the freezing classroom vanished; the fluorescence dimmed, and for those few fearful minutes, I led them into forbidden places. We journeyed through the damp, dreary, forgotten corners of the most macabre regions of imaginations, and saw the fervent madness of creation.

We went in search of death to find life.

"You mean—" a student paused "—he like tortured them…while they were still alive?"

"Sick," Charles said with a veiled smile.

"Ugh," Anita shivered. "That's fucking gross. Frankenstein was a dick."

The bell rang, and I dismissed them. "Someone please wake Jeff up so he isn't late to his next class."

Someone screamed his name right into his ear, forcing him yet again to jolt suddenly awake.

"That Frankenstein guy was sick," someone said on their way out.

"I can't believe he tortured animals."

"While they were still alive. Insane."

It made me smile a little bit.

Jeff was the last to leave, his sweater still imprinted on one side of his face.

After World Literature, I walked across the hall to see Wilson. "Let's grab food. My former boss emailed to let me know that I have an observation after lunch. If we go eat, we can stay out until the bell rings and then there won't be time for any meeting bullshit before class starts."

"I got the same email, looks like I'm after you, and there's no way to escape this one. Lunch sounds good even though I think our friendship is making me fat."

"Take up running," I suggested again.

"You know my thoughts on that."

"I'm tired of being observed," I said, standing in his room, waiting for him to get ready. "It makes me feel like I'm a fish in an aquarium or like some kind of test subject."

"Maybe you can ask Ritz for some one-on-one coaching instead? I bet you'd like that."

"You noticed?" I said, surprised.

"You're practically drooling every time you see her. And when she's in the room talking to you...well, let's just say it's uncomfortable," he joked. "Tension. So much tension."

"She's married," I said quietly.

"So much tension," he repeated.

105

"Anything's better than more meetings and observations."

"Welcome to teaching. Complain when you've been doing it for fourteen years, and they're still walking in to make sure you're doing your job."

"I can't imagine that," I said. It wasn't just the thought of having observations after fourteen years that bothered me, but I couldn't seem to wrap my head around the idea of even teaching for that long. "Speaking of traumatizing, we finally started chapter four."

"How did that go?"

"I read to them the whole period. It felt like story time, and they probably hated it."

"Lecture is important," he said, turning to go back to his classroom.

"Not according to my teacher training," I said, following.

"I'm sure that works for some schools, but these kids have really low reading levels. A lot of them need to have reading modeled for them."

"Model reading? They're teenagers," I said.

"You'd be surprised. Having you guide them through helps a lot. You created an experience for them. They'll remember that, even if some of them tuned out. Did they pay attention?"

"Some of them," I said, then added, "maybe."

"Some is good. Having some enjoy it is better than none. None is the norm for this school."

"I know I could do better," I said. "I could do more. I'm going to have them read at home. We're at that point. And I may have to have them read over the break so we can get caught up. I need to do other things in class besides read. They're behind on everything."

"Go for it," he said. "See what happens. You need to find out what works for you in your classroom. Don't cling to your teacher training. It's there to give you a few ideas, but the reality is what you experience every day in the classroom. And don't be too harsh on lecturing."

"They'll complain that it's boring," I replied.

"Who cares? Handling boredom is a skill. Working through it is a skill as well. They'll have to sit through meetings and take notes just like we do. When was the last meeting you went to that wasn't boring? It's not always fun and games. They have to be prepared to handle that."

"True," I said. He finished up at his desk while I waited in my jacket and hat, hoping my former boss wouldn't turn the corner before we left.

"How's your schedule looking?" he asked.

"I need to finish chapter ten by the time we come back from Thanksgiving break."

"What chapter are you on?"

"Four."

He laughed.

"I'll see how far I can get them this week. What we don't finish, they'll have to read for homework. I'll print out copies."

"And you think they'll read over the break?" he said with a look.

"If I threaten to test them, they will."

"Be prepared that most won't do it."

"Then they fail," I said, trying to act like that didn't bother me.

He put on his jacket, and we left his class and started walking towards the door. It opened suddenly, startling me.

When I saw who it was, I said, "Holy shit! What are you doing here?"

CHAPTER THIRTEEN

An Unexpected Visit

"We brought you lunch!" Matthew said. He held a plastic bag full of Styrofoam containers.

"It's Chinese food," Taylor said.

"Hi!" Zaliki smiled, exposing her braces and white teeth that contrasted her dark brown skin.

"We'll talk later," Wilson said, and vanished out the door.

I gave them each a hug. "Let's go in my room."

"It's fucking cold outside," Taylor said.

"We were worried that we'd show up and you wouldn't be here," Matthew said.

"I was just about to grab lunch with my friend. Perfect timing. This is awesome! Wow." I was trying to process everything that was happening. "No student has ever actually brought me...anything before."

"We heard you were here but didn't believe it," Taylor said as I unlocked my door. "Some people said you were fired."

"I didn't get fired," I lied. "I switched schools."

Inside my room, we pulled some desks together while Matthew started unpacking the containers. They started catching me up on their lives as juniors.

"We all hoped to see you this year, but then we saw some

other guy replaced you, and then the rumors spread," Matthew said.

"Why didn't you tell us you were leaving?" Taylor asked.

"It's complicated."

"We've got time!" Taylor said. "And you better have a damn good reason for coming to this shit-hole instead of staying with us. We miss you."

"Believe me, if I could've stayed, I would've," I said, looking at her hair. "What's with the blonde? No blues, purples, or reds?"

"Nah. Just ordinary blonde. I got tired of all the colors," she said.

They were part of my best class at my previous school, and they were the only ones that spent lunches in my room. Seeing them there made me realize how much I missed my old school. Well, parts of it anyway.

"Why are you *here*?" Matthew asked.

"They needed an English teacher here, so they moved me," I said. I felt bad lying.

"Of course there'd be a job here. I went to this shitty school for half a year and hated it," Taylor said.

"Did you really?" I asked.

"Yeah. This place is ghetto. My parents let me switch schools because everyone was fighting and getting pregnant. It was a joke."

"Why didn't you tell us you were leaving?" Zaliki asked.

"I wanted to, but I couldn't. It's boring office politics. Anyway, what's new with *you*. What's going on in your lives? You're juniors now! Upperclassmen. How does that feel?"

I sat there chowing down on noodles soaked in MSG and soy sauce with chunks of what might have been pork or beef or dog, whatever they put in affordable takeout food those days. I dodged the vegetables and personal questions as we caught up.

They told me about the students that had dropped out, who was dating whom, and how glad they were to have a new principal. They hinted at the parties and other illicit activities.

"Careful. I'm still a teacher," I smiled.

"I may get a job," Zaliki said.

"Wait. You're going to work?" I said in disbelief.

"I can work!" she said.

"But who'd hire you?" I teased.

"Rude," she said. "I'm actually a really good worker."

There was another silence.

"Awkward," Taylor said.

We laughed.

"You seem to be doing pretty well considering—" Matthew stopped.

"Considering what?" I asked.

More silence.

Zaliki looked at Matthew. "You weren't supposed to talk about it."

Taylor rolled her eyes. "Really, Matthew?"

"I'm sorry. I knew I'd mess it up," he said. "I'm just going to eat my food quietly. I'm an idiot. Sorry, Mister. I didn't mean to bring it up."

"What do you mean?" I asked.

"The breakup," Zaliki said.

"We heard," Taylor said.

"Wait. That's why you're here?" It clicked. "You guys came here on your day off of school to check up on me?"

"Yeah," Zaliki said. "We heard you broke up with your girlfriend. We knew how much you loved her and wanted to make sure you were okay."

I didn't know what to say, "I'm...wow...um...Thank you. That means a lot."

Zaliki said, "We don't feel sorry for you, but we do miss

you. And that's why we brought you food!" She smiled and then quickly covered her braces.

"I owe you guys," I said.

"You've already done plenty," Zaliki said.

"Yeah, my writing is much better because of your class," Matthew said.

"Mine too," Taylor said. "I mean, only a little bit. It's always been pretty fantastic as far as I'm concerned."

"Right…" I said. Laughter, eye rolls, and heavy chewing followed.

"And we owe you for letting us BS in your class during lunch, so we wouldn't have to eat with the plebs," Matthew added.

I looked at them. "I don't know about all that. If I were any good, I wouldn't be struggling so much here."

"That's because this school sucks, and it's full of assholes," Matthew said.

"Truth," Taylor followed.

"It's not *that* bad," I replied. "It's different. I won't lie about that, but I think I can make a difference. There's potential." I think I believed that if I kept saying it, maybe it would become true.

"Do they still draw dicks on everything?" Taylor asked.

"Shut up. They draw dicks?" Matthew giggled.

"Oh boy, you got him started," said Zaliki, looking at Matthew.

"You know about that?" I asked.

"*Everyone* knows about that. This is the dick-drawing school. It's kinda funny because we're supposed to be the art school."

"Not sure it qualifies as art," I said.

"At least they're expressing themselves." Matthew was still laughing. He turned away from the table as his face reddened.

"You want to see if they have an opening here?" Zaliki raised her eyebrow at him. "I think Matthew is interested in brushing up on his hidden talent."

"He does love the dick," Taylor said.

"Anyways," I laughed. "We'll let Matthew deal with that transition when he's ready."

"We're glad you're doing okay, even if you're working here. Everyone misses you," Zaliki said.

"Not everyone," Matthew added, dabbing away tears. "But the ones that don't miss you are probably the ones you don't miss either."

"The feelings are mutual," I laughed. "I'm doing okay. It's been a little rough, but I'll survive."

"We heard you cried," Taylor said. "Look who has a heart after all."

"Word gets around. That's false. It was raining. There were allergies. A bit of insulation blew in through the vents and landed on my face. There was no crying. Not me."

"Uh huh. Raining. Inside," Taylor said.

"I don't have emotions. I am a cold-blooded English teacher, destroyer of dreams, assigner of essays. The only emotions I feel are in the form of rage brought on by misplaced commas."

"He *is* the Slender Man," Matthew said.

"Oh god. I forgot about that. If the suit fits," I laughed. The kids at my first school had called me Slender. They had even drawn pictures with me as the infamous Slender Man that I put up on the wall behind my desk.

"Do you miss her?" Zaliki asked.

She wasn't asking for me. She wanted to know what it was like to break up with someone you loved. Everything was a lesson. You never stop being a teacher.

"I miss the idea of her," I said. "She changed. People do. It's hard from time to time, but it's getting better. But yeah, there are some things I definitely miss."

"I bet there is," Taylor said.

"Awkward," Matthew added.

I ignored it. "When you're with someone, you grow together, and learning how to grow on your own again...that can be hard. I take it one day at a time. I miss the comfort of coming home to someone. Looking into the eyes of someone who loves you, knowing they feel the same way you feel about them."

I paused. The rush of emotions wasn't there. There was still pain, sure, but it wasn't as sharp.

"But people change. In the end, it needed to happen. And as much as it sucked, it's not all bad. I'm learning that other people care about me, like you guys. Like all this." I pointed to the food. "This is amazing."

"We are pretty badass," Matthew said.

"Yes, we are," Zaliki said.

"I've always known that I was pretty incredible," Taylor added.

"I'd say all around, we're probably your best students," Matthew said.

"Okay, okay, calm down," I said, smiling. "You guys are alright."

"We brought you Chinese food. I think that makes us number one," Matthew said.

A freshman of mine appeared at the door. "Mister, I have a question."

I looked up from the food. "Sorry, can't talk. Important meeting."

He looked at me, looked at the students, then walked away.

We were laughing when I saw someone else appear at my door. "Hello. Oh, this is a surprise! What are you all doing here? Don't you have school today?"

In an instant, the room went quiet and cold. It was my ex-boss.

"No," Taylor said.

Silence.

After setting down the computer and materials for the observation, my ex-boss turned to my former students and asked, "How are classes?"

"Fine," Taylor said. She didn't even try to hide her disdain.

"Good. Everything going well with the rest of you?"

"It's great," Zaliki said, then took a bite.

Matthew mumbled something as he chewed his food.

"Great. That's good to hear. I'll be right back." My former boss left the room.

The kids began packing up the food, and I realized that our moment had ended.

"We better be heading out," Matthew said.

"Talk about ruining lunch," Taylor said. "You have to deal with that?"

"It's a long story. You guys should get out there and enjoy the rest of your day."

Zaliki cringed. "Yeah. It's time to go. I don't want to answer any more awkward questions."

"No worries. I understand." I whispered, "Take me with you?"

"Sure, we'll just throw you in the back of the car," Zaliki said. "There's room for four."

"Ugh, I wish," I said only half-joking.

They each gave me a quick hug and started to leave. Matthew turned around at the door. He looked out and then back in. "Good luck with that," he said, gesturing towards the direction of the bathrooms and making a face.

A couple of minutes later, my former boss returned and looked around. "Oh, they left?"

"They had to go to work." It was easy to lie.

"That was nice of them to show up."

"Yeah. I need to wash my hands before class starts," I said, and walked out.

"I'll set up in here. I hoped we could have a few minutes to discuss what I'll be looking for before class begins."

"Great," I said.

I didn't hide my complete lack of enthusiasm.

Sea otters are necrophiliacs.

I hate to ruin the image of the cute little pond kitties for you, but they're vicious little bastards. They've been known to drown prey and then haul the carcass around for a few days, fucking it in their free time.

I would have rather listened to the high-pitch squealing orgasm of a sea otter splashing into yet another violent climax, the sloppy slapping sounds of wet fur against the matted remains of some bloated, lifeless plaything forcefully sloshing against the waves than ever listen to my ex-boss again.

CHAPTER FOURTEEN

Homework

Two eighth-graders had asked to stay after class to work on assignments. They had argued that they would only be skipping art. They had told me that they were worried about their grades, but I think it had been more because they didn't like their art teacher. I didn't like their art teacher either, so I had agreed and had sent an email.

It had been on the condition that they wouldn't talk to me during my plan. And sure enough, they had worked through the whole period in a corner of the room, eventually turning in their essays at the end.

Now, they were trying to stay longer.

And I was kicking them out.

"Alright. You two gotta go to your next class. The bell's about to ring," I said.

"No, Mister! We want to stay in here," Sofía continued to plead. "Your class is way cooler."

"Right...You're not hanging out in here all day. I gotta teach, and you gotta go learn. Art was one thing, but I'm pretty sure you have other important classes. So...on you go," I said, shooing them away.

Zooey turned to her friend. "Bitch, let's go."

I looked at her wide-eyed, "Interesting nickname."

"She's my number one bitch," Zooey laughed, trying to drag her friend towards her.

"No. You're my bitch," Sofía said, resisting playfully.

"Duh, bitch," she replied. "We're each other's bitches. Now, let's go." Her long, curly hair waved wildly with each fake tug.

"Let's keep it somewhat professional here. You're in school." I shook my head. My class was starting to fill up with freshmen, and I gestured to the door and stood up. "You're going to be late."

"Come on, bitch. He's got stuff to do," she said. Then for good measure, she repeated, "Let's go, bitch."

Her tiny friend gave in and followed her to the door.

The bell rang.

They both stopped, turned around, and asked in unison, "Mister, can we have a pass?"

I rolled my eyes, pulled out my green pad, and scribbled on it. "There. Now go," I said, handing it to them.

"Thank you, Mister," Sofía said.

"Alright, lez go already," Zooey said, pulling her friend away.

As soon as they crossed the threshold, I turned to my class, and my entire demeanor changed. "I need a volunteer."

Anita raised her hand. I nodded, and she stood up. I handed her a thick stack of packets that I had stayed late after school the day before making.

They were intimidatingly massive, flopping onto the desks when she dropped them. Unfortunately, they weren't large enough to wake Jeff up when one bounced off his head. He rested beneath it, searching out oblivion.

"I thought we weren't using packets anymore?" Chelsea asked. She pulled her chemically destroyed blonde hair behind one ear and held her head in frustration. The amount of product in her hair produced a comical result as the patch she had just touched jutted out to the side under its own volition.

"We weren't. But I can't ask you to read at home without giving you the story."

"Is this like the whole novel?" Sallie asked.

"Wait. We're reading at home?" Chelsea stumbled towards understanding.

I rolled my eyes. "It's chapters five through ten. Let me explain."

Without any money left in my budget, I had been forced to set a forest ablaze and make copies of the novel Wilson gave me. I had only photocopied a handful of chapters, but they had still needed industrial-grade staples to bind the heavy packets together. It had been a lot of work for something that would most likely only be abandoned, forgotten in the bottom of dark, unfrequented places: in backpacks, underneath desks on the metal holsters that hung there, on the tables of other classrooms, or, and this was the most likely scenario, inside the nearest trash can.

There was a sudden knock at the door before it slowly opened. "Sorry to interrupt. We got a gift for you." It was Steven, the head custodian, with another custodian. They carried in what appeared to be a new whiteboard. "I hope you don't mind if we put this up," he said.

"Go for it." I stepped out of the way and closed the door once they were inside, trying to hide my enthusiasm.

Sad, I know.

"There's no easy way to put this. You're going to have homework over the break."

Period Four capsized in swooning undulations of disbelief like a small rowboat caught in the middle of a lake during a summer storm.

I waited, ignoring the mounting protests and vigilant

cursing. Hands flailed in pantomimed melodrama. I looked back at the custodians as they went about measuring the wall and marking where the anchors would hold up my new board. They paused and watched the reaction. Our eyes met, and I shrugged my shoulders.

"No. No. Fuck this. I ain't doing shit over the break," Charles said.

"This thing is huge," Kelly said, examining the packet.

"That's what she said," Joaquín giggled.

"Really, Joaquín?"

"I had to, Mister."

"You're here today," I said to Kelly. I was shocked, unsure when she had last shown up to class. "It's been awhile."

"Good to see you too, Mister," she said, pushing up her thick glasses.

"I'm not doing it. I don't care if I fail," Charles said.

"I would expect nothing less from you, Charles."

The complaining continued, but it was dying down.

"It's not as bad as it sounds, if you let me explain."

The complaints rose again.

"Or keep complaining. That's cool, too. I'll wait while you continue to waste your time and remind me why I had to do this in the first place. I wonder how long this will take…"

I leaned against a desk and crossed my arms.

"Shut the fuck up, everyone. Shut up. He's waiting," Anita said, pounding on her desk. "The reason why we have homework is because you people can't shut up and listen."

"Kiss ass," Charles said.

"Fuck you. I'm a kiss ass because I actually want to finish high school? Remind me that I'm a kiss ass when I graduate on time and your dumb ass is still here pushing forty, struggling to graduate because you can't count past ten."

He mumbled something.

"What was that, bitch? Say it to my face. What?" She threw

up her arms.

"Anita," I said.

She continued, "You're all quiet now. That's what I thought. You sit there, keep drawing, and keep your mouth shut. Dumbass motherfucker."

"Anita," I said, louder.

"I know. I know. I'm sorry, Mister. I can't help it. He pisses me off."

"Don't sweat the little things. It's not worth getting in trouble over. You're better than that."

The class finally grew quiet.

I continued to wait.

"You going to talk?" Sallie asked me.

"Oh. Are you ready for me to explain now?"

"Just say whatever you wanted to say," she said.

"If you insist. I would hate to keep you waiting," I said. "You see, that's your problem. You think everything revolves around you. It doesn't. That's not how this works. We have a schedule to follow so we can finish on time. We should have started reading ten minutes ago. Instead, you want to complain. And then I'm supposed to start when you tell me? No. No, no, no. That's not how this works."

I pushed off of the desk and continued, "You come in here, and you waste time. You waste time getting ready. You waste time talking. You waste *a lot* of time complaining. I have to get that time back." I paused to let it sink it. "And the only way I can do that is with homework."

Adolescent aggression continued to simmer. "Period Nine is only on chapter three. They mess around *a lot*. They're horrible. They may make it to chapter five. Maybe. And what they don't finish will be homework over the break. You all work...most of the time." I looked at a few of the slackers. "If you start chapter five today and read a little bit for homework each night, we could get close to the end of the packet before the break. If that happens, then you'd only have to read a chapter, maybe. That's only eight pages. That's a page a day for the whole break, ten minutes of your time. Maybe. Or it could be more. The choice is yours. We're behind. This is how we catch up. We have to finish this novel on time. Until we're back on schedule, you're going to have homework. Get used to it."

The bitching and complaining erupted again only to be occluded by the sudden high-pitched squeal of a drill as the custodians set the anchors in the wall for the new board.

"You waste time every day," I said over the drilling. "I never wanted to be the teacher that gives homework over the break, but you've made me that teacher. If anything, I should be mad at you."

"I ain't doing it." Bob crossed his arms and rolled his entire head in protest.

"If only there were some way for me to make sure you did the reading over the break…" I pretended to ponder in the most melodramatic of ways. "Oh, I know, a test the Monday you get back. Excellent idea. Thanks, Bob."

"That's fucking stupid. Just like this class," Charles said, pushing the packet off his desk.

The drilling stopped.

I walked over and picked it up. The top page was nearly torn off. I set it down neatly and placed my hands on either side of his desk and leaned in. "I understand that growing up is a challenge for you. Some people need a little more time to mature. I've been patient, but now I'm done. I don't care… look at me. I don't care about your opinion. You *will* do this, or you *will* fail."

I let go of his desk and walked back into the middle of the class. "You can hate me all you want. You can hate this class all you want. But if you want to graduate, you'll do what I ask."

The custodians finished mounting the board up on the wall and grabbed their things to go. "Thanks, gentlemen. That's amazing. Let Mr. Nimitz know—" I turned to look at Charles, and his eyes widened "—let him know that I greatly appreciate it."

"Is there anything else we need to let him know?" Steven asked.

"No, that should be enough," I said.

I waited for the door to close. "To graduate, you need sixteen quarter credits of English. That's four full years of English. That means you cannot fail this class at all. You need me to graduate. Otherwise, you'll find yourself in summer school." I turned to Charles. "Or worse."

I picked up another stack of papers and began passing them out. "One more assignment."

"How many forests do you destroy a year?" Anita asked.

"Enough for Leonardo DiCaprio to send me death threats."

"Huh?"

"Can someone wake Jeff up?" I asked.

Anita yelled across the class, "Jeff! Wake the fuck up!"

"Anita," I said.

He slowly picked his head up. "I wasn't even sleeping, Mister."

"Aside from the reading that you will be tested on, you have an assignment on imagery. This should be a refresher." I finished passing out the papers. "Who remembers what imagery is? Sallie?"

"I don't know."

"Great. Let's try that again. Sallie, what is imagery?"

"I don't…"

I interrupted. "Try. Break up the word. What word do you see in imagery?"

"I dunno," she said.

I walked to the back of my class and wrote "imagery" on

the new board. The new, perfect surface glistened around the darkened marks I had made there.

"What word do you see there, Sallie?"

"I dunno," she repeated.

"Image," Anita offered.

"Thank you, Anita. I was talking to Sallie, though. What word do you see in there?"

"Image," Sallie repeated.

"Good work. Based on that, what do you think imagery means?"

I waited. Nothing. "Can anyone help Sallie out?"

Anita rolled her eyes and defined it.

"You're so smart," Bob said.

"It's written on the paper in front of you," Joaquín said.

"In bold," someone else added.

"Oh," Sallie said. "There it is."

"Idiots." Charles was already drawing a pentagram on the handout.

"The details for the assignment are on the paper I handed out, including the due date, which is the Monday after the break. I'll collect these before the test. You're to pick a scene in any of the first ten chapters. You'll draw out the scene, and then you'll write an organized paragraph in response to the question: How does the author use imagery in this scene effectively? Follow the instructions I provided. Pay attention to the details," I said. "Oh, and no stick figures. I hate stick figures."

"I can't draw," someone said.

"When do we get to the monster?" someone else asked.

"Good question," I said, pulling out my phone to check the time. There wasn't much. "Alright, everyone. Open your packet to chapter five," I said.

I began reading.

CHAPTER FIFTEEN

Student Apathy

The time before the break moved by slowly and painfully, like elderly people fucking.

Period Eight was reading chapter six. There had been mild progress, but I was doubtful that they would actually do any reading on their own. First quarter had taught me that.

"Let's discuss Frankenstein's breakdown. You all have hopes, dreams for the future. Right? What would you do if the dreams you spent your whole life working for suddenly became nightmares that haunted you?"

No answer. I sat there on the desk kicking my feet back and forth, waiting. Everyone seemed to be in a daze.

Is my class this bad? I thought.

"No thoughts at all? Come on, tell me what you think," I said.

"This class is so boring," David sighed. "That's what I think."

"Boring?" I asked.

Student teacher does not handle apathy well.

"Yeah. Reading this book sucks," David said.

I grew angry. It was boring because they weren't trying. "What do you find interesting?" I tried to remain calm.

"I dunno," he said. "Not this."

"'I dunno' is not good enough. I want an answer. What interests you?"

"I dunno. I play Xbox and…oh one time, I ate a slice of pizza while I pooped. That was weird. I didn't like that." He stifled a giggle; the oversized shirt that draped around him billowed a bit.

I waited for class to quiet down. "Thanks for the share. Back to my original question, what interests you? That'll help me make this class more enjoyable."

"Read a different book?" Zac said under his breath.

"I wasn't talking to you, but thanks for the suggestion. I'm more curious as to how we can make *Frankenstein* enjoyable. I'm open to ideas. If you have one, write it down on a piece of paper, and leave it on my desk. Or, you can speak to me. And not only about the book, but you can give me suggestions on how I can improve my class."

"Reading sucks, Mister. It's not your fault. I don't think you can do anything to make it better. It sucks. It's boring. I hate it. You can't change that," David said.

"Just stop so we can get back to work. I don't want homework over the break," Helen said.

"If you all gave this class a chance, it could be amazing."

"Movie day!" someone shouted.

"That's not an option. We have that discussion every day you come to class. This is an English class. Reading and writing are part of it. If you want to sit there and complain, then you're just whining. You want to do something about it? Give me a suggestion. That's how we improve and grow."

"You want us to do more work," someone complained.

"If you want this class to be enjoyable, then you need to do some work. And you need to give me some ideas to make it more interesting, more entertaining."

"Isn't that your job?" Zac questioned.

I laughed. "To entertain you? No. Nowhere in my contract does it say I have to make class fun. I want you all to enjoy being here, but you don't even want to try. You just sit there and space out. You don't care about anything."

"I dunno, man. It's not you," Emily said. She rested her round face on her hand, squishing her cheeks in a way that made her look like a dying fish trying to breathe. "I've always hated reading."

"It's really boring, Mister," another student added.

Several more chimed in with similar opinions.

I used to daydream how badass I would be as a teacher. I had had the pathetic, lazy teachers in high school who had taught me English through boring worksheets and multiple-choice tests. They had been the same ones who had only cared about standardized tests. I had thought they were a disgrace to education when I was a kid, and still felt that way as a teacher.

And despite all I learned and how hard I was trying, they still found my class boring.

I was pissed. I should have never decided to teach *Frankenstein*. It was stupid. Another book would have been better. We would have had more free time to do other things. Or maybe they'd still be bored because that's what they were: boring. I was angry at them for not doing the work. I was angry with their families for not caring if they did the work. I was angry with the district for not doing the work to get us the basic resources that we needed.

No one seemed to give a fuck.

So, I sat there on the desk in silence, thinking, listening to seconds tallied by an absent-minded clicking of a pen, wondering what I could do.

I was beyond exhausted from finding a new place to live, working a second job, trying to get over my ex, and popping Xanax like vitamins.

I wanted to quit, to pack it up right there and leave, flipping them the bird on my way out. But I couldn't. I had to succeed. I couldn't leave a failure.

The quiet slipped into bitching that continued to grow louder until I couldn't stand it anymore. "Enough! You're bored? You're bored? You're boring. You're lazy, lackadaisical, uninspiring, and pathetic. You want me to make this interesting? You don't deserve interesting. Almost all of you refuse to do any homework. Most of you don't care. I could put extra hours into my lessons, but it wouldn't change the fact that you wouldn't do anything. Do you think I became a teacher to sit down with a bunch of lackluster fifteen-year-olds and have fifty minutes of story time every day? No. But you refuse to read at home. So rather than coming in here and gaining a deeper understanding of your world while developing your voice, you choose to constantly whine like you're on a family road trip packed into a minivan without air conditioning."

Student teacher does not handle apathy well.

"You're not gaming. You're not at some party. You're not surfing YouTube at home in your pajamas. You're in an English class.

"I get it. There's work. But instead of trying to find some joy in becoming better people, you sit there spacing out, munching on snacks, waiting for class to end.

"Your attitude needs to change. Until it does, you're always going to be bored, and school is always going to suck. The problem isn't school. It's you."

As a student teacher, I had this one professor, a little old lady who must have taught when Kennedy still enjoyed convertibles, stop by my classroom regularly to watch me teach and grade my performance. After each conference, she'd point to the last line on the evaluation paper over and over again: *Student teacher does not handle apathy well.*

That had been my reaction when one or two kids out of an entire class didn't care. How was I supposed to handle a whole grade that didn't?

Who could I turn to for the answers? Where could I turn? Was the answer in some ancient text on education?

Those college books sell because teachers remain ever hopeful. Seasoned professionals leave their little microcosms of experience at the end of their careers, believing they have it figured out. They write down their knowledge to pass on to new teachers like Prometheus handing over the torch. But what they fail to realize is that every school is different. What works in one classroom often fails in another. There is no perfect answer.

The idea of the perfect classroom was no different than a poster of a swimsuit model a teenage boy might hang on his bedroom wall. It was this ethereal object in the distance that was secretly hoped for but never obtained.

The books served as hope. They were ideas from other teachers dropped in like reinforcements and supplies behind enemy lines.

Education is trench warfare. Teachers hold the line. Somedays gaining ground, others losing it. Each teacher was trying to survive until the next happy hour, the next break, the next year.

In each classroom, we raged war against lethargy, apathy, and ignorance. Each year we struggled to survive the friendly fire of misguided community involvement and political pressure. And then we limped home and bandaged our wounds and tried to heal enough before returning to the fight.

When did teaching become about survival?

Student teacher does not handle apathy well.

Nothing I learned prepared me to work at that school. I knew how they spent their evenings. I heard the stories in the hall, the too loud whispers of sex, drugs, Rock & Roll. Parents nowhere to be found. They were living life in the fast lane before they were even tall enough to see over the dash.

Others passed the night playing video games.

And still others left school only to go home and play mother or father while their parents were out working or whoring or drinking or whatever it was they did that forced their eldest children into their places.

It was a culture of absence and poor decisions.

How was I supposed to make a difference?

Could I blame them? If I had grown up like that, would I give any fucks about some bullshit novel from the 1800s?

"You pissed him off, David. Way to go," Helen said.

"I am pissed. But it's not why you think. Imagine you slip and fall on the stairs, breaking your ankle. It's twisted backward, and the bone is sticking out. You lay there, writhing in agony, flipping around this mangled leg, wondering if you'll ever walk again. Thick tears pour down your face. Your family rushes your broken body to my hospital, and I come out to look at the wound. I'm a trained professional. I need you to trust me. But instead of letting me do my job, letting me take care of you, you fight me. Every time I get close to you, you kick at me with your broken foot, the cracked bones grinding loud against one another. You're yelping and flailing in the air all while blaming me for your agony. What would you think of someone like that?"

"That they were pretty stupid," someone said.

"And yet, that's what it's like to be a teacher."

Silence.

"Then when your wound heals broken, bones poorly fused because of how hard you resisted, you blame me. You hold me responsible when every time you try to move a white-hot river of pain surges through your poorly healed body.

"You look at me. You're angry. You're confused. You need

someone to blame. So you keep coming back to me." I gazed at them. "How long until I give up?"

Student teacher does not handle apathy well.

"I'm sorry that you're bored. I am. I love this stuff, and I want you to enjoy it. I want you to succeed. This goes beyond preparing you for college. I'm trying to prepare you for life.

"I get it. You're bored. You think reading sucks. You think writing sucks. You think this class sucks. You think I suck. But maybe if you took a step back and looked at it differently, you'd see that it's not as boring as you think it is.

"Maybe, just maybe if you tried to think about what we read and apply it to your life, you'd see a connection. And maybe, just maybe if you did that, you'd find something in these lessons for you.

"I want this class to be amazing, but I refuse to spend hours and hours of my time if you aren't willing to do the work. If you show me that you care and that you'll try, then I'll do everything I can to make this class more enjoyable. If you won't, then why would I spend hours coming up with ideas that you're only going to ignore?

"You need to care about your education and your future. Otherwise, no matter what I do, you'll always end up bored. The choice is yours."

CHAPTER SIXTEEN

Broadway Productions

"Mister, do we really have to act?" Carl asked.

"Yup. Today's the day."

"Ugh." He pouted and walked away. "This is supposed to be an English class."

"Oh come on," I said. "This is much better than tests. And it's *Hamlet*. You have to act out *Hamlet*. It's not meant to be read like a novel."

"Whatever, Mister."

I was actually excited. It was World Literature, a pause in the chaos. There were only a few juniors in the class, the rest were seniors. This meant that there were no freshman shenanigans to worry about.

"I had a question first," Olivia asked. I was walking over to take a seat at the back of the class. The bell had just rung.

"What's up?" I plopped down on top of the desk and surveyed the room. There were only about twenty students in the class.

"Polonius…is he for real? He seems like kind of a joke."

"His character is ironic. Think of him as your naïve uncle that talks constantly but doesn't listen to any of the advice he gives."

"Oh, so that's why he rambles on about a bunch of bullshit?" Olivia asked.

"Pretty much. He's a blowhard."

"A what?" Her eyes widened.

"A blowhard," I said again, checking attendance with ticks on my clipboard.

"Blow-heart?"

"No. Blowhard," I spelled it out.

"Blow…hard," she repeated slowly, trying not to laugh.

"Is that how you like it, Mister?" Corey asked.

"That's how your mom does it," Solomon yelled across the class.

"Oh snap," Olivia said.

"Corey…not appropriate. Solomon, the freshmen usually don't show up until next period. You're early." I tried to regain composure, my face still warm. "It's a word. One word. All together. It means someone who talks and brags a lot." I let out a heavy sigh.

"I'll just google it."

"No!" I said a little too loud. "Just use a dictionary."

"Google image it?" Solomon asked.

"Oh god," I said with a laugh. "Do what you will with your free time. You guys are terrible. Aren't you supposed to be juniors and seniors?" I finished attendance. "Who's ready to act?"

"Can we skip acting and keep embarrassing you?" Solomon asked. "This is fun."

I rolled my eyes. "I'm thinking a solid 'no' on that one. It's your turn to be embarrassed. Who's first?"

Our "stage" was really just the space in the middle of the class between the five columns of desks (three deep) that faced each other on either side of my room. I managed to push the giant metal cart into a corner.

"Which one of you blowhards wants to go first?" Solomon

asked.

"And you say you never learn anything in school," I said.

"Alright, blowhards. Let's do this," Corey said, standing up. I was unnerved by him volunteering. The kid wasn't going to pass the class. Not because he wasn't smart, he just never did anything, but I wasn't going to keep him from trying. I kept my mouth shut and watched him lead his team to the "stage".

Corey limped up with his foot in a brace. Candice followed with her punk rock swagger. Solomon threw back his long, dirty blonde hair and skipped up to the front.

It was an interesting group, a party boy, a philanderer, and a girl who had been forced to switch schools.

It started out simply enough. Solomon was Hamlet, crying about the loss of his father to Candice, his mother, who patted him on the back while trying not to laugh. "It's going to be okay," she said between awkward pats. It looked like she was trying to save him from choking but in slow motion. They were all wearing black, not for the sake of costumes, but because that's how they usually dressed.

Corey staggered towards Solomon and said, "What's up, son? Why you crying like a bitch?"

"You're not my father!" Solomon replied.

"I don't know about that. I fucked your mom last night. That basically makes me yo daddy."

"What?" Solomon pretended to be mortified.

"I fucked your mother. Last night. You didn't hear the bed shaking? The moaning? You know what they say, 'when the castle's a rock'n don't come a knock'n.' Oh come on, I know we were loud. The guards started banging on the door because they hadn't heard screams like that since we took Norway. She's a screamer, your mother. Yup. I hit that harder than a castle siege. Again and again and again. She can't get enough. Guess what I was doing this morning? Fucking your mother. You know what I'm gonna do tonight? Fuck your mother. And if there's time after lunch, I'll be fucking your mother. Face it. I'm your daddy now, son."

It was ridiculous. I was laughing. I shouldn't have been, but I was.

Solomon howled in grief, "Why!?"

Candice put her hands up in the air. "Scene."

I was trying not to laugh, but it was too much.

"You okay over there?" Olivia asked.

"That was, uh," I chuckled, "pretty accurate."

If you're wondering why I wasn't as harsh on them as I was on my freshmen, it's because they weren't freshmen. These kids had already failed at least one semester of English. That class was there to help them graduate. They all hated reading, but at least this way they were getting some exposure to it and having fun. It was my one chill class. No tests. No major writing projects. No drilling over the basics. My only goal was to make literature enjoyable for them. I hoped that at the very least they could leave school thinking that books weren't that bad. If they at least tried, I was happy.

"Well, that covers that. Solid effort. *A+*." They celebrated. It would be the only assignment some of them did all quarter.

The next group consisted of three girls that mumbled through their scene in a confused mess.

"Umm...that was the...best thing I've ever uh...yeah," I said over the uneven, lackluster clapping.

"You're such an asshole," Victoria said.

"Yup," I shrugged.

"What was our grade?" she asked.

"Next?"

"Our grade?" another asked.

"Who's next?" I repeated.

She called me an *asshole* under her breath a second time.

Miller stood up, "I'm ready, Mister.

134

"Where's your group?"

"It's just me."

"Impressive," I said. "We're ready when you are."

He crept to the front of the class. And for a moment, I was worried that he would freak out because he seemed so nervous. But he took a deep breath and said, "I'll be doing the scene where Hamlet talks to his mother about how sad he feels."

Once I said "action," his entire presence changed.

He walked around the room talking about his feelings, "Mom…my pain is so dark, so deep that I cannot express it to you. I—" he paused "—I wish you could understand the loss I feel in my heart, in my soul…

"You think these clothes reflect my feelings in their blackness? No. They don't touch on the iceberg of my pain. I've hidden away so much."

The class was quiet, drawn in. He continued, his shy facade fading away with every line he uttered. "You think a pathetic absence of color could possibly illustrate my feelings? *No.* It's only a fraction of the complete oblivion and dark expanse of my soul. If only you knew, if only you could understand the true extent of my pain, the pain I feel for the death of my father."

He went deeper into the role, and for a moment it was like I was watching someone on a real stage. "I just want to stop it all! I want to blow myself!" He stopped suddenly.

Laughter erupted.

"I meant," he stammered, his eyes wide, "I meant 'blow my head off!'"

But it was too late. Everyone was roaring.

"Blow yourself!" Solomon said.

"I meant blow my head off…I…" He put his hands to his head. "I'm so sorry."

I leaned back in the desk and crossed my arms, shaking my

head. He had done really well until the end.

He called, "scene," then went back to his seat and stared at his desk, avoiding eye contact while stifling laughs.

The comments tapered off until the room slowly returned to mostly normal.

"Looks like we got ourselves a blowhard here," Corey said into the silence, and everyone started laughing again.

Eventually, the laughter faded and the room again quieted down. The class turned to me, waiting.

"Do you have to ask? *A+* for effort," I said. "Shakespeare would've been blown away."

CHAPTER SEVENTEEN

Nemesis

"Malcolm, stop flirting. Start reading," I said from my desk, the coffee taking longer to kick in than normal that morning.

It was a Thursday, and every Thursday was "Study Hall" for the eighth-graders in my Advisory. We were supposed to have planned activities, key word being "supposed." I used it to mentally prepare myself for the day while hoping no one would talk to me until "real school" started.

If you haven't heard of Advisory, then you're lucky. In short, it's a complete fucking waste of time. It was a class that wasn't a class; think homeroom, but more of a waste of time. And we started every day with one.

Malcolm pulled out a book from his backpack. But instead of reading it, he held it like a safety blanket in front of his chest and leaned forward on it.

"No. You need to be reading," I said again.

"I am reading," Malcolm said, leaning back to show me that he had his book in his hands.

"Have you ever used one of those before?" I asked.

"Yeah."

"Typically, they're supposed to be opened first."

"Oh yeah," he laughed to himself and then opened the

book.

"No. Not randomly in the middle. Usually, it's good to start on the first page."

With attitude, he flipped to the beginning of the book.

"It's upside down," I said. "Is this a first for you?"

He rolled his eyes. "I hate reading, Mister."

"Maybe if you pretend to flirt with it, it'll be more enjoyable."

He sighed, kicked his feet, and dropped the book on the desk. "This sucks."

"You're going to hate me when I teach you next year," I said. I didn't teach him during the day. He was one of Wilson's eighth-graders.

"I won't be here next year," he said.

I wanted to say something biting back like, "don't get my hopes up," but instead I took a swig of coffee and stared back at my computer.

You're probably wondering where I'm going with this. Maybe you're thinking, "we get it. the kids didn't like reading, they were a challenge; move on already." Well, there's a perfectly good reason for this chapter…

Suddenly, Nemesis walked into my class.

There it is.

"What are you doing here?" I asked. "You're supposed to be in your Advisory. You don't have me till Period Nine."

The kid limped to the back of the class and grabbed one of my markers. I cringed. I hated when the students touched my markers. That's how "artwork" ended up on the whiteboards.

The kid wrote, "Nemesis is Mister's frind" on the board in the back.

"Friend?" I suggested.

"Yeah. You like it?"

"Friend has an 'e' in it," Malcolm said.

"I know," Nemesis said. "I was testing you, duh."

The kid corrected it, then limped over to my desk, and stood right next to me. Loud hip-hop music blared through one free headphone that dangled over the kid's shoulder. The other was plugged into the kid's ear and fueled the bizarre and uncomfortably close gyrations.

"Can I help you?" Still tucked into my desk, I leaned away.

The kid was already famous at the school after several trips to the office, meetings with parents and teachers, and a day spent under the constant supervision of the principal. The limp didn't help. I didn't know if that was what made Nemesis act out or if it was the other way around.

My students were a lot of things: lazy, unmotivated, ill-read, probably diabetic (a result of dumping 7-Eleven nacho cheese into a bag of hot Cheetos for lunch every day), but they weren't bullies. Wilson explained to me that the community was very closely connected and accepting. The school had its share of kids with hygiene issues, mental deficiencies, and alternative lifestyle choices that would have been targeted at a typical suburban school. And I had prepared myself for potential bullying, but nothing ever happened.

Except with Nemesis.

It was like the kid wanted to be isolated. Nemesis constantly acted out, and the other students would talk. The stories kept piling up.

"Nemesis, can you back up a little bit?" I asked calmly. Goosebumps spread uncomfortably over my skin.

"Hey. Hey," Nemesis said. Not moving. Still dancing.

I leaned further away towards the wall. "Why are you here? You don't have my class till the end of the day."

"Good morning, Mister. You're my favorite teacher. You know that?"

"Um, thanks. But you got to get to class," I said.

"OMG. I was talking to my..." Nemesis began to talk about

whatever dramatic situation the kid currently had been experiencing. I tried not to pay attention. I never asked my students about their personal lives. There were nosey teachers, teachers who thrived off teen drama like they were watching Spanish novellas. I preferred not to know.

I needed the kid to leave, but I had to be careful. Nemesis was known to unravel into a kaleidoscope of vitriol when teachers approached sternly. The kid would explode on staff when they tried to reinforce normal expectations. Nemesis created problems. I wanted to avoid problems. So, I did what I could to avoid the kid. I was patient, understanding, and I let a lot of stuff slide. Wilson had told me to pick my battles, and in this case, I listened. Instead of pushing the issue, I hoped the kid would grow bored and leave.

Admittedly, I was also slightly afraid.

Nemesis continued to talk.

"And like this nigga comes up to me…"

"Excuse me?" I said in shock.

"Nah, Mister. It's cool. I'm black."

"I would appreciate it if you'd refrained from that word," I said. The kid was unfazed; the kid was also not black.

The longer Nemesis talked, the less I paid attention. All I wanted to do was update my grade book. Instead, I imagined walking out of my classroom and onto the soccer field behind the school. I pictured finding a place on the slightly frozen field to kneel down and pull out an old sacrificial blade. I imagined the blade glistening in the sun as I held it in front of me with extended arms before suddenly slamming it into my chest, gutting myself in a plume of steam as my organs exhaled into the chilly, morning air. I saw the blood from my gaping wound gushing out over the frozen blades of grass, dyeing the field a darker shade of red as I paid my entry fee into the sweet release of death.

"What do you think, Mister?" the kid asked me.

"I'm sorry, what?"

"Were you even listening to me?" Nemesis's mouth dropped open.

"Of course I was. I've been sitting here the whole time."

The kid smiled. "Duh. I knew you were. I was testing you. I asked you if I can stay in your advisory?" More awkward dance moves. Too close. No sense of personal space.

Uncontrollably, my whole body shivered the way it does when you see someone's teeth scrape against a fork. I pushed out of my hard plastic chair and walked to the back board, pretending to be busy.

"Are you cold mister?" More dancing.

"No."

"Can I stay?"

"Unfortunately, that's not allowed," I said.

"Come on, please! Mister!" The kid pouted.

"This isn't your class right now. If you stayed, I would get in trouble. Big trouble."

"Oh, darn. One of these days I'm going to stay in here all day. You'd like that, wouldn't you?"

I forced a laugh, "You wouldn't want to be in here all day. There's a lot of reading."

"I don't mind. I love reading."

"You gotta go," I said. "I'm sorry. I'll see you in class later, okay?"

"Fine," the kid said. "See you later, Mister."

Nemesis slowly limp-danced towards the door. I waited. When the kid finally reached the door, *they* bowed and nearly screamed, "Bye-bye!" before limping away.

Malcolm started giggling to himself; he slapped Larry in the chest and said something.

They started whispering.

"ENOUGH!" I shouted.

"You heard me?" Larry said.

Viktor James

"Of course I heard you. I'm not deaf."

CHAPTER EIGHTEEN

A Striking Feature

I was skimming over an email about something that had gone down with Nemesis while Period Eight worked on their journals. People were nearing the end of their patience, both students and staff. The school psychologist wanted to try a system she created to help deter the bad behaviors. I was in the process of trying to understand how much extra work that would entail when Kiera spoke out in frustration.

"I don't get the journal."

"You what?" I turned in my chair to look at her.

"The journal doesn't make sense."

"Did you understand it when class began five minutes ago?"

"No. Why would I understand it then and not understand it now?"

"Why would you wait so long to ask for help?"

"I forgot."

"Forgot what?"

"To ask for help."

"*Right.*" I closed out of my email. "It says, 'Why do you think Frankenstein had a mental breakdown? What do you think the consequences will be? Be specific.' Think about what Frankenstein has experienced, all the traumatic and stressful events. That's where you start. And then from that, try to predict what will happen to him. Does that help?"

"Oh, okay."

"Next time you don't understand, ask me. Don't waste time. I'm here to help."

"Okay, Mister." She went back to work.

I began to walk around and inspect what they had written.

Less than a minute later Kiera asked, "I still don't get the journal?"

"Was that a statement or a question?" I asked.

"What?" She pushed her lip up with a pen and gazed blankly at me.

"Oh my god. He just explained it," Emily said.

"Shut up," she said.

"No, you shut up," Emily replied. "You should have paid attention, dumbass."

"I wasn't." She laughed.

Emily shrugged her shoulders.

"You want to explain it to her, Emily?" I suggested.

"Sure. So, you remember that like Frankenstein is tripping out because of how ugly his creature is? And like his mom has died. And he basically has no friends and just spent his whole life trying to make this monster, but he didn't really want it to be a monster, and so now he's dealing with that and freaking out. You gotta like look at all that stuff and then try to figure out what'll happen. Like, imagine what would happen next if you were Frankenstein."

"But I'm not the Frankenstein," she said.

Emily replied, "Ugh! Pretend, dumbass! Mister, I don't understand how you do this."

"I drink regularly."

"Why don't you pretend to be the Frankenstein," Kiera replied.

"I did, dumbass. That's why I'm writing, and you're confused."

"You already are the Frankenstein," she said.

She kept saying "the Frankenstein" for some reason.

"What are you talking about?"

"I'm not stupid. I know you're just trying to get me to act all..." She held her hands out like a zombie. She had a piece of red licorice in her hand that she bit into after she finished her pantomime.

"What are you talking about?" Emily asked. "That's the creature, dumbass. The creature isn't Frankenstein. Have you even been paying attention?" She rolled her eyes.

I looked at the two girls. "You sure you two are friends?"

"Yup," Kiera said, gnawing on another piece of licorice.

"Even though she's basically an idiot," Emily said.

"You love me. Want some licorice?"

"Hand it over, dumbass," Emily said.

Kiera zombie walked over to Emily and handed her some licorice, "Look, I'm the Frankenstein." She mimicked the monster from the movies.

Emily facepalmed with the red twirl in her hand, "Really?"

"I meant the creature. I meant the creature!" She started laughing at herself and sat down.

"I think we're done with the journal," I said. I sat on an empty desk beneath blasting cold air that was for some reason being pumped into my room even though it was freezing outside. I shivered and began. "Where are we? Frankenstein's freaking out. He's in total meltdown mode. Right?"

"Cause he's a lil bitch," David said.

"Yeah," Kiera said between bites of her burrito. "Why he would run away from his creation? What an idiot." Part of the tortilla was dangling from her mouth.

"Where did you get a burrito from?" I asked.

"It was in my purse. You want one?"

"You have another burrito in your purse...never mind. I'm good, thank you. So, Frankenstein doesn't handle the whole parenting thing very well. Can you blame him?" I walked past Kiera's desk and picked up the aluminum foil wrapper that had fallen to the floor.

"Thanks, Mister!" she said, her mouth half-full of the burrito still.

"No worries." I rolled it into a ball and tossed it back in forth in my hands.

"He sat there and made the damn thing. He should take care of it, not run away," Emily said.

"He's a little bitch," David chimed.

"Let's make predictions. The idea here isn't just to read the book like a robot. We want to be involved. Remember, we're approaching the story like a crime scene. We want to figure things out before the author tells us. The clues are all here on these pages. The more we pay attention, the more we can figure out before we're told. It'll help us process the story better, and it makes reading more interesting. So, what do you think'll happen?"

"Frankenstein's gonna kill himself," David said, looking up from coloring on his shoe, clothes still draping, hair still a mess.

"Why do you think that?"

"Because he's all like depressed and shit. His butt buddy Henry has to hide all the sharp things from him 'cause he's like freaking out and seeing shit."

"Okay. Write it down. Exactly like you just told me."

"For real?" He looked up at me.

"Yeah. They're your notes. Not mine."

"But you grade them."

"I do. And I look to see that you're trying to think about the book. Write it down in a way that'll help you. I'm not going to take points off if you curse in your notes. You should see my notes from college. Good ideas. Write it down. What else? What about the creature?"

Silence.

"Come on. Picture it." More silence. "Let's try this. Um. I need a volunteer. Mario?" He looked up at me and shook his head slowly in a way that said, *do not fuck with me today*. "Um, Selena?" I had taught her when I had subbed at the beginning of my first year. I figured I could leverage that to get her to volunteer.

Her head tilted with this *"really?"* look on her scrunched up face.

"Come on," I pleaded.

I set the aluminum foil ball down on one of the empty desks and said, "stand here."

"You asked Mario to volunteer first. He should do it," she said.

"He's having a bad day. Just trust me on this. It'll be quick and painless."

She reluctantly gave in and hunched over to where I asked her to stand, hugging herself.

"Okay, pretend she's my daughter," I said to the class.

"Ew," she said.

"You keep talking like that and you're grounded," I said.

"Uh…whatever, Mister," Selena rolled her eyes.

"Don't give me any attitude!"

"Pfft. Whatever." She flung one side of her neatly parted hair over her shoulder. "How about *you* don't give me any attitude?"

"Too real," I said.

"What?" She smiled awkwardly exposing braces.

"Never mind. I need you to act like you're excited to see me. Be like, 'Hey, Dad!'"

"That's weird…"

"Trust me. It's way weirder for me. I am way too young to have a daughter your age."

"But you're like forty," Selena said.

"You just failed for the semester."

"I didn't mean it!"

"And I'm twenty-freaking-seven."

"Your hairline says otherwise," Mario added.

"You want to volunteer?" I asked. He shook his head. "And that's because I spend forty hours a week around you guys."

"Can we hurry this up?" Selena asked.

"Okay, so you're my kid, and you're acting surprised to see me. Go!" I said.

"Uh…" She hesitated. "Hi…Dad?"

"But with your arms out! Pretend to be nice. Act like you're about to ask me to go out with your friends even though you're grounded because you failed English," I said.

"Rude," she said. With reluctance she opened her arms and shouted, "Dad!" and took a step towards me.

I screamed instantly, "EW! GROSS! GET AWAY FROM ME!" and ran from the room. I tried to slam the door behind me, but it was on a pneumonic lift, so instead, it closed slowly as I tugged on it, awkwardly trying to speed it up.

The door finally clicked shut.

Out of the corner of my eye, I saw Nimitz standing with his thermos, an eyebrow raised at me, "How's it going?"

"Good. In the middle of a lesson," I said, "trying to make a point."

He nodded and turned back to talk to Wilson in the hall. I burst back through the door. Selena was still standing awkwardly in the middle of the classroom where I left her. "Now, imagine what it must feel like to be the creature. As soon as the creature was born, he reached out to his creator, and Frankenstein just ran away. The creature had no one to

148

prepare him for the world. Selena's had years to deal with being a monster. No big deal for her," I joked.

"Rude!" she said again.

"You're a natural," I told her. "Good job."

"Really, Mister?" She rolled her eyes, kept her arms crossed, and said, "Whatever."

"You can stop acting now," I said.

She stuck a palm out at me as she turned towards her desk and sat down.

"Thanks for volunteering," I said.

"What!? You made me!"

"That's not how I remember it. Is that how you remember it, Cesar?"

"No, Mister. The way I remember it, she said, 'I want to be the monster. I think I'm a natural.' And I'm sittin' here thinking, that's a little weird, but mad respect to you for helping her live her dreams."

"I will cut you," she said to Cesar.

"Loser," Mario scoffed.

"You're the loser! I only had to do it because you were too chicken to go up there," she said.

"I wasn't chicken. I just had a headache," he said and mimicked his head hurting. "Ow."

"A headache my ass," she said. "I hate you both."

"I want you all to imagine experiencing what Selena just acted out. Imagine you walk home, open the door, and see your parents. You try to hug them and—"

"Pfft, my parents don't hug me," Mario said.

"He said to pretend, nigga," Cesar said.

I kept going. "And you go to hug them, and they freak out. They start calling you a monster, telling you that you're ugly, yelling at you that they wished you'd never been born. What do you think your reaction would be?"

"That would fucking suck," Kiera said as she opened a bag

of chips.

"That would be awful," Emily agreed.

"That monster gonna kill some shit," Cesar said.

"Mister, is that what it was like for you growing up?" Helen asked.

"Oh, burn!" Cesar said. "Someone needs to go to the nurse and get this man some ice."

"Ouch," I laughed.

"Just kidding, Mister. Don't fail me. But seriously, why does he run away?" Helen asked. "I mean, Frankenstein knew what he was making all that time. He couldn't look down and be like, 'damn, that's ugly?'"

"It's 'cause it smelt like fish. You know, 'cause he was just born. Get it?" said Zac.

"Ew. You're fucking gross." Emily said. "He didn't come out of anyone. Why would he smell like that, dumbass?"

"Your mom smells like fish," Kiera said, giggling as she bit into a cracker.

"Where did you get crackers from?" I asked her. The chips were nowhere in sight.

"My purse. You want one?" She offered me the roll.

"But you have…chips? Where did the burrito go?" I asked.

"It's still in there," she said with crumbs falling out of her open mouth.

"I am so confused. Anyways, Frankenstein runs away from the creature because it's hideous. He's terrified."

"I still don't get why he would make him so ugly if he would be afraid of it," Helen said.

"He didn't want it to be ugly," Kiera said, still spurting out crackers. "He was just like really into what he was doing. He was like obsessed. Right? He didn't see what he had done until the creature was alive and then he like freaked out."

"Did you just actually make sense for once?" Emily asked.

"I'm not an idiot."

"You're dropping crackers," I said.

"Coulda fooled me," Emily said.

"Burnnnnn," Cesar added.

"Anyways…then what happens?" I asked.

"You must poop all the time. Like massive dumps," David said.

"*David*," I said.

"What, Mister? She eats constantly."

"She does take big nasty dumps," Emily said.

Kiera sprayed crackers in a fit of laughter and started coughing. I got worried for a second. "Oh, please don't die. I don't want to clean up that mess."

"I do *not* take big nasty dumps! I just have a fast metabolism!" She looked down at all the crumbs that covered her desk, hoodie, and notebook. "I almost choked to death. Give me some of your water."

Emily walked over to her and handed her a water bottle. "Don't put your mouth on it. I don't want your germs."

"Back to the question," I said. "You see…wait. What were we talking about?"

"The creature runs after Victor. Victor runs away. He freaks out. Butt buddy has to take care of him. Kiera takes fat, nasty dumps," David said.

"I do not!"

"Oh. Predictions. What do you think happened to the creature?" I asked.

"I dunno," David said.

"Does he have clothes?" Kiera asked.

"It doesn't say," I said.

"Where did he go?" Helen asked.

"Think about it. Where would he go?"

Silence.

"He definitely stands out in a crowd. What's the first thing people would notice about him?"

Suddenly, without hesitation and with a great deal of pride, Kiera yelled, "His balls!" A perplexed look crept over her face as she slowly realized that something about her answer was off, "Oh wait..."

"What *the* fuck? You're too stupid," Emily said.

"His...what?" I tried to process, "Wait. Why would—"

"Cause, he's like naked..." she said, giggling. She stuffed a few chips into her mouth as if it would save her from answering any more embarrassing questions.

I shook my head. "No. No. Someone step in, and save Kiera here. What's his most noticeable feature...aside from... that?"

"He's huge. He's like tall and has muscles," Emily said. She looked to her friend. "His balls? You're too stupid."

"I dunno." Kiera was snickering.

"This is what I want you to do: think about the creature's reaction. Where will he go? What will he do? Take a minute to write down your predictions."

As they began to write, I picked up the aluminum foil ball I had set on the desk and bounced it off Kiera's head.

"Hey!" she said.

"Really?" I said, shaking my head.

CHAPTER NINETEEN

Period Nine

It was Period Nine, the last obstacle before the break. I've been putting off talking about them. No other class perfectly encapsulated my failure as a teacher more than the one that took up those final fifty minutes of every day.

Attendance was quick. A third of my class was missing. I felt relief ooze over me. It wasn't the best reaction for a teacher to have.

I wanted the day to be over.

"Are we reading again?"

There were exasperated sighs.

"I thought we finished yesterday," Ricky whined, poking his firm hair spikes into his large arm.

"You finished chapter five yesterday."

"I knew we finished it," Ricky said, still playing with his hair. "Where's Kate? I need Kate!"

"You'll survive," I said. "We finished chapter five. The other classes are almost to chapter ten. And no, we're not done, not even close. There's like thirty chapters."

"I'm sick of reading," Ricky continued to whine, placing his head on a palm. With his jellied fingers, he continued to play with the spikes on his head. "It's all we do."

"We aren't reading today," I said. I wasn't about to spend the last hour before the break trying to get them to read. I needed to survive until 3:20 p.m.

That was my only goal.

"We're not?" His head shot up. "Yes! What are we doing?"

"Movie?" Justin grinned.

"No. When will you all tire of asking me that question? We're working on the Imagery Assignment."

"Ugh," Justin moaned and leaned back in his chair like someone had just shot him.

"You do realize that it's mostly coloring a picture?"

"But there's writing too," Ricky whined.

The kids who barely spoke English sat off in a group by themselves. They looked around trying to figure out what was happening. One kid shrugged to the others.

"It's a paragraph," I said. "One. Single. Paragraph."

"One paragraph too many," he said.

I rolled my eyes. "Get out any work you completed on the Imagery Assignment. Most of you started on Wednesday. Some of you left yours in here; I put them on the table in the front. Hunter, can you please translate that for them?"

"Sure," he said. While he was often late, did very little work, and was probably stoned most classes, he didn't mind translating for me.

"Where's Ms. Perón?" Emma asked.

"She's been in meetings all day," I said. "She should be back after the break."

"That's not what I heard," Ricky said.

"It doesn't matter what you heard. That's where she is." I had been shutting down rumors all day.

Ted said something in Spanish.

"I heard Nemesis accused Ms. Perón of —"

"Enough!" I glared at Ricky. "There's no place for that kind of talk in this class. You keep it up, and I'll send you to the office where you can find out for yourself. Or, you can get out your Imagery Assignment. If I were you—"

Suddenly Nemesis burst into the classroom with an exaggerated limp. "Mister," the kid said in a strange accent. "Sorry, I'm late. It's not my fault. They let us out late in P.E."

"No, they didn't," Ricky said. "I have P.E. with you."

"Uh, I got out late. Whatever. Mister, I need to go change; I'll be right back."

"You were supposed to change in class," Ricky said.

"The teacher wouldn't let me," Nemesis said.

"Liar," Ricky said.

"I was in the middle of teaching. Please, if you're late, try to enter quietly."

Ignoring me, Nemesis said, "I'm so tired from running around in P.E. I'm sweating." The kid began fanning away sweat with a hand. Someone said something in Spanish. Nemesis glared at them, then looked at me and said, "I'll be right back."

I waited for Nemesis to leave. I needed Perón there.

Nemesis whirled back into the class before the door fully closed and smiled. "Everyone. My new name is Fabulous. You have to call me that from now on."

"What the fuck?" someone murmured.

"Shut the fuck up," Ricky said.

"Seriously. My new name is Fabulous."

"Please, hurry up," I said.

Nemesis stood by the door, not moving. Waiting.

"Please," I cringed and felt death spread a little further over the remaining black shards of my soul as I said, "please, hurry up...*Fabulous*."

"I'll try," the kid said, leaving.

Had Perón been there, she would have worked her magic and taken care of Nemesis. I needed her in Period Nine. Say what you will about special education teachers. They're a bit quirky, blunt, and at times, oppressively obstinate. But, at the end of it all, they're fucking lifesavers. No way I could have done what Perón did on a daily basis. She essentially followed around Period Nine from class to class and kept them in line. At least, she had until recently.

Once the door closed, I went back to directing the class. "I want you all to be focused on—Justin, I'm talking. You need to make sure—" I stopped, glaring at him. "What you need to do is—Justin, can you give me like three minutes to go over a few things, then you can talk all you want. I know the break is almost here, and believe me, I want it just as badly as you do, probably more, but I need a minute to start class, then the rest of the time is yours."

"Yeah," he said, his mouth gaping like a fish tasting fresh air for the first time.

"Thank you. Please make sure you—Justin. Speaking in Spanish is still speaking," I said.

"I wasn't talking," he said.

"This is why it's bad to drink and do drugs during pregnancy," I said under my breath.

"Huh?" he stared at me.

"He just called you a crack baby," Ricky said.

"You're a fucking crack baby. Pinche Madre!" he said to Ricky.

"Speak English! No comprende, señor," Ricky mocked.

Justin fired something back in rapid Spanish.

"Justin. Please. Once I'm finished, you can have the whole class to talk. Fair?"

"Fine."

"Be sure to get—" He spoke again. "You know what? Fine. I don't even care. Figure out what you need to do on your own." I started laughing. "When you don't pass, make sure you switch schools because I don't want to teach you again next year. The rest of you, I'll come around and make sure you're on the right track. Get to work."

The door opened, causing me to shudder.

"Sorry, I'm late, Mister. I was in the nurse's office." Kate walked over and handed me a pass.

"No worries," I exhaled. "We just started."

The door nearly closed before it shot open again as an eighth-grader named Larry burst in and hurled a snowball right into Kate's face. She screamed instinctively. Snow fell from her as she surveyed the damage. She scooped up the snow from the carpet and took off after him. I followed, yelling for them to stop.

It was actually a quiet day for Period Nine.

It took a few minutes to sort it all out. I told Kate to go clean up. And then I turned to Larry and began to tear into the poor kid. I did the whole, "you could've blinded someone" gig. Nemesis zipped by us and went into my room.

Larry was supposed to be in Wilson's class. So when I was finished talking to him, I knocked on Wilson's door and told him what had happened. Wilson gave me a reassuring glance, and I left it at that.

I walked back into my classroom, picked up some resources I had printed off for them and began handing them out a little too heavily. Soon, Kate returned, her face still red from the impact, her hair matted wet. By the time I made it over to the other side of the room, Emma was quietly crying.

"What happened?"

She shook her head.

I asked again.

She mumbled, "Nothing."

"Fabulous was making fun of her," Ricky finally said.

"What?" I said.

"Fabulous called her retarded," Ricky said.

"And some other mean stuff." Kate reached forward and rubbed her on the back.

The headphones blared "S.O.S." as the kid danced and drew at the desk. I tried to get Nemesis's attention, but the only reaction was a tapping to increase the music's volume.

I couldn't understand how anyone could make Emma cry. She was a sweet, quiet girl.

"Nemesis. Nemesis. Nemesis!" No response. I walked over and made eye contact. Nothing. I reached forward and tugged the cord from one of the headphones. It hit the desk with a clank.

"Go outside," I said.

"What? Why?"

"You know why."

"I didn't do anything."

"Nemesis, you need to go outside. Now," I said.

"I'm not Nemesis! My name is Fabulous!" the kid nearly yelled. "I'm working. Leave me alone!"

"That's not even the assignment." I lost it. "That's a love letter. Stop what you're doing and get the hell out of my class before I call someone to take you out of here."

"I am working. This is for my new girlfriend," the kid said, bobbing around to the music, nearly unfazed.

"Stop and go outside." I was out of patience. I grabbed the letter from the kid's desk. Nemesis reached for it causing the paper to rip in half.

And I was glad. I had to try hard not to smile because I knew exactly what would happen next.

"NO!" Nemesis screamed at me. "You ripped it! That was for my girlfriend!" Then came the tears. And the screams. And the profanity. Lots of profanity.

"I'm going to call the office," I said.

"NO!" The kid stood up. "You niggas always comin' at me like I owe you somethin'. You all teaming up against me! All y'all! Fuck this. I'm done! Fuck you!"

Hunter was laughing, whether it was because he was

probably still high or because of what was happening, I wasn't sure, but Nemesis wasn't pleased. The kid picked up a pencil and threw it at his face. His reaction time, delayed for obvious reasons, caused him to jerk back seconds after the pencil cartwheeled towards the floor. "Ow! What the fuck!?"

Nemesis stormed out of class. I went to Hunter. "You okay? Are you bleeding?"

"Nah," he said, pulling his hand away. "That fucking hurt though."

A little red spot of blood formed from where the pencil had impacted his face.

"You're bleeding."

There was a loud crash from the door down the hall that led outside.

"Go to the bathroom and wash it," I said.

"Nah. I'm cool, Mister." He kept touching where the pencil struck him.

It took some time to calm down after I called the office to let them know what happened. Eventually, I walked over to the front table and grabbed another stack of packets. I also picked up the box of tissues. I passed the packets out. When I reached Emma, I handed her the tissues.

"Really, Mister?" Ricky said, eyeing the packets in my hands.

"Relax. It's the SparkNotes." I had stooped that low. "You don't have to read it. It's just something to help you out if you get confused."

The phone rang to let me know that the office had Nemesis. They also wanted me to send Hunter and email a report. *Great, more paperwork.* Hunter pleaded to stay, his bloodshot eyes looking for clemency. "You're not actually in trouble," I said.

"I'm fine, Mister."

"You just caught a pencil with your face. Go to the office

and have a nurse look at you. Tell them what happened."

To make sure the kid gets suspended, I thought.

He rolled his eyes, then grabbed his stuff and sulked away.

I was halfway through the incident report when I noticed Justin had nothing out in front of him. All the papers I had just handed him were underneath his desk, and he was murmuring to his friend.

I listened.

When I said there was no bullying at the school, I may have lied a little bit. There was some. Some students had been teasing a new kid, Carlos. Last week, while he was sitting at his desk, someone tossed an open condom in his hoodie. When he had gone to pull the hood up, it had fallen on his head.

No one knew how it got there, so nothing came from it except a lecture.

I finished the email and clicked "send." Then I continued to listen.

Justin leaned over to Ted and was whispering about Carlos in English. The kid whispered about as well as he followed directions. From the other side of the room I heard him say, "He likes big, hard meat. Cock sucking faggot."

Carlos looked around and smiled, trying to understand the words.

"Justin, grab your things. Now! You're sitting next to me for the rest of class."

"Nah," he said.

"Let me rephrase that. You need to move *now*. I'm not giving you a choice," I said, nearly yelling.

"Nah. That's okay. I'm not feelin' it."

"Do you think I care? I'm not asking."

"What? Are you going to make me move?" He laughed.

I banged my hand on the desk. "I'm *not* giving you an option!"

160

"I'm fine right here," he said, cool as ever. "And making me sit next to you is kinda weird. I'm not really into that."

At that point, rage flooded my mind. I wanted to say things that would make the kid crumble; I wanted to break him in front of everyone. I wanted them all to see that cocky smile fade into streaming tears. Instead, I walked over to him. I put my shaking hand in the middle of his desk and leaned forward until I was only a few inches from him, glaring at him.

He leaned back.

I leaned closer and nearly whispering said, "Would you prefer I call the principal and your parents and tell them you called a student a 'fucking faggot?' Do we need *another* meeting? I'm sure your father will *love* that." His eyes widened. "That's what I thought. Now move."

Huffing and puffing, he took his things and moved seats.

The rest of the class was uneventful. Justin stayed mostly quiet, though it didn't stop him from occasionally making faces at his friends and shouting an obscenity or two in Spanish. Very few people colored or drew. A ding from my computer notified me that they had suspended Nemesis for the week after the break. And Emma regained composure enough for me to take the box of tissue back. I patted her on the shoulder and gave her a slight smile.

Then the bell rang, and I let them go.

Just another day in Period Nine.

"Carlos," I beckoned for him to come over. I called Kate over as well.

"What's up, Mister?" she asked.

"Can you tell Carlos that if anyone gives him any problems to let me know, and I'll handle it?"

"Okay," she said and spoke to him in Spanish. He thanked me, then gripped the straps of his backpack, pulled them tight, and left.

I hid in my room cleaning rather than performing the required hall duty. I picked up the remnants of wrappers, papers, and the occasional pen that had found its way to the floor. Cleaning up after them annoyed me, but it was better than dealing with more students.

Once I was sure they were all gone, I strolled out of my room and walked down toward the open doors at the end of the hall. I stood there watching the trailing exodus over the snowy field as the cold air chilled the building.

Looking out at the sea of trailing backpacks and black hoodies kicking up the fresh powder, I sighed audibly. It was time for Thanksgiving break.

The teacher next to me turned away from the door and walked down the hall shouting, "I made it through the week without killing anyone!"

CHAPTER TWENTY

Shit-Talking

I had fucked up. Big time.

The moment I opened the door to the annex, a group of eighth-graders swarmed me, shouting at me. I tried to ignore them, pushing passed and nodding as I moved to unlock my door.

I set my stuff down on my desk, turned around, and said, "Alright, alright, let me have it."

I hung my head in shame.

Ellen stood proudly in her Patriot's jersey, grinning. "Why are you here? I thought you said you were going to move to Canada if the Broncos lost."

"I'm making arrangements as we speak." I took off my coat and shook my head. "That game was garbage and you know it. We were so close." Some Thanksgiving that had been, screaming at Manning as the Broncos lost...to *them*.

Ellen laughed. "Go, Patriots!"

"This is what I get for talking crap." Hating on the Patriots had turned into my Monday morning M.O.

Let me back up and say that while I was struggling with my ninth grade classes, eighth grade was a lot more chill. They were learning that if they wanted to avoid work on a

Monday, they just needed to ask questions about football. I was often too hungover on Monday morning to protest.

"You're in the wrong part of the country to root for the Broncos," Ellen said.

"Pretty sure jerseys aren't part of dress code," I joked.

"Whatever, Mister! We're allowed to wear them after game day. Duh!"

"Tom Brady? Really?" I rolled my eyes.

"He's the best!" She showed off the number. "When's your flight?" Ellen laughed. "Wait. Don't leave. Not yet. We need to make fun of you more and then you can go."

"This is going to be a long day."

Calvin walked through the eighth grade horde, wearing bright orange, and took a seat on a desk next to mine. He was one of the few ninth grade boys that spoke to me outside of class. I think the rest were too scared.

He waited until the haters pattered out and then said, "You watch the game?"

"Nice jersey," I said. "Finally some colors I respect. And yeah, I did. Sadly."

"We had them the entire first half."

"I think I lost my voice screaming at the TV. Now I get to deal with this. I should have called in sick today. Or maybe this week," I said.

"Don't worry, Mister. We'll get them next time."

"Definitely. How was your break?" I asked.

We talked about the holiday while I began to ease back into things.

After a week of waiting tables, finding a new place to live, buying a new car, and yes, finally, a new pair of shoes, I was ready to get back at it.

Until I remembered the test.

I knew it would be a disaster. I actually wanted not to do it. I hated tests, but they didn't give me a choice. It seemed to be the only way to get them to do anything. And I had to stick to my guns. I decided to make it incredibly easy. They had to read five chapters. The test was five questions, each one asking for a chapter summary. That was it.

How hard could that be? I thought.

I should have known better.

Someone yelled, "Go Patriots!" from the hall, and I turned to see another glint of a blue and silver.

Calvin was talking about his break when the light from my projector hissed and popped.

Calvin paused. "Did the bulb just go out?"

"I think this piece of shit finally broke," I said, trying to turn it on and off.

"Like your heart did when the Broncos lost," Brutus said, standing at the door.

"I don't have a heart," I said. "The Patriots ripped it out during overtime."

"Is that why you're still single?" Brutus joked. His friends Alfred and Ezekiel looked astonished at the brazen nature of their friend.

I laughed it off, wanting to say something about his mother, but remembering where I was.

"Don't worry, Mister," he said in that thirteen-year-old, sure-of-himself way. "I'm sure there's a woman desperate enough to settle for you, a woman sad enough to like bald men."

Again, I thought of a joke about his mother; again, I refrained. "Kid's got jokes," I said to Calvin.

"Not very good ones. Why do you put up with that, Mister?"

"He's an eighth-grader." I paused. "They're…special."

"I was never rude like that."

"That's because you're an incredible kid."

Brutus laughed. "You know I'm just joking, Mister."

"Mister, did you watch the game?" Alfred appeared at his side. He paused after each word as if it were a sentence of its own.

"Did I watch the game? Alfred, we've been talking about it the whole time you've been standing there. Are you awake?"

"Yes. I am. Awake?" His eyes drifted away.

"You don't sound too sure," I said.

"Why are you a Broncos fan?" Ezekiel said from behind his friends.

"Because I love disappointment," I said.

"Is that because you're so used to it by now?" Brutus asked.

"Only from teaching," I said.

"Ouch," Calvin said.

"I'm joking," I smiled. "Somewhat."

"I'm ready for the test today, Mister," Calvin said.

I stuck out my fist, and he bumped it.

"I knew the Patriots would win," Alfred continued, unfazed. Robotic. "They are my team."

"How do you handle all that disappointment, Mister?" Brutus asked.

"Life is full of disappointment, then you die." I walked to the whiteboard in the back, forced to write the lesson down because the projector broke. "I didn't know you were a football fan. I thought you liked soccer?"

"I am a Patriots fan," Alfred almost seemed to ask.

"You don't sound too sure about that," I said. The kid probably couldn't name a single player on the team besides Brady. He was just there with his friends to annoy me.

Someone yelled, "Broncos suck" from the hall. I sighed, pulled out a red marker and wrote, "Talking about last week's game will result in an automatic 'Fail' for the year" on the board.

"Really, Mister?" Brutus asked.

"How was your break?" I asked, not caring.

"It was good. I played a lot of PlayStation."

That wasn't surprising.

"How was your break?" Alfred asked.

"It was good. I did some shopping, hung out with friends, and I bought a car."

"What was it? A '97? Can you even afford a car?" Brutus mocked.

"Shut up, stupid. Do you even have a car?" Calvin said, glaring at the kid.

"Surprising, isn't it?" I said to Brutus. "It's even a shiny one."

Brutus continued to tease, and I mostly ignored it.

"I gotta go before I'm late to class," Calvin said. "See you, Mister."

I nodded goodbye. As soon as Calvin left, Brutus, who was apparently too scared to say anything before, spoke up, "That kid thinks he's *so* cool. Mister, do you let him stay in here because it makes you feel like you have friends?"

"Brutus, chill out with the insults, man. I'm trying to be patient with you. But enough."

"Careful, careful," he taunted.

"You sound jealous," I said. "I'm sure some people enjoy being around you."

"Yeah. Your ex-girlfriend."

I looked at him. Rage burned for a second, but then I just let it go. It's a weird situation. You could talk shit back and easily "win," but what kind of victory is that? He was thirteen. Sometimes you just had to let shit slide.

They waited for a reaction.

"I get that you're trying to upset me. I'm not sure why. If there's something that's bothering you and you need to talk, please let me know. We're here to help you." I glared at Brutus.

"Alright. I get it," he teased. "I hurt your feelings. I'm sorry, Mister. Let's go so he can cry."

They moved out into the hall.

A few kids started pouring into my class for Advisory. Those who hadn't had the chance to talk crap about my team did so to pass the time until the bell rang.

Then we escorted our eighth-graders down into the main building and had our Community Meeting. Something we did every Monday morning. We packed all seventy of them into one room and tried to provide a sense of community while talking about current events and concerns. Wilson led the meetings. Another teacher and I kept the peace.

Wilson was berating their performance. "Your grades are falling. You only have three weeks left of the quarter before the break. You need to work harder." That was the mantra for this school.

Suddenly, it hit me. I had three weeks left to teach the novel. There was no way to finish *Frankenstein* in time.

"Go to the office! Now!" I heard Wilson yell, shaking me from my thoughts. "I have had enough of you three. I'm finished," he said. Then he looked at me, "Can you walk them down there?"

I led the boys into the hall, a little startled myself. Wilson could be terrifying if he wanted.

Once we were all outside, Brutus said, "I don't know what Mr. Wilson's problem is."

"We were just talking," Larry said.

"He's stupid," Ezekiel said.

"You disrespected him in there. How do you not see that? He's tired of it. That blows my mind considering all the extra work he does for you."

There was silence.

I continued as we walked down the hall and through the small cafeteria that bumped up against the main office. "He lets you keep your stuff in his room during lunch. He lends you books. He gave you all a soccer ball to use. The guy is after school every day tutoring you guys when you need it. And then you show up and run your mouths while he's trying to talk. I'm surprised he didn't yell at you sooner."

"You think we're all stupid," Ezekiel said.

I stopped.

"If I thought you were stupid, I wouldn't teach you. I'd leave. I'm not here to waste my time," I said, then kept walking toward the office. "You're not stupid. Don't get me wrong; you do a lot of dumb stuff that pisses me off. I'll admit that. I have a hard time understanding the culture here. You have people that care about you, but you push them away. It blows my mind."

"He just constantly talks. He's boring," Brutus said.

"He expects the best out of you. He keeps telling me that you guys are the best kids he's ever taught. I don't see it. But he's insistent. Then you act like this. You don't care. You're rude. You run your mouth. You piss him off." I opened the door to the main office and pointed at the chairs. The kids each found one.

I started to walk away, then stopped and turned around. "Stop hurting the people who care about you."

CHAPTER TWENTY-ONE

Lower Expectations

I was walking back from the printer in the main building when I saw Larry and Justin roughhousing in the doorway to the bathroom.

Larry popped out and said, "How's it going, Mister?"

"Where are you supposed to be?" I asked, trying to figure out what was happening.

"We have Art, Mister," Larry said, as if it mattered.

"You do. Justin is in the ninth grade. I imagine he has a different class."

"I was in P.E.," Justin said, appearing next to his friend.

"And now you're hanging out. In the bathroom. Together," I said.

"He was trying to wrestle me, Mister," Larry said.

"You're not helping your case," I said.

Justin pushed Larry's shoulder. "Shut up. You were trying to wrestle me."

"Wrestling..." I said.

"I was giving it to him, Mister. Hard," Larry said with a hearty giggle.

"WOAH! No. No. Just...go to class. I don't need to hear anymore," I said.

Justin's eyes widened. "Mister! Naw. Mister. Mister."
I started walking away.
"It ain't like that. We ain't gay."
I shook my head and held up a fist. "Stay proud."
"He just called you gay," I could hear Larry say.
"Nah, Mister. It's not like that," Justin shouted again.
"You're so gay," Larry laughed.
"No, you're gay," Justin said.
"You're gay," Larry continued to laugh.
"You're fucking gay," Justin said again.
"Quit flirting and get to class!" I yelled behind me.

You might be thinking, "why not take them to the office? Why not have them serve detention? Inaction only makes things worse!" Remember that a girl had threatened to stab Wilson with scissors and had returned to class after twenty minutes. Taking them to the office would have done nothing.

Wilson had said to pick my battles.

And I had shit to do.

When Period Four began, I was waiting with the tests while they found their seats. Students gloated over the Patriots victory. They tried to coax me into reminiscing over the Bronco's Thanksgiving failure. None of them seemed to notice my warning on the board in the back.

"As much..." I paused until they quieted down. "As much as I would love to continue having this conversation, you have a test today." There were groans.

"Oh shit. He was serious," Charles said.

"I hoped he'd forget," Bob said.

There were more curses and complaints.

"But before we get to that, first things first, I need your Imagery Assignments. Pass them up to the front row and then down to me please."

There was another general murmur of complaint.

I waited for them to sort all that out, and when there was a small stack of papers on either side of the room, I began passing out the test. "Put everything away except your notes, a sheet of paper, and a pen."

A general murmur rose.

"Do *not* write on my tests. This is a class set." I repeated the completely useless command. Useless because you know how that ended; people wrote all over them.

"Mister, I got this," Joaquín laughed.

"I'm sure you do," I said doubtfully.

Anita calmly put her things away and opened her notebook.

Jeff was already asleep. I placed a copy on his head.

"You have the whole class. It shouldn't take that long. It should be easy, as long as you did the reading," I said.

"I didn't fucking read," someone muttered.

"When you finish, continue reading. We'll review the chapters you read over the break tomorrow.

"Mister, I haven't read the chapters," Sallie said.

"Probably shouldn't tell me that." I went and sat at my desk, putting together lessons for the week while they struggled with the test.

Joaquín finished fast, Anita followed. The rest worked until the end. You could almost hear the kids racking their brains, trying to figure out how to answer. I couldn't help myself. I looked out at their frustrated faces and said, "Had you read, this would have been really, really easy." Some gave me scowls; a few put their heads down in exasperation.

"I need the tests and your answers before you leave," I said as the bell rang. "And if you haven't already, don't forget to turn in the Imagery Assignment!" I shouted over the sudden cacophony of students packing up.

I finally looked through the small stack of assignments that maybe seven kids had completed. Over twenty zeroes. In one class. On an assignment that mostly involved coloring.

When Period Nine staggered in, I had five more completed Imagery Assignments, and most of the tests I had glanced at were failures. I sputtered out the instructions one last time. Then, I handed out tests covered in scribbles. Some might have had answers on them at that point, but I didn't care. They could have used all the help they could get.

"Ugh. I don't want to do this," Ricky whined.

Justin said something in Spanish that I ignored.

Kate read over the test. "This is so hard, Mister."

Nearly everyone complained, except Emma. She thanked me and went to work.

Justin said something to Ted.

"There's a test out, Justin. If you speak, you'll get a zero, and I'll send you to the office."

With Nemesis gone for the week, I welcomed the silence that followed.

Hunter looked at the test, thought better, then put his pencil at the top of his desk and let it roll down towards him. Over and over again.

I watched Justin's struggle to sit still grow increasingly difficult. He started tapping out a beat. Our eyes locked and the beat grew louder as a smile widened on his face.

"Justin. Here. Now." I pointed to the desk next to mine. He didn't fight me this time. He just rose up, took his things, and scooted over.

"You left the test on your desk," I said.

"I'm done."

"We just started."

"I'm done."

Student teacher does not handle apathy well.

"Did you do the reading?"

He laughed.

"I know you didn't do the reading because you left all your papers in class before the break."

I thought back to a similar situation my previous year.

"I don't have the essay," he had said to me. I could see the tears building up in his eyes.

"It's worth a third of your grade," I had said.

"I'm sorry, Mister. I know. I know it's important. Please, give me an extension. If you don't, I can't play football."

I had hesitated before saying, "Okay. Get it to me when it's finished."

A few days had passed, and he still hadn't given me his essay. A week, two, nothing. On his way out the door, on the last day of the semester, I had stopped him and had asked if he had finished it.

He had laughed, "You didn't actually think I was going to do it, did you?"

"No," I had said. "I didn't."

"You didn't? But you still let me have the extension?"

"Yes."

"If you didn't think I was going to turn it in, why did you keep asking me? Just to annoy me?"

"No," I had said. "I had hoped I was wrong."

I sat the answer key down on Justin's desk along with his blank test. "Use this. If you at least try, you'll pass."

I went back to my desk and tried to figure out what to do with *Frankenstein* before winter break. I was still at a total loss when the final bell rang.

I thought about the day, all the assignments that weren't turned in, all the tests that would fail. I just sat there in my shitty plastic chair, trying to think of what to do. So many people were going to fail. So many. I wondered what Admin would think when I handed in zeroes for more than half my class.

Justin had left his test on the desk. I went over and picked it up. There was half a sentence on the paper. I crumpled it up and tossed it toward the trash. It missed and rested on the floor with some other garbage there.

Fitting.

Despite just finishing a week-long break, I was ready for another.

Wilson came into my room, "Everything okay?" Then he stopped and saw the massive space in the middle of my room. "Where'd your projector go?"

"It burnt out earlier today. Steven came and wheeled it away."

He looked at me. "You sure you're okay? You don't seem fine."

"No. We teach a bunch of..." I paused. "The tests were horrible. No one did the reading. I think maybe fifteen out of all my freshmen turned in an assignment that required them to draw. They don't give a fuck. And if they don't give a fuck, why should I?"

He smiled.

"What?"

"Fifteen of them did it?" he asked.

"Yeah, something like that."

"That's better than what I thought," he said.

"That's not good enough," I said, angry.

"Look, this school is tough. You have high standards, and that's a good thing, but they're going to resist. Most of these kids made it this far without doing homework, and they're expecting it to stay that way."

"How can I teach if they won't read the book at home? How can I get them to learn if they refuse to do anything? I've made copies of the book you gave me. I'm handing them the SparkNotes for fucks sake. If they would read the fucking book, if they would fucking pay attention, if they would fucking do what I asked them to, we'd be almost done by now."

"So, that's what this is about?"

"Yes! I can't fail them all. I have to make a choice. I have to do something. We aren't going to finish the book. I don't want to give up. I refuse!" I leaned back and threw my pen down on my desk. "But it seems like I may not have a choice."

"What do you plan on doing?"

"I don't know."

"We've got less than three weeks now, right?"

"Less than that. I need the last week of school to prepare them for the final. They *need* a final. I did the math last period. I have nine days. Nine days. Fourteen more chapters. It doesn't sound like a lot, but it took them this long to read ten chapters. It's not possible. There's no way. I can't finish. I'm fucked. They win."

"Not quite." He put his leg up on a chair and rested his head on his hand, thinking. "Why not continue teaching it next quarter?"

"What?" I was blown away. "I can't do that. In what school does an English teacher take two quarters to teach *one* novel. That's insane."

"If you're going to teach here, you have to stop using every other school as a guideline. You're *here*. You have to do what works best *here*. And I've been *here* long enough to know that what works best *here* doesn't always make sense or seem reasonable. *Hell*, sometimes it isn't even sane."

"But taking like four fucking months to read a novel that is 185 pages long is beyond insane. It's idiotic. The audiobook is only eight and a half *hours* long," I mused. "Isn't that worse? Doesn't that make my class seem pathetic?"

"Why? We're here to help them learn and grow, but you have to know how to adapt, too. You're right. You can't back down. They've had teachers backing down and moving on since they've been here. That's what they're expecting you to do."

"So what do I do instead?"

"Push through. Stick with it. The freshmen will see that their whining isn't getting them out of work, and they'll give in and try harder. They're stubborn, but they're not insane. They think they can break you. They're pushing you there. Don't give in. Stick with the plan.

"You need to teach the novel. That's what you set out to do. You just need to adapt to figure out how to make this last two quarters instead of only one."

"And what will Admin think?"

"They'll think you're doing what's best for the kids."

I thought about it. "That might work," I said. "I'm not ready to give up."

"Good."

He thought I was talking about the novel. But I was talking about my career. Each day I walked into my classroom pushed me closer to the edge, but it was nice to have someone there that wanted to keep me from jumping.

CHAPTER TWENTY-TWO

Eighth Grade

"You're late, *Mister*," an eighth-grader said with the exaggerated melodrama found mostly in thirteen-year-olds.

"Someone's all sassed up today, Aviana," I said.

"I don't like waiting, *Mister*," she said.

"*Fresa*," I said. It was one of the few Spanish words I learned at the school that wasn't something that would lead to me being punched in the face if I used it in a bar.

"Very late, Mister," Alfred said robotically. "We've been patiently waiting."

"I was teaching you a lesson on patience," I said, unlocking my door.

"You get mad at us for being late, but you're late to your own class," Brutus said.

"Maybe your bad habits are rubbing off on me," I said. "I was with my Advisory working with our little buddies, and we lost track of time." In reality, I had lost time bullshitting with the Kindergarten teacher about Marvel movies while my students read to his students.

The eighth-graders found seats as I stood in the middle of the class waiting. Finally, without warning, I fell to my knees, "WHY CAN'T WE GET JUST ONE SNOW DAY!?"

178

The class went quiet, staring. I stood back up, straightened my vest and tie. "Sorry. I had to get that out of my system."

"Mister, you're weird." Sofía arched an eyebrow at me.

"I think we're making you crazy," Zooey said.

"Truth," I said. "I need someone to pass out the books." I went to the board in the back to write down the focus question for the day. When I finished, most of them had their notebooks out, pens ready, and books opened to where they needed to be. It was vastly different from ninth grade.

"Let's think back to yesterday," I said with a smile.

"Hey, Mister!" Sofía stifled a giggle.

"Yes?"

"You wrote 'tits' on the board," she said, bursting into laughter.

An eyebrow raised, I looked at what I had written: "about" followed by "its."

I rolled my eyes and stifled a laugh, "Wow. Thanks for reminding me that this is eighth grade."

"Tits," Alfred said with a smile. "Tits. Tits. It's funny… because…tits."

"Keep it together." I was shaking my head. They continued to laugh. "What's next? Fart jokes."

"I like fart jokes," Alfred said. "Farts are hilarious, Mister."

"Back to yesterday's reading," I said. "Brutus. Careful with that book. They're new."

"I'm not doing anything."

"You're bending the spine. We just got these. You gotta be careful, man."

"They don't look new," he said.

"They're new for us. Wilson used his own money to buy them. Let's treat them with respect."

"Maybe he could have bought newer ones," Brutus said, tossing the book down.

"Be grateful he cares enough to spend his own money to

help out," I said, "and *please* don't bend them."

"I wasn't bending it," Brutus said.

I shook my head. "Anyways, so if you remember from yesterday—"

"You're such a fucking liar," Aviana said.

"Aviana," I said.

"I wasn't bending it. Why do you have to accuse me?" Brutus asked.

"I saw you fucking do it," she said.

"Aviana, language," I said. "Brutus, I'm not trying to call you out. I'm just saying to everyone in general: please try and take care of these books. That's all."

"He's such a fucking liar," Aviana said.

"At least I'm not ugly," he said.

"You're fucking ugly. No one likes you!" She shot up out of her seat.

It really was that drastic, the change in moods.

Brutus said something to her in Spanish.

"For the last time, I'm not fucking Mexican! I don't fucking speak Spanish!" She was more than a little angry. "Say it to my face, you little bitch. Say it."

He said something else in Spanish.

"Enough!" I called, standing between the two of them to keep them from looking at each other. "Aviana, outside. No. Go. No. Go outside. I don't want to hear it right now. I'll talk to you out there."

She left in tears.

"You," I said to Brutus, "if you ever call anyone ugly in my class again, I'll send you out, and you won't come back."

"She started it, Mister. She called me a liar."

There was a smile on his face hidden beneath the façade of remorse. "Get into your groups. You're looking for words you don't know. Five of them. Define them. Dictionaries are under the desks. You can use your phones, too. Fill out a word map for each one. I'll be right back."

"Mister?" Alfred asked.

"Yes?"

"Can I…define…horny?"

"What?"

"It's right here," he said, holding open the book.

"Did you have that bookmarked?"

"No. I just found it." He smiled wide.

"That fast?"

"Yes."

"If there's one word in that book I am certain you know—"

"But Mister, other kids might not know what it means."

"Really?"

"Please."

"Well, because you said 'please,' I guess."

"Really!?"

"*No.* Write down the words you don't know. I'll be right back," I said.

Aviana was still in tears when I went out into the hall.

"What's wrong?" I asked. I felt like something must have been happening for her to react like that, that there was something she wasn't telling me. But she didn't reveal anything other than annoyance.

"Brutus is such a fucking idiot. I fucking hate him," she said through tears.

"Hold on a second." I went back inside, grabbed some tissues, then went back out and handed them to her. "You don't need to cry. It'll be okay."

I hated tears. I wasn't really sure what to do with a crying kid. The only thing I knew was that I should get them to stop crying, but it wasn't like there was an off-switch for teenage emotions.

"Take a few deep breaths. Can you stop crying?"

She shook her head.

"If you don't, I'll start crying. And if you want to know what ugly looks like, imagine a giant bald baby bawling uncontrollably. It's horrific."

She laughed a little through the tears. I thought I had achieved success, but then she began to cry again. "Brutus called me ugly. And I hate that they talk in Spanish around me. It's fucked up. They say shit about me all the time because they know I can't speak it."

"You don't speak Spanish?" I asked stupidly.

"I'm not fucking Mexican," she said.

"Okay. Okay. I'm sorry. Please, don't curse at me."

"Sorry."

"I know you're upset, but don't let Brutus get to you. He acts like that because he doesn't want people to realize that he's hurt inside. I'll talk to him. I won't put up with bullying in my class. If anyone's giving you crap, talk to me, and I'll sort it out. Okay?"

"Okay."

"But it needs to be me that talks to him because if you curse at him, then you get in trouble, and that doesn't need to happen."

"I want to punch him in the face," she said.

"He probably likes you. That's how eighth-grade boys are. They tease the girls they like."

"I would rather jump off a bridge," she said.

"Into his open arms?" I suggested.

"Are you crazy? No way. More like into an ocean filled with acid and sharks that want to eat me alive with landmines that are on fire." The tears trickled.

"That's going to be a hard ocean to find," I said. "Remember, when people make fun of you, it's most likely because something's wrong in their lives. Not yours."

She nodded, face buried into tissues as she tried sorting out emotions.

"I'll talk to him. You stay out here and compose yourself. Take some deep breaths. I want him to apologize to you."

"No. It's okay, Mister."

"This isn't an opinion. No one calls anyone ugly in my classroom. I hate that word. It's disgusting." I knew all too well what it felt like to be called ugly. Somethings, no matter how hard we try, we can't change. If I could stop someone from feeling *that* pain, that disgusting tearing sensation that a word like that brought to the soul, even if only for a little bit, it would be a small victory.

Once back inside, I called Brutus to my desk. He stood up reluctantly, pushed away his notebook, and stomped over.

"What you said hurt." I spoke in a low voice. I had made sure his back was facing the class. I didn't want him laughing off what I said because he caught sight of his friends. "Do you realize that?" He tried to look back at his friends. "Hey. Look at me. Here. I'm talking to you."

"Whatever, Mister," he said.

"Not whatever. You called her ugly. That's not okay."

"She called me a liar. I'm not a liar."

"You lied. I'm not an idiot. I saw what you did. This isn't about that." He started to protest, but I interrupted him. "You *will* apologize."

"But, Mister." He dropped his arms to his sides and sagged his shoulders. "What about her?"

"What about her? We're talking about you. This is your chance to be a man. Take responsibility for your actions. Don't worry about her or what she has to do. What *you* said was extremely, extremely hurtful. Do you understand that?"

"Whatever." He rolled his eyes.

"Not whatever. Do you understand that?"

"Yes. I understand," he said, exasperated.

Everything was relatively calm after the drama had sorted itself out. Alfred even found a different word besides "horny."

Strangely enough, I was looking forward to my eighth-graders more than the other classes. They seemed somewhat reachable.

When the bell rang, class thinned out into the hall. It appeared that I would have time to plan. That is, until I saw that Sofía and Zooey had stayed behind.

"Can I talk to you?" Sofía asked.

"I can't let you skip art again. Ross was pretty upset with me for doing that. She sent me an email," I said. There were tears in her eyes, "What's up?"

Zooey patted her friend on her back

I grabbed the box of tissues and asked her to take a seat. I was learning that as a teacher, all the shit you do with the books and tests and lessons was secondary.

I didn't like it.

I became a teacher to discuss literature, to share my passion about a subject that I held in my heart. But the longer I worked at that school, the more I realized that there was a lot more to teaching than prepping kids for college.

Every student has a story.

And at that moment, she needed to share hers.

CHAPTER TWENTY-THREE

Firecracker

"Do you know why we are here?" Ritz asked Helen.

"Yeah, I kinda think so." She was still embarrassed.

We were packed into Ritz's small office around a table with a fake wood veneer that reflected the lone fluorescent ceiling light above. Everything in the office screamed, "I'm an office!" Bright brown facades, degrees posted up on the walls, pictures of family, semi-comfortable chairs, and a small plant on the desk. The blinds were open, letting in the gray from outside.

"I'll go over it just in case there's any confusion," she said. She was overly formal. Given the circumstances, it made sense. It wasn't the time for jokes. She turned to me. "Thank you for taking time out of your plan to be here."

I had almost given up on trying to use my planning period.

"I'm here to act as the mediator so we can resolve this issue," she continued.

"Issue" was an understatement. Helen had lost her shit in class.

"You'll both tell your side of the story. Then, we'll work out a solution to resolve the matter and restore the disturbance in the community."

*Bringing balance to the force...*I thought, trying not to laugh.

I really didn't care about what happened the day before. It's not like Helen actually did anything that upset me. Unfortunately, it was because of *how* she acted that made it necessary to do this.

"Helen, start by telling us your side. What's your understanding of the events?"

I flipped out like a raging psychopath, I summarized for her in my head.

"I feel so stupid. I'm such a dumbass. It's just...he was handing the tests to us yesterday, and everyone was failing. And I was pissed. Not at him. Well, kind of at him. But, I was also pissed off at myself because my grade was bad, like really bad. No one did the homework over the break, and we all deserved to fail. And he was nice enough to let us have more time to work on the project to improve our grade because nobody did that either...I guess I just felt overwhelmed, and I just kinda snapped because his class is really hard, and I'm trying, but I feel stupid because I guess I'm not trying hard enough, and when he handed me the next set of chapters to read, I guess I kinda just freaked out and threw them at his face and started saying a lot of really mean things...and then I stormed out of the class."

She inhaled.

Screaming. She forgot about the screaming.

"Do you remember the mean things you said?" Ritz asked.

I believe it was, *Fuck you. You bald piece of shit.* That was then followed by a string of random curses from *asshole* to *fucking-bitch-shit-asshole-cunt* or something like that. Sadly, it lacked the eloquence of a genuine insult.

"I cursed a lot. But I don't really remember," she mumbled.

"Does this sound accurate to you?" Ritz was looking at me.

"Normally, there are two sides to every story, but I think Helen about summed it up," I said. "I appreciate your honesty." I just really wanted to leave.

She looked down.

"Do you remember what she said? Was she cursing *at* you?"

It was the first time Helen looked directly at me, and I knew what she was asking.

"It's all kinda fuzzy. There was a lot of yelling. I don't think she was cursing at me. I think she was just cursing in general." It was a small lie.

In all fairness, I was trying not to laugh when I passed back the tests. It was hard not to after failing more than fifty students on an open note test when they could have just gone home and read the SparkNotes. It felt like a situation that merited laughter, either that, or curling up into a ball in the corner and crying.

"That's important. Cursing at a teacher would make things a lot more severe," Ritz said. "Remember that both Nimitz and I wanted severe consequences for your actions. I need you to understand that. Cursing and throwing things in class is *unacceptable*."

"It's simple, Helen. You messed up," I said. "I need you to set things right before you can rejoin my class. I need you to give an official apology. You don't have to write anything down. And I don't need or want you to apologize to me. I want you to apologize to the class for being disruptive. That's it. Do that, and you're welcome back."

She nodded.

"And in the future, if you're upset, you have the right to go into the hall and calm down, get a drink of water, take a few deep breaths."

"Oh, I will, Mister. And I'll apologize to you in front of the class. I don't mind. I'll write something up."

"You don't have to do that. Focus on setting things right with the other students. They need to know it's okay to be around you."

She nodded again.

"Look. Freshman year isn't easy. You're getting used to being in high school, and it keeps getting harder. You'll have to adapt and overcome the challenge. What you're feeling now, that's growing pains. You're allowed to be annoyed. You're allowed to hate me at times. You're even allowed an outburst or two, but when you throw something at me, we have a problem."

"I understand," she said. "I lost my shit." She quickly covered her mouth and looked at Ritz. "Sorry! I didn't mean that."

Ritz nodded this time.

"I am so sorry. I feel embarrassed by the whole thing. People are calling me a firecracker now."

To be fair, she exploded.

"Actions have consequences," Ritz said. "They're probably a little on edge after what you did. The apology will help put that at ease."

"Thank you for not suspending me," Helen said. "My mom would have killed me."

"Suspended?" I laughed. "No. My job is to keep you in my class so you can learn and grow." It was the right thing to say with Ritz there. I really just wanted my plan back. I would have said anything to have ten minutes to make a few copies.

"Do you think that's fair?" Ritz asked her.

"That's not enough. I deserve a worse punishment," Helen said. "I fucked up—sorry—my stupid mouth is always getting me in trouble. I mean, I messed up."

"That'll be plenty, just make sure next time instead of launching projectiles at me, you grab a drink of water or take a walk or something. I don't want to start wearing my helmet again."

She laughed a little too loud. "No, Mister! It won't ever

happen again. And. And…and I want to write *you* a letter too. I want to explain myself. I'm so sorry. I feel like an idiot. You're my favorite teacher, Mister."

Doubtful. But I didn't blame her for saying what she needed to say to get out of trouble.

"If you want to write a letter, I don't see why not," Ritz said. "Does that work for you?"

"Only if you don't get behind on your other work. I'd prefer you focus on that," I said.

"No. I really want to," she said.

There was an awkward pause. Ritz ended it by saying, "I think that wraps things up."

"I'm happy if you're happy," I said.

"Thank you, sir," Helen said.

"Jesus. Don't call me sir," I said. "I'm still in my twenties, dude."

"Thank you, Mister," she said.

"I think you can head back to class," Ritz said.

"She looked like she was about to break down," I said to Ritz after Helen left.

"They always do when they're in here. She can be a handful, that one. And look at that; you're her favorite teacher." She smiled at me, a light glimmer highlighted her freckles under the ambient office glow.

"*Great.* I can't fail her now. Or I *need* to fail her? I'm not sure how that works."

She laughed. "That's not the first time I've heard that from a student."

"They need better options," I said.

"You don't give yourself enough credit. You're a breath of fresh air. It's nice to hear your class is challenging, too. They need that. They may hate you now, but they'll thank you later."

They hated me now, that was for sure.

CHAPTER TWENTY-FOUR

Soccer

"How's the head?" Wilson guessed.

I felt like I was on a ship at sea during a storm. "I may vomit," I said, looking out at the gym, glad for a little extra time before "real school" began. It was Advisory, again. We had decided to make it a free day instead of doing the traditional meeting. Wilson had suggested the gym.

"On a Monday? Brave start. Next time wait till Thursday. Makes it easier to get through the week."

I stifled a gag. Our students were running around, cracked out of their minds on freedom, hitting and kicking balls, screaming, laughing. We stood off to the side and talked.

"Talk to me about the girl. Who's the lucky lady?"

"No girl. Just some co-workers," I said. "And my friends, the ones that let me stay with them."

"So no woman?"

I was holding a bottle of orange-flavored Pedialyte in my hand with the label ripped off. I was pretty sure the kids didn't know what it was, but I wanted to be careful. I took a sip. "Are you kidding? I don't even have furniture. My bed is a sleeping bag on a hardwood floor."

"Find one that likes camping." He nudged me in the ribs.

I almost vomited.

"Oh, sorry," he said, then yelled something at one of the kids.

When I regained composure, I said, "There was a girl. Kind of. A blonde I was dancing with, but she thought I was gay."

"No way?" He laughed.

"To be fair, I had followed my friends into a gay club and didn't realize. I had been surprised this girl was dancing with me. She was pretty hot. I went and told my buddy when she went to the bathroom. He said, 'She thinks you're gay.' I didn't believe him. So the turd walks me over to her and asks. And she says, 'Oh my, yeah. I did. I'm so sorry. I thought you two were together.' Then my friend goes, 'Nah. Even I have standards.'"

He laughed, "Did you feel at home there?"

"I was wearing a sweater, too."

"Wearing a sweater in a gay club? That'll do it," he said. "And you were surprised?"

"I was surprised she talked to me," I chuckled, regretting it.

"When do I get to see the new place?" he asked.

"Not going to happen. It's a dive. I have no furniture so it's uncomfortable, and it echoes. It's temporary, just until summer."

"Why only summer?"

"I just want to make it through the year," I said. I didn't tell him that I wasn't sure I would stick around. There was also a very pathetic part of me that hoped that things with my ex would change.

"Where's it at?"

I told him.

"You enjoy being around hipsters and crackheads?"

"It's all I could afford. There's a lot of other stuff around there, though, like microbreweries, concert venues, coffee shops."

"Crackheads, needles, the occasional guy swinging his shirt around his head at three a.m.," he paused, "Also known as crackheads."

"After teaching here, I'll blend right in," I said.

"Is there a pool or anything like that? I need to know if I should plan on coming over and meeting some of your female neighbors in the hot tub."

"It's a tiny studio with like this eastern religion theme or something. The only amenity might be someone doing yoga in the hallway."

"Could be fun," he said, watching the eighth-graders run around the gym.

"A soccer ball is like crack to these kids," I said. "How do they even keep track? There's like forty goddamn people playing with—" I counted "—three soccer balls...and we're in a gym. My brain physically hurts trying to follow what's going on here."

"These kids love soccer," Wilson said.

"You'd have to love it to play like this. Where are the goals?"

"I'm not sure."

The gym was a mess with people. Misako, the eighth-grade math teacher, was hitting a volleyball with some girls in a circle. There were some kids on the sides shooting hoops, others sat with friends on the bleachers, talking. A few of the awkward kids were in a distant corner playing with something on the ground.

Advisory at its finest.

The gym looked like any other school gym: a shiny wooden floor, retractable basketball hoops, brownish bleachers to one side, and banners on the wall bragging past victories: district champions, state, nationals. Another lifetime. Then there was the stage; you know the one. It was the place where you performed as a beanstalk in your second-grade play, the one where you were worried that you'd forget your lines even though your mom kept reminding you that you were playing a plant and that plants don't talk.

I pulled myself up onto the stage and took a seat, legs dangling. Wilson joined.

I watched the eighth-graders running around, tunnel vision on the game. "This is insane."

"I'm telling you, these kids are passionate about soccer. Some of them are really good. A couple may even play in college if they keep their grades up."

"I get that they may be passionate, but at this point, it isn't even a game. It's a mosh pit."

"Think outside the box," he said to me.

"What do you mean?"

"You gotta just take things the way they are here. They're different. They're always different. Whatever school you work at, it'll be different. That's how it goes."

I nodded and took a sip of the orange goo.

He was wearing an old, blue blazer with matching slacks, and stylish but old black shoes. Contrasting this was the school t-shirt that he wore in place of a dress shirt, the faded emblem of the district resting on the left breast.

We sat on the stage, watching insanity unfold with each punt or sudden steal. One kid would skillfully out dribble someone else, but then another would come up from behind and kick it out between the legs.

"You won't see your ninth-graders out here doing anything like this. That was my problem with them when they were in my class," Wilson said. "I couldn't connect with them because I couldn't find their passion."

It sounded like there was regret in his voice.

"If I had brought them in here to do this, they would have

just stood around. At least with these kids, they have something I can relate to, sports. And if they have something like that, something you can understand and can relate to, it makes it easier to show them how other things, like school, is important."

"My ninth-graders are content with existing," I said, pausing as another wave of nausea washed over me.

"These kids are different," he said. How he talked about them with such pride, it's how I imagined a loving father would talk about his children. "Last year, I used to have fresh water bottles in my class for them after they practiced during lunch. And for the ones who were really into soccer, I had a former student who had played professionally train them for a session last summer."

"I won't even lend them a pen," I said. "But that explains why all the boys talk to you. There are like two boys out of all my classes that actually talk to me. I think I scare most of them away."

"They're intimidated by you. Did you play sports?"

"No. Never."

"You look like an athlete."

"Genetics," I shrugged.

"A lot of these kids have had abusive experiences with the men in their lives. Having a tall, bald, intimidating teacher who looks like a bouncer can be scary."

"I read poetry, and girls at bars think I'm gay. I'm hardly intimidating."

"Again, you're thinking in a box. To these kids, you might be. Keep that in mind when you talk to them. You may not feel all big and scary, but to a few of them, you are."

"That's stupid."

"It's not stupid when you think about it. They push you away because they feel threatened, even if they don't realize it. They'll warm up to you after a while."

"I'm only a threat to their GPA," I said.

"If you want more of the boys to be open to talking to you, try being more approachable," he said.

"I never wanted to be a mentor. I struggle with that," I said. "When I was in high school, I never asked for help. I just did what I needed to do and moved on, unless I had a question. I just want them to come in, learn, and leave."

"Mentoring is a huge part of teaching at this school. These kids don't have much in the way of positive role models or discipline. The longer you teach here, the more they'll come to you for advice. You don't just work at this school; you're a member of their community.

"Why don't they just talk to a counselor?" I said, forcing down another big sip.

"Think about it. Who would you rather go to for advice, a teacher you see every day or a counselor you've only met once?"

"True," I said.

"Being a school counselor is a useless job unless you're dealing with severely distraught kids, and then those kids probably should be in a different environment."

"I don't know about all that," I said. I'd rather the kids talk to the counselor. I thought of the tears and shivered. "How come they're not scared of you?"

"I'm *not* intimidating, not in the way you are."

I got it. People were scared of me. My professors had warned me in university that kids may feel intimidated by my stature. I had tried to be less terrifying. But aside from altering my genetics, I wasn't sure what else to do.

"I wish I could intimidate ninth grade into reading."

"How did they take the news about spending next quarter on *Frankenstein*?"

"You heard what happened with Helen."

"Oh yeah. That sounded intense."

"I also handed back the Imagery Assignment. I gave them two more days in class to work on it. But now, I'm turning them into presentations and adding a grade. More are doing it, so that's better."

A ball whizzed by and nearly hit us. Wilson got up and ran behind the stage to grab it. He threw it out to them. "How are their grades now?" he asked after he sat back down.

"Better after the retest, but still a lot of zeroes. We're getting there. Hunter's one hell of an artist. Kelly, too. I just wish they weren't...indisposed...most of the time. They have talent."

"That's good to hear."

"But you were right about eighth grade. They're growing on me."

"I told you." He smiled. "I know these kids."

Misako walked over to us and held up her watch. "Is time."

"It's time?" Wilson asked.

"You call dem? I don wan to yell." She was the math teacher in the class next to mine. I laughed at the idea of her not wanting to yell. I could hear her screaming through the wall most days.

Wilson kicked off the stage and took care of it, screaming at them that Advisory was over.

Once we were settled back into class, school began. I was handing out copies of the novel to my eighth-graders when I heard the tail end of a conversation that made the hair on my neck stand up. I pretended not to listen as they continued whispering, thinking that I couldn't hear them.

I listened a little longer until I knew for sure.

"Ezekiel, Derrick, and Kyle!" I yelled. "Get the hell out of my class. Now!"

Their faces froze as if they had just handed their phones over to their grandmothers without clearing their browser histories.

The room stayed silent even after they left.

"What happened, Mister?" Alfred said slowly.

I ignored him. "Continue reading where we stopped yesterday while I handle this."

I called the office, demanding the principal come immediately. My body shook with rage as I opened the door, not exactly sure what I was going to say. I should have stayed calm. I didn't.

"You three have got to be the STUPIDEST kids I have ever taught!" I was shaking. "Seriously. I've never, EVER had a student, let alone three, be so stupid. You want to deal drugs in *my* class? In front of me!"

Their eyes widened.

One started to speak.

"No! You say nothing!"

Wilson came out into the hall. "Everything okay?"

"No. We are so far from okay right now." I looked down the hall. A couple of other teachers came out to see what was happening.

I turned to Wilson and told him.

"Are you serious?" He put his hands on his hips and leaned forward, the school emblem jutting toward them.

I thought I was loud.

No.

Wilson was much, much louder.

I saw how much Wilson cared as I listened to him. He was angry because he was disappointed. He let them know they had let him down. Whereas I had been insulted because they had disrespected my classroom, he felt slighted because they had disrespected themselves.

"What's the problem?" Nimitz appeared behind us, coffee thermos in hand.

"They were talking about buying and selling drugs in my

class," I said.

Without pause, I saw a complete change in Nimitz's composure. "Gentlemen, come with me. Now." And with that, he led them outside.

It must have been thirty degrees out, and two of the kids weren't wearing jackets. The boys shuddered from the cold as the door opened. Nimitz followed without so much as a shiver.

Once they were gone, I turned to Wilson. "I think I spoke too soon."

CHAPTER TWENTY-FIVE

Your Mother

The countdown on the board in the back broadcasted, "6 School Days Before Break" in red dry-erase marker.

Some days were great. The students were interested in the story. They learned the differences between the novel and the film versions. They were intrigued by the history of the murdering monster. They grew to resent Frankenstein's failure as a father. And in those moments, I felt that the story finally hooked them.

And then without warning, everything changed. I would find them constantly off-task. I would take cell phones at an alarming rate. I would send kids into the hall for being idiots.

Some couldn't give a fuck, regardless of what I did. Some stared into oblivion, waiting for class to end. Others scribbled aimlessly in their notebooks. And some didn't bother showing up at all.

Jeff still slept in class.

There were days with decent discussions and a few thought-provoking questions. And there were days where I had to explain things like the fact that Buffalo wings were made from chicken, not buffalo.

We pushed on.

Joaquín approached me as people walked into class. He spoke quietly. "Mister, I wanted you to know that my mom is a little worried about me."

"Why?" I asked. *Had I pissed off another parent?*

"I told her I wanted to read instead of play video games. I'm really far ahead in the book. I can't believe the creature kills Henry," he said.

"Woah." I smiled. "That's awesome. But be careful not to spoil it."

"It's really good, Mister. Thanks for picking it. My mom can't believe I have a 'B' in your class," he said, grinning.

The bell rang.

"I'm not surprised," I said. "Keep it up." It appeared he had made some progress from the apple-bearing asshole I had wanted to bean over the head when we first started the novel.

"Let's get started." I said after attendance. "A couple of things we gotta talk about. You'll notice there's no journal. That's because your final is next Friday. We'll be spending an entire week preparing for it. That starts today.

"And, to clear the air now: the rumors are true. You will have to read a little bit over the break.

"I have made—stop complaining. This will help us finish by the end of the third quarter." *If it takes more than two quarters to teach one novel, I'm going to hang myself,* I thought.

The complaining escalated. I waited.

"Shut up," Anita said. "You know he's not going to change his mind. You're wasting time. This is why we always fucking have homework."

"She's speaking the truth," I said.

"I'm ahead," Joaquín bragged.

"Teacher's pet," Charles said.

"Shut up," Joaquín fired back.

"I'll shut your mom up," Charles giggled as he drew in his

notebook.

"That doesn't even make sense," he said.

"I think you know it does," he said.

"Charles. Enough," I said, confused myself.

"Mister, he's got a pretty hot mom," Charles said.

"Fuck you," Joaquín said. "You soulless bastard."

I had a hard time figuring out that friendship.

"She actually *is* pretty hot," Anita said.

"Gay!" someone yelled.

"Enough. Joaquín's *hot* mom aside, we need to talk about the final," I said.

"Oh damn, Mister said your mom's hot," Charles said.

"That was sarcasm." I shook my head.

"So, you don't think his mom's hot? You think she's ugly? Damn!" Charles said.

"I didn't say that." I was annoyed. "Can we move on?"

"Hey, Mister," Charles said. "You got a girlfriend, yet?"

I looked at him, unamused.

"My mom found a man. At least for now," Sasha chimed. "You missed the boat on that one."

"If you're still single, you can move on Joaquín's mom," Charles laughed.

"We talked about this," I said. "I'm not dating anyone's mom. Let's focus."

"If you're ever feeling lonely," Charles said, "She usually works until three a.m."

"Eat shit and die," Joaquín said.

"I changed the question for our final discussion," I shouted.

"Sometimes there's a line, so you need to come early," Charles said.

"Oh fuck," Anita said.

Joaquín was glaring at his friend, lips pursed. "Dead. You're dead." He threw his pencil down on his desk.

"Focus!" I said. "Stop talking about moms and focus on the assignment. The question is a little different, but it's still the same."

"Wait," Sasha said. "You're telling me that if you had some fine-looking mom coming after you that you wouldn't hit that?"

"Can we...talk about the final?"

They continued back and forth, Charles pushing, tip-toeing.

"Charles. Enough. Or I'll have to send you out. I'm trying to be patient. But there's a line."

"Sorry, Mister." Then he looked at Joaquín. "Sorry...for keeping you up last night."

"Douche," Joaquín said.

"But to be fair, the group that came in after was much louder," Charles added.

"Charles. Out. Now."

"Come on, Mister. Please, one more chance," he said.

I turned to the class. "We're going to do something called a Socratic Seminar for a final." There was bitching. I fought through it. "Guys, it's a fifty-minute conversation about the book. That's it. I gave you five articles. You're going to read them and try to use those facts to support your views in the conversation."

The bitching continued.

I waited. It was supposed to be a fun alternative to a test. Less studying. Less stress. It was just a conversation; it was easier to grade and easier to pass, which a lot of them needed. My other school had loved them.

"Is medical experimentation justified?" I said, explaining the question.

"Yes!" someone shouted.

"No. I mean, that's the question you're answering."

"Huh?"

"It'll make more sense by the time you finish the articles. They're about cutting open living bodies to see how they work, digging up and stealing corpses, and performing experiments on animals."

"Why do we always read?" Sallie asked.

"That's your question? After what I just said?"

"Yah..." Her mouth hung open.

"Because I enjoy watching you suffer," I said.

"You're mean, Mister."

I looked at her mangled red eyes, "What have you been doing, Sallie?"

Shocked, she looked away.

They had a week to read, prepare, and write a paragraph explaining the reasoning behind their beliefs. That paragraph was their ticket to the discussion.

"At the beginning of class on Friday, you'll turn in your ticket to gain entry into the debate. No ticket, no debate. No debate, no grade. No grade, no credit. No credit, no college, *and* you drop out of high school and bag groceries until you're thirty. You need to make sure you do this. You need to make sure you write that one paragraph. It's just one.

"Every time I do this, people who don't write the paragraph sit on the edge of class, listening, getting frustrated because I don't let them participate. Every time. So make sure you do it. Are there any questions?"

"We have to read *all* of this?" Sallie asked.

"Oh my fucking god," Anita said. "If you weren't so fucking high all the time, you wouldn't be so stupid."

"Anita," I interrupted. "Thank you, but I got this. Sallie, you're reading one article in your group today, just like we did at the beginning of the quarter. Do you remember when I broke you all up into groups?"

"No. I don't think I was there that day," she lied.

I rolled my eyes and explained the assignment again.

"Ugh. So it *is* just more reading," Sallie whined.

"This is an English class," I said, growing frustrated. I spent a lot of time trying to find interesting articles that were at their grade level. I wanted it to be fun. "You read. It's required. You don't complain about having to do math in Algebra or exercise in P.E., do you?"

"I don't like doing any of that," Sallie said.

"Then why even come here?" I asked, annoyed.

Student teacher does not handle apathy well.

"I'm here because my mom doesn't want me to join a gang," Joaquín said.

"Ironic," Charles said.

"Why's that ironic," I asked, stupidly. "I'm glad he's not in a gang."

"It's ironic because his mom is," he said.

"What?" I said.

"Not like a real gang. Mostly just gang bangs," Charles laughed.

"Motherfucker!" Joaquín yelled.

A poor choice of words.

"Out! Now!" I said.

This time he went without complaint.

CHAPTER TWENTY-SIX

Dismissed

When the bell rang, I followed Period Eight into the hall. I was having a harder time than usual that day trying to find the strength to care.

"Look who's finally doing hall duty," Mack taunted. He was the other teacher across the hall, next to Wilson.

"Someone finally learned how to read emails," Wilson said. They stood next to each other outside their classrooms like two tall ivory totems as students flooded around them.

"What email?" I asked.

Wilson, arms crossed in front of him, shook his head.

"I'm only out here to avoid Period Nine," I said.

"Are they really that bad?" Mack asked.

I started listing students.

"That's how you end your day?" he asked.

"You want to trade classes?"

"That's all you, buddy. I'm done. Last period plan," he said.

"I want to go home," I said. I stood next to them and watched students trickle into my class.

"Oh, it's not that bad. You only have, what, twenty people in there?" Wilson asked.

"Enough to make me consider how late a late-term abortion should be," I said.

"Oh damn," Mack said, covering his mouth.

"If you see me walk into my class with a coat hanger, stop me," I said.

Kids moved about us, oblivious.

"I don't get it," I continued. "I teach the same thing three times every day. And it's a manageable wreck until Period Nine, and then it's a shitshow. Every single day."

"Are you using all the different learning styles?" Wilson teased.

"Really?" Mack looked at Wilson. "Is he cracked out of his mind?"

"Hey, this is the Golden Boy." He pointed to me, taunting because Ritz had praised me at an after-school meeting. "You're standing in front of a soon-to-be legend. We should be asking him for advice."

"Calm down, Mary Poppins. You're the one with the food truck equivalent of a public library in your classroom," I said.

"Oh damn," Mack said. "You two going to throw down? English vs. English?"

"We just might." Wilson mockingly put up his fists.

"I don't hit the disabled," I said.

Their mouths dropped. I threw my arms up and shrugged. "And with that gentlemen, it's time for me to get this shitshow started."

"Stay sane," Mack said.

I slipped into my class as the bell rang and closed the door.

With each step, I felt happiness seep from my soul. I turned to see slumping, distraught teens waiting for me to begin.

I took a deep breath and tried to fake it. "Happy Friday. You'll notice there's no journal on the board," I began, "That's because—"

The door boomed back open.

Nemesis limped in melodramatically. There was no apology for being late this time. The kid no longer liked me.

"Fuck," Ricky complained.

"I was hoping the kid was absent," Kate said.

I was not happy to see Nemesis, either. A lot of drama had happened with the kid after the suspension. It turned out that Nemesis had lied about the events with Perón, hurting the one person at the school willing to help.

Where did that leave the rest of us?

Nemesis was going to the office more and more for pissing off students and going off on teachers.

I was angry for Perón. She would never be. She never took anything personally. She had only wanted to help Nemesis. Instead, she was thinking about abandoning her career, a career she had spent a lifetime building, all because of one child.

Teachers aren't supposed to hold grudges, but like with everything else, Nemesis made that a challenge.

The kid dropped a bag down but didn't take a seat. I think it was supposed to be a makeshift backpack. It was a grocery bag. I guessed that the kid's parents couldn't afford a real book bag, or the kid had misplaced the real one and that was the substitute. You never know unless you asked, and I never asked.

The kid was dancing again, Bruno Mars blazing into the room through tiny, generic headphones.

"That kid is so fucking annoying," Ricky said.

"Yeah," Kate said. "I wish the kid would just leave."

"Enough," I said. "Any more comments like that and I'll send you to the office. We need to begin. As I was saying, you'll notice there's no journal on the board. That's because for the next week..."

Moments like that sucked as a teacher, having to say one thing while believing another. Nemesis was intentionally annoying; everything was about drawing in attention, no matter the cost. It infuriated me, but I had to remember that the kid was probably dealing with some shit. Every student has a story, after all. And so, I forced myself to try and care.

Those moments illustrated a different side of teaching. They highlighted a truth: You could only do so much. You could only help so many people. Sometimes you clicked with kids; you found out what worked, and you pushed them to succeed. Other times, you'd clash. Kids would annoy you, piss you off, but you'd adapt and drive them to succeed. And then some kids were just unreachable; they isolated themselves, building up walls until they turned into anathemas. Teachers like Perón pushed passed those barriers. They went to war for those kids, and sometimes, as was the case with Nemesis, the ones they fought for would stab them in the back.

I was naïve when I started out. I wanted to be the teacher in those stupid movies. I wanted to inspire, to be someone students would climb to the tops of their desks at the end of the year for, cheering, "Oh! Captain, My Captain!" But life isn't a movie.

And *that* wasn't teaching.

Nemesis continued dancing by the chair, refusing to sit down, listening to "Waterfalls" loud enough for me to hear all the way at the back of the classroom.

Ted said something to the kid in Spanish. Nemesis glared back.

I continued even though Nemesis and the music distracted everyone. I knew the kid was on edge and if I said anything, there would be another "outburst". I won't lie. It was tempting, to push buttons for just a little peace. But I refrained and left Nemesis alone.

I had made the final easier for Period Nine. And as I was explaining it to them, most drifted off to those familiar places where they typically stayed until the final bell. Everyone except Ted, Hunter, and Justin. They were whispering in Spanish to each other, pausing, glancing over at Nemesis, whispering more. Snickering.

I finished up the instructions without much in the way of confrontation. And they only complained a little when I told them they would have homework over the break. More relief washed over me. *Maybe it would be an easy class?* I thought stupidly.

Nemesis eventually sat down.

"We're going to start with an article on body snatching. It's the first article in the packet I gave you," I said. I learned that I couldn't trust them to work in groups, so I would have to go through everything with them, holding their hands.

The boys continued whispering.

"You need to be looking at the packets with your notebooks out, writing down what you think is important. I'll write notes on the board. Please copy what I write," I said.

Heavy sighs and murmured protests followed.

"Let's go," I said, snapping my fingers. "I know it's Friday, but focus. This is for the final. We only have forty minutes to work before the bell rings."

Only forty minutes...

As the rest of them tugged out their notebooks with great effort, Ted leaned over and caught Nemesis's gaze. He said something to the kid in Spanish. They locked eyes like two feral animals in a territorial dispute. Nemesis suddenly shot up out of the chair.

"Have a seat please," I said.

"What, bitch?" Nemesis glared at Ted. "What did you say? Say it to my face?"

Ted smiled and shook his head.

"Fucking say it to my face, nigga! Say it to my face!" Nemesis moved towards him, and I stood in the way immediately.

"Nemesis. Nemesis." I blocked the kid. Nemesis tried shooting around me, but I was probably three times the kid's size. I also wasn't limping. "Why don't you go outside and get some fresh air, okay?"

"Fuck you."

"That's not the best response," I said. "Let's go outside."

"Fuck all of you. I'm fucking done with this school," the kid said.

Ted said something back in Spanish.

I focused on guiding Nemesis to the door.

Out of the corner of my eye, I saw Ted pretend to stagger while sitting down and making a face at Nemesis. The kid didn't need to speak Spanish to know what he was saying.

"You want to fucking fight? Let's fight, bitch. Fight me. Let's go. I'll fuck your shit up." Nemesis tried to move around me, but failed.

"Nemesis," I said, moving the kid closer toward the door. It went back and forth as I used my mass to guide the kid out of my class. Rarely will a kid touch a teacher, most are smart enough to realize that's a big no-no. I used that to my advantage.

Ted said something else in Spanish as Nemesis and I made it into the hall.

"Nemesis," I began but the kid flipped the bird and limped away toward the exit.

"Wait," I whimpered as I stood still and watched the doors behind Nemesis close.

I made the call.

Back in my room, Hunter, Justin, and Ted were laughing. "Enough! I'm through. Ted. Outside. Now. The rest of you read. The next person that pisses me off is out of here."

Ted sulked out into the hall.

Outside, I waited as Ted walked back from the water

fountain. I kept the door to my class open because even though there were only fifteen people in my room, I couldn't leave them alone.

Ted leaned against a dented corkboard on the wall. He started picking at a hole there, waiting for me to speak.

"Look at me," I said.

He made no eye contact.

"Look at me!"

He turned slightly, his lower lip hanging out, a bit of drool falling from it. He wiped it away. Pimples formed ridges and peaks over his forehead.

"You intentionally pissed Nemesis off."

"Yeah. So?"

"If you're going to start fights every time you're here, then I don't want you here."

"I don't want to be in there," he said.

Me neither, I thought.

I wish I could whisk together some inspirational tale of how, out there in the hall, I talked to Ted about what he did and why it was wrong. I wish I could say, "We shared a moment. It was a small one, but enough for him to change his ways." But that wasn't the case.

I talked, and Ted picked at the board. I knew he had antagonized Nemesis, pushed the kid to leave the class. And I was glad that he did. The kid had left. And telling me to fuck off meant that Nemesis wouldn't be coming back for a while.

Maybe you're reading this thinking, *What a shitty teacher.* You're right. I was new, inexperienced, and ill-prepared to deal with that school. I was annoyed that he had pushed Nemesis to pop, but I was also grateful. And I hated him for making me feel that way.

After I lectured him in the hall, we went back into the classroom. I knew what I said wouldn't have much of an impact. My heart wasn't in it. Besides, he gave no amount of fucks about what I had to say.

I went over to my desk and wrote both of them up. Going through the motions, I reprimanded the other two kids as well.

By the time I was back at the board teaching, we were almost out of time. I walked them through the first article with ease. There was no interest, no debate, no discussion amongst the groups as there had been in the other classes. There were only bored faces floating in the ether waiting for that final bell to ring.

A phone call interrupted to let me know that they had found Nemesis and that the kid would be staying in the office. *No shit,* I thought. They mentioned something about a counselor and new strategies while I impatiently pretended to care until they hung up.

I went back to my board and pretended to teach. I had a professional responsibility to those kids, so I went through the motions, but my heart wasn't in it.

It sucked because not all the kids created problems. Ricky, Kate, and Emma were fine. They did what they could. They tried. They may not have liked my class, but they respected me. And for them, I forced myself to let things go and try to teach.

Halfway through the second article, I heard Ricky say, "Why are they packing up? We have like ten minutes left."

"Ugh. They're stupid," Kate said.

Emma was shaking her head.

I followed her gaze to see Ted, Hunter, Justin and a few others sitting at their desks with their backpacks on, waiting.

"What the hell are you doing? There's still ten minutes left of class. Did I tell you to pack up? Why do you have your backpacks on? Why are you sitting at your desk with your backpacks on? Do you realize how ridiculous you look?"

I was blown away by the audacity. We were almost

halfway through the year. They knew better.

"You don't think any of this information is relevant? You realize this is for the final?" I was nearly yelling.

Student teacher does not handle apathy well.

No response.

"You come in here and do nothing but waste my time and theirs," I said, pointing to the few students who were still working.

There was no response, only dull, cow-eyed expressions.

"Put your stuff down. Put it down, and stand up. Stand up. Now!" I yelled.

Ted looked at me like I was reciting the original *Beowulf*.

"Ted. Up. Now," I yelled.

He looked at me and smiled.

"You have two options. Get up or get out."

His grinned wide like a jack o' lantern.

"Get the hell out of my class," I yelled. "Out!"

"I'm standing," he said in the silence. He rose and placed his hands in his pockets.

"No. You lost your chance. Go! Now! Get out!"

He grabbed his stuff and left, more annoyed than angry.

"Anyone want to join him?" I asked. They stared back at me. "You think this is a game, don't you? You think that none of this matters?"

There was only quiet.

I noticed trash around their desks. "You can't even sit in one place and not make a mess. Look at the floors around your desks."

There were protests.

"I didn't do that," Justin said.

"Yes. Yes, you did," I said. "It's from the packet you were tearing up. The packet I handed you. The packet that's still torn up on your desk. Don't tell me it wasn't you. There's trash everywhere from you guys."

They avoided my eyes.

"Leave your stuff at your desks," I said.

They slung off their backpacks and stood still.

"No one leaves this class until you finish cleaning up every single piece of scrap paper and trash off this floor. You can come in here and ignore me if you want to, but you won't come in here, ignore me, AND trash my classroom."

"I don't want to," Justin said.

"Do you think I care what you want? You think your boss who hires you out of pity because you're not qualified to do anything else will care what you want? You think your parents will care what you want when they finally kick you out of their basement at thirty? Are you smiling? You think this is a joke?" I grinned like a maniac. I may have come a little unhinged in that moment. "Justin thinks this is funny." I laughed. "Everyone else is going to think it's hilarious when I keep them in here after the buses leave because you decided not to do what I asked you to do. They'll think you're *hilarious*."

The students who were sitting there realized what that meant and started shouting at the kids to clean.

"Quiet!" I said. "The only sound I want to hear is them picking up trash."

Slowly, like drops of rain falling from a cloud before a storm, they began to follow instructions.

The bell rang.

"Stay seated."

Once they had finished, we stood there, staring at each other.

Half a minute passed in silence.

"If you think this sucks," I finally said, "imagine doing it every day. Imagine this is the only job that you can do because you don't have any other qualifications. Imagine working long, exhausting hours, laboring as your muscles tire and your back aches. Imagine your bodies growing old, and still, you struggle to work because it's the only way you can bring money home.

"You don't have to imagine. You know why? Because I've seen your parents, and I know what they do."

It was still quiet except for the bustle of students moving about the hall on the other side of the door.

"Think of your parents. You think this is the life they want for you? When you go home tonight, look your mother or your father or your grandmother in the eyes. Look at them when they come back from work or before they go to their next job. Stare into their eyes. That could be you.

"They're doing that for you, so you don't have to do this. You think this is a game, that I have nothing to teach you, that none of *this* matters. EVERYTHING MATTERS!" I yelled, slamming my fist on the board behind me with every syllable.

I let it sink in.

"My job—" I cleared my throat, raspy from the yelling. "My job is to help you improve your lives. But you come in here with your bullshit attitude and you think you can break me?" Eyes gazed toward the door. "I'm over here!" Heads turned. "You push me, and I'll push back ten times harder; I swear to God. You will NOT move me.

"Your parents work their asses off to give you a better life. You should work hard for them in return. And if you don't care about your parents, then do it for yourself. Do it because you know you deserve better.

"You can come in here watching each minute tick away in misery, or you can change your attitude and try to learn something. Think about *that* over the weekend. This assignment, the final, is hope. It's a chance for a better future." I knew they didn't care. I knew they weren't listening. I knew they just wanted to leave. But I had to try, if not for them, then at least for me. I wanted to feel like what I did meant something.

The sounds from the hall quieted as most of the children left.

We waited in silence before I shattered it with one sharp word: "Dismissed."

CHAPTER TWENTY-SEVEN

Fears

You will, at some point, ponder what would happen during a school shooting.

It's unavoidable.

Not all the time. Most days pass by without a thought of it, even for a hyper-anxious person like myself. But then something happens, and it bubbles to the surface.

It could be a story in the news, a friend mentioning something, or even a look a kid gave you that makes you wonder, "Would he?" And then you began to ask yourself, "What would I do?"

I knew I didn't want to die in my classroom. Maybe in my first year, in the beginning, when I still thought of teaching as some noble, glorious profession, I would have stood in front of a bullet for my kids. But what about at a school where I constantly questioned coming back to work?

Definitely not.

That was the thing. I would sit there sometimes and imagine myself in that situation, hoping I could follow through and do what needed to be done.

You might ask, "Why the fuck would you think of something like that?"

My youth had taught me always to expect the worst. It had helped me prepare for the inevitability that something would go wrong.

And so I would think about it. I would weigh the possibilities out in my head, preparing myself for any situation just in case shit went south. At least, that's what my anxious brain told me.

I would sit at my desk in silence long after the students left and a deep purple dyed the sky and imagine how I would react if I ever found myself in that horrible situation. Half-graded papers would lay abandoned as my thoughts carried me away. And when I had grown sufficiently unnerved, I would shake it off like an uncomfortable nightmare and return to work, flipping through an endless stack of subpar papers.

The thing is, I didn't want to die in my classroom. But I also know that if the situation ever occurred, out of instinct, I would take a bullet for those little bastards.

And that annoyed me.

Many of them hated me. Many of them talked shit about me outside of class. Many of them probably even wished someone *would* kill me. Some of them probably wanted to do it themselves. I had seen that look a few times, the look a kid gives you when you're struggling with him, eyes betraying thoughts of violence. You could almost see it dancing across their corneas as the fantasy played out in their minds.

You never forget those eyes.

I looked out at Period Nine.

Where they worth it?

When you think about sacrificing yourself for someone, you want it to be someone you love, respect, admire. I could barely tolerate them during the fifty minutes we spent together every day.

I cared about kids. I wouldn't have been a teacher

218

otherwise. I just didn't feel like I cared about *those* kids. How can you care for someone who doesn't give a shit about you?

No, they weren't all bad. And, yes, I get that it wasn't all their fault. There was no way you could look at Nemesis and blame the kid. There were too many other variables at play.

But in a life or death situation, where I needed to act instantly, I'd be lying if I said there wouldn't be some hesitation.

When I was a teacher, every time there was a school shooting, the world felt weird afterwards…fuzzy for a few days, like nothing made sense. That feeling would ultimately fade, at least until there was another one.

Earlier that week there had been a school shooting. Two kids were dead.

I should have known that it was coming.

The intercom blared, "Attention all students and staff, we are now in a lockdown." Instantly, my stomach twisted as my heart tried punching its way out through my throat.

I stood up and walked briskly to the door. With my key, I locked it from the outside, turned off the lights, and then forced the door closed against the resistance generated from its pump until it clicked shut. I nearly shouted at Period Nine. "Everyone please find a seat on the floor in that corner," I said, pointing to the far back corner of the class.

I turned around to see that they had listened and were slowly sulking over to the corner to sit down. With the door locked and lights off, the only thing left to do was close the blinds. Luckily, I hadn't pulled them up since August.

I joined them on the floor.

"3 Days Until Christmas…" glistened on the board in the back above their heads in red dry-erase marker.

"What's going on?" Ricky asked.

"Is something happening?" Kate followed.

"Please, I need everyone quiet," I said.

You never know if it's a drill or not.

Justin turned to talk to Ted.

"Stop talking," I hissed.

That was the lockdown protocol. We had trained during the summer in case anything happened. Sadly, it was perhaps the only training that really mattered.

There were two types of drills: lockdowns and lockouts.

A lockdown was the most serious. It meant that a threat was inside the school. We had to secure our classroom and wait for the all clear, which was either the principal or the police unlocking the door. You did nothing else except wait until that happened. There was no talking, no phone calls, and no texting. You sat, and you waited. Even if you heard a student or a staff member knocking on the door, you were to do nothing. You couldn't trust anyone.

Lockouts were less severe but still serious. It meant that there was a threat in the area. Admin locked all the outside doors, and no one was allowed to move between the buildings. Class still carried on though. Nothing much changed except you couldn't go outside or let anyone inside.

In that neighborhood, there were a couple of real lockouts that happened because of neighborhood crime. One time several people were killed in a house nearby before school even started. The police arrived and secured the scene, but while they were doing that, we had to hang out in the cafeteria for a few hours, waiting.

That day it was a lockdown, and I was with Period Nine.

"Put your phones away," I said as I sat there on the floor next to them. They looked at me, hesitated, then slid the phones back into their pockets. To be honest, I was probably more anxious than they were, and I hated myself for that.

Ted snorted at something Justin said.

I snarled at him, and he stifled the giggle with an eye roll. I knew that if someone burst through that door somehow, I'd be really fucking annoyed at having to take a bullet for any of those fucktards.

"Is this a drill?" Kate whispered. "What if it's for real?"

"I'm not sure. They don't tell us, but we'll be okay," I whispered.

"There was a school shooting the other day," Ricky said.

"Quiet," I hissed.

We sat there on the floor and waited in silence as the minutes passed.

It was the worst possible situation. I was in a locked, darkened room, with Nemesis, Ted, and Justin. And they couldn't do anything else but sit there. I began to wonder, *What if they start fighting? What if Nemesis tried to storm out of the class?*

It made me wish they had decided to suspend the kid for more than two days. I thought for sure it would have been at least a week, but apparently telling a teacher to *fuck off* wasn't so bad.

Each minute was a footstep on broken glass. I didn't know what I would do if they behaved like they usually did. Would I have to fight the kid? I knew I couldn't let Nemesis leave if something happened. That was for sure. No one could be allowed to open that door. Suddenly, I wished I had the forethought to ask Nimitz those kinds of questions.

Would I sacrifice myself for them? I thought.

I looked at each kid. I hated teaching them. That was true. But I didn't hate *them.* Every day they came to my class was a chance for change. Maybe they would take longer than others. Maybe some of them would never change. But every day they came into my room was a chance.

We continued to wait. Some of them laid down to take a nap, completely unfazed. Others picked at the carpet. Hunter drew quietly. Nemesis listened to inaudible music. Justin picked at himself. Ted gazed at the gray light that seeped in through the spaces around the blinds.

I leaned up against the desk and slid my foot forward, watching.

Waiting.

CHAPTER TWENTY-EIGHT

The Moment of Truth

The lockdown turned out to be a drill.

I sat in the shower, beneath the steam, watching the water circle down the drain. Steam billowed over the curtain. It was hard to breathe, yet soothing at the same time.

I closed my eyes, focusing on the pulsating water. It had been a long day followed by a long night. And while the long hours wrecked me, at least when I was waiting tables, I didn't have to worry about school shootings. Having an alarm clock rip me away from a sleeping bag I barely warmed was a small sacrifice for that security.

I was tired of working two jobs. But it would be years before I quit waiting tables, my class keys handed over long before I retired my apron.

Waiting tables was easier than teaching, and it paid more. And unlike teaching, the only thing that haunted me when I left that place was a few flaky food stains that came out after a pass through the laundry.

Staring into the reality of what that lockdown meant, I began to question more and more if I wanted to keep teaching. And as the pre-shower coffee slowly percolated in my veins, I looked to the flowing water, a river carrying away the filth from the night before, and wondered.

Can I live without teaching? I thought.

It was constantly there. Everything was a lesson. It didn't matter where I was or what I was doing.

If I was at a baseball game and a guy dropped a $20, I would pick it up and hand it to him, knowing I could come back to class the next day and use it as a teachable moment.

If I had a weird night at the restaurant, I would show up at school the next day, ready to share.

I saw lessons while waiting in traffic on the drive home, rolling silverware at the end of a shift, watching the bubbles in my beer pop and fade. And I even saw lessons as I sat in the shower, hoping the hot water and the caffeine would pull me together in time for another long day.

I wanted to be the best.

I know that based upon my story so far, knowing what you know about me now, that it may seem hard to believe, but I truly wanted to be the best. In those moments, working towards the holidays, teaching was all I had.

I had already lost one love. I wasn't ready to lose another.

I felt overwhelmed. It was too much. Too constant. My goal was too impossible. All I had ever wanted to do was help people. That's why I chose to teach. And there I was, a teacher at a school that needed me, but instead of embracing me, they fought me, cast me out, attacked me. For the first time, I truly contemplated quitting. Not the passive-aggressive, "I'm going to quit. I'm over this" reaction that's more of a whine than an actual threat.

No.

I contemplated surrender.

I wanted to call the office and say, "I can't do it anymore" before disappearing out of all their lives. Other teachers had done it, had simply disappeared. The kids came back wondering what the hell had happened. It was easy to surrender. You just…stopped.

But when I reached for the phone, I thought of the people I would let down. Not the students, though I knew deep down, they needed me. No. I thought of Wilson and the others, Nimitz especially. The man defied the district when he invited me to teach at his school.

I won't lie to you. If I could somehow warn my younger self, even to this day, I would tell him not to teach. Without hesitation. And by the time I finish this story, you'll understand why.

Just know that at that moment, staring down at the drain, exhausted, trying to build up enough pressure to push through my day, I still had fight left in me.

I stayed in the shower until the water ran cold.

As I put on my suit, I thought about what that day meant for me. It was the moment of truth. Our big discussion. The final.

I grabbed my bag and shotgunned another cup of coffee, then filled up a thermos with more and tossed in plenty of basic bitch creamer for good measure before heading to the door.

I looked back at my apartment before I left. It was more a hovel than a home. There was no furniture, only a sleeping bag resting on a hardwood floor. What few belongings I had were in plastic bags. And two flipped open suitcases held a haphazard collection of all my clothes. I needlessly locked the door behind me and left.

At school, I went straight to my room to set up for the seminar. As I moved desks into a makeshift circle, I exposed bits of paper, candy wrappers, and the odd Cheeto bag that I kicked aside. The result was a disfigured circular shape of desks, all facing each other. Along the walls rested several extra desks for the students who failed to prepare.

"1 Day Until Christmas" stared at me in red as I wrote the

"big question" on the board.

"You ready for the big day?" Wilson strolled in and took a look around. Behind him, students trailed down the hall. "Excuse me," he said before I could answer. "I'm sorry, guys. The bell doesn't ring for another ten minutes. I know it's cold out there, but you can't come in here until the bell rings. We've talked about this. I know I know. But teachers need the time to prepare. I know. I'm sorry."

"Still no word on keys?" I asked when he returned.

"They won't give us any."

"I don't get it," I said. "They hate being here, but they come in early."

"It's warm. It's safe." He shrugged. "Today's the day. Are you excited?"

"If by 'the day' you mean a reminder that we couldn't even read a hundred pages in two months. Then, yes. Today's the day."

"Oh come on, don't be so harsh. Look at it this way. At least you know what you'll be teaching next quarter," he teased.

"Are you always so optimistic?" I asked.

"Annoyingly so, I'm afraid."

"It's a shame you have the same plan as I do. Otherwise, I'd invite you to watch."

"You want to show off some of your 'Golden Boy' tactics?"

"You're not going to let that go, are you?"

"Nope.

"I'm not trying to show off. It's just that the ones I've done in the past have been really cool."

"Just remember, this isn't your old school. Don't get discouraged if it doesn't turn out how you imagined it would."

I nodded.

"Either way, good luck today," he said and moved toward

the door.

"Wilson. Have you gotten any emails from my ex-boss?" I asked when he reached the door. "It's been a while since we've had to hide during our plans."

He smiled wide. "Nope. Nothing."

"I was just curious," I said.

"I don't think we'll have to deal with that anymore."

"No?"

"You'll soon learn that these things come and go."

"And this one's going?"

"I believe so," he said. "Have a good day." And with that, he turned and left. It appeared that students weren't the only ones who struggled with follow through.

As soon as he entered the hallway, a tiny seventh grader appeared out of nowhere and followed him into his room asking him questions. A few more people followed. I could hear Wilson lead them all back outside.

Once the bell rang, the masses flooded into the building. They usually only trickled in, but it was below freezing that day, so every few seconds, a booming slam from the heavy metallic doors would bang echoes down the hall.

I sat in my room, waiting for my computer to come to life.

Suddenly, I heard a much louder slam as the door hit the railing outside. Then there was a very high-pitched caw that could only be Nemesis. I held my breath as the kid stomped past my door and down the hall.

After Nemesis passed, I realized I had been clenching and forced myself to relax.

Students continued to move in and out of the building. Many of them had several plates of food; some had gifts; a few had balloons. It was the last day before break, and many of them would be passing out presents to their friends or favorite teachers.

From my desk, I could see them darting in and out of

Wilson's and Mack's classrooms, and I imagined they did the same with the classes down the hall.

No one entered my class.

I wasn't surprised.

Soon there was yelling right outside. I logged onto my computer, thinking it would pass, that it was some middle schooler cracked out on sugar, ready for the break. The noise grew until it was the only thing I could hear.

I recognized the voice.

I moved from my desk to the hall, stumbling into the worse case scenario: Nemesis was arguing with another kid named Donnie.

Nemesis and Donnie were too similar and too opposite. Donnie was much quieter, but if he was ever pushed to his limit...he would react. It was rare, but when it happened, a staff meeting typically followed.

Donnie was nearing Vesuvius in terms of volatility when I reached the hallway. I immediately jumped in. "Donnie. Donnie, calm down. It's okay. What's wrong?"

"You can't do that! You can't do that!" Donnie was repeating, pointing at Nemesis. I had no idea what had happened, but I moved quickly.

"Donnie," I said again, standing between him and Nemesis. He was looking through me to Nemesis, body shaking, spit forming at the corners of his mouth. I hadn't seen him act like this before.

Nemesis's voice screeched around me, and I knew I needed to get Donnie out of the hall before he snapped. He was the kind of kid that would start hitting and wouldn't care who he struck.

"It's okay," I said. "Hey, buddy, talk to me. Talk to me."

"It's not okay. It's not," Donnie said.

"You're right. You're right. That's not okay. Here. Sit with me in my room. We'll hang out in there. You can vent to me.

228

It's okay. Someone will handle the rest."

The kid was muttering curse words under his breath, spit slushing at the corners of his lips.

Nemesis started shouting something at him. Donnie twitched and suddenly tried to lunge at the kid. I quickly stood in his way, trying to get him to look me in the eyes, trying to distract him.

I had absolutely no idea what the fuck I was doing. Slowly he turned to look at me but avoided my eyes as so many of them often did. "Hey, buddy. Let's talk in my room. Come on," I said. "It's okay."

In my mind I was thinking, *please don't punch me in the face.* It would have made a fitting but unfortunate end to the quarter.

He was returning to a simmer.

We walked into my room. He sat down muttering curses under his breath as he rocked back and forth.

The other teachers handled Nemesis. I could hear yelling in the hallway. Donnie didn't seem to notice. He just sat there, rocking and back and forth, waiting.

I stood there next to him until Ritz arrived with the school psychologist. It took some coaxing, but they eventually took him away.

That had been enough hall duty for me that day. I sat at my desk and spaced out for a few minutes, trying to process what the fuck had just happened.

"Mister," I heard a voice say.

I looked up, "Yes?"

"I need to talk to you," Helen said suddenly, breaking my concentration.

"What?" I said, more curt than intended.

"I need to talk to you," she repeated.

"Oh. Yeah," I said, still feeling slightly unnerved.

"I asked you yesterday if it was okay at lunch to talk with

---

you. You said to come by today in the morning," Helen said.

Did I? That was stupid, I thought. Then I noticed she was crying.

I wasn't sure why she came to me. I wasn't a counselor. I wasn't qualified. Most of my students couldn't tolerate me. Still. She needed someone to listen.

Every student has a story.

She cried. I told her it would be okay. After a while, she calmed down, as much as anyone could in her situation.

"I appreciate you coming to talk to me. It means a lot that you trust me," I said. "But you also need to speak to someone at the school. I can make you an appointment if you like?"

"I don't want to talk to a therapist."

"I get that. I do. But, I'm not qualified to answer these kinds of questions," nor was I qualified to deal with emotions, especially ones covered in tears.

She nodded.

"You'll be in good hands," I said. I honestly had no idea. I had never spoken to the school shrink. Different circles.

Helen wiped away fresh tears and asked, "Can I have a hug?"

"Um," I paused. "Sure. I guess."

Wilson had told me that opening up to them about my problems would help them see me as human. I didn't realize it also meant they would come to me with their problems.

I shook off the feeling. I was there to teach. The final was that day. That was my focus. Everything else was secondary.

When the day ended, I moved around my room, slowly putting the pieces back together. I should have listened to Wilson and lowered my expectations. The final had been a disaster. Too many kids had been absent. Of those that had shown up, many didn't do what they had needed to do to participate. Of those that did, they hadn't said much. It had been a failure.

230

I had been a failure.

My class emptied, and I took a seat on my shitty plastic chair, trying to process the fact that we were only halfway there.

CHAPTER TWENTY-NINE

Cougar Den

Wilson decided to take me out for a drink. And after my week, it was well-deserved.

It was the Wednesday after the Winter Break.

He had been going on and on about the place for a while, but I had always shied away from the offer. He had said it was a great place to meet women, but I was still hung up on my ex. Things were different now, much different.

"If any of these ladies want to take you home and fuck the shit out of you, don't let me stop you," Wilson said, looking at me.

"There isn't a woman under forty in this place," I said.

"And they're willing to show you they're still young." He winked and held up the shot of whiskey the server had just dropped off. "To you not dying!"

"To me not dying," I said and clinked my glass to his. I threw the shot back and ignored the sharp ache in my neck from the sudden tilt. I grimaced. Whether it was from the bourbon or the accident, I couldn't tell you.

"That's my drink right there," he said.

"Ugh." My face cringed. "It tastes like it was poured out of an old shoe, filtered through charcoal, and then zested with gasoline."

"Elixir of the gods," he said.

"If you say so." I was still cringing. As a server in a restaurant, you meet a lot of "men". Bastards with big beards who drink whiskey like milk. If that was what being a man was, I was far from it. "I'll stick to beer. Preferably right after Period Nine or during. If we could have someone walk by and hand me an IPA, like a bomber, a big fucking bottle, I would crack it open, take a huge gulp, then look at them and say, '*You* did this to me.'"

"We've all been there." He looked around our table. "Not a bad spot, right?"

I surveyed the scene.

It had the feel of an old hunting lodge but without the creepy stuffed animals. The place was dimly lit with dark, heavily dented wooden tables. Every surface in the joint was made from thick, heavy wood (maybe that's why there were so many older women there) that dampened the noise and made it easier to have a conversation, despite the place being fairly crowded.

We had found a table off in the back with huge, worn leather seats. Books lined the shelves on the far wall, and flames licked fake logs inside a fireplace to our side.

"Assuming that the woman in the corner over there with the rapey eyes doesn't drug me and drag me out of here, I'd agree."

"I'd encourage her to," he said, smiling.

"You creepy fuck," I said. "Not normally my type of place, to be honest. I tend to hang out near the city center."

"Hipster," he taunted, shaking his head. "This is more my speed."

I was learning that about Wilson. He was maybe only eight years older than me, but the man had refined tastes. He hated pop culture. He loathed technology (he didn't even have a smartphone). And he was more inclined to listen to Sinatra than one of the countless bands bubbling up on the charts.

I leaned back in my chair to straighten my vest, more as a twitch than a necessity.

"I can't believe you worked today," Wilson said.

"The accident wasn't that bad."

"And you say you aren't the Golden Boy."

"I'm not. I only came in because I don't have emergency sub plans."

He laughed. "You were supposed to do those in August."

"I never got around to it. Besides, hanging around my shitty apartment all day would be more painful than teaching with whiplash." I thought about my car and how mangled it was. "Fuck. Now I gotta figure out when to buy a new car. I only had the thing for about six weeks."

"And it was her fault?"

"Yeah. She got a ticket at the scene. It was kind of intense. There were like two fire trucks, a few police cars, a traffic jam, two tow trucks, and pieces of car shit all over the road."

"And you're not in any pain?"

"My neck hurts. But a few more of these and I'll be fine." We tipped our glasses together, and I took a swig of my beer.

"When's your doctor's appointment?"

"Earliest I could get in was Friday. I'll have to function until then," I said.

"Rough day, man. And you said the cunt is with someone else?" Wilson asked nonchalantly.

"Yeah," I sighed. That had been how the day had started. "She's already moved on. It's time I do the same."

"That's why I brought you here," he said.

I looked back at the room. "To steal someone's retirement?"

"They're not that old," he said.

I had made the mistake of looking at her social media. She had posted pictures of her celebrating Christmas with her new boyfriend. We had only been broken up for two months. It still hurt, a dull pain that occasionally spiked until I knocked back a glass or crushed a Xanax. We had been together for years. She had talked about kids. And in two months, she had moved on to someone else. It was stupid to snoop, but I let curiosity get the best of me.

I had left my house feeling hurt, and then the car accident happened. It had been like life was trying to bitchslap some sense into me. I was stubborn, so it would take an automobile to have the desired effect. I needed to pull my head out of my ass and move on. There hadn't been any hope of reviving that relationship, not after what she did. It was over. I had to understand that the person I fell in love with was gone. She had changed.

It was time to move on.

"Well, look, man. I didn't just bring you here to let these sexy broads distract you." He nodded to a crowd that looked like they were waiting for a game of bingo to begin. "I don't live too far away from you. I can give you a ride in while you figure out the car situation."

"You don't have to do that. Besides, I don't want to be a burden."

"No burden. I wouldn't offer if it were. You're on my way."

"But I have to work at my other job in the evening."

"I'll take you there too," he said. "Really, I don't mind. You can sling some of that tip money my way for gas, and I'll give you a ride until you get a car."

How could anyone be so generous?

"I don't know what to say," I said.

"Just drink. Cheers!" After we put our glasses down, he added, "Besides, it's about time some good luck came your way."

I wanted to change the subject. "Tell me about this 'Dart Night' of yours. I've heard a few people mention it, but no one ever goes into detail. People keep asking me if you've taken me to one. When's that going to happen?"

"When you're ready,"

"*I'm* not ready?"

"Not for dart night. I need to see if you can hang."

"I wait tables. That basically makes me a professional alcoholic," I said.

"That may be the case, but I need to know you can hang."

"Uh huh," I said.

"You know that's how I got my job."

"Darts? Fuck. If we were hired based on any sense of athleticism, I'd be fucking unemployed. I can barely piss in a toilet without missing the bowl."

"Not by winning darts," he laughed. "I met Nimitz at a dart competition. I stepped outside to smoke a cigar and started talking to him. I told him I used to be a teacher and that I was looking for a job. He told me he was a principal looking for an English teacher. We talked for a while, and then he asked me to come by for an interview. He hired me the next day."

"From darts?"

"From darts."

"I'm more than a little envious. I always hear stories about people easily slipping into teaching. That's never been my case. I think Nimitz hired me out of desperation. Even when I first started in the district, I was a Hail Mary hire. I was pulled from a school I was subbing at to teach at the main campus because the teacher there was having seizures. I'm everyone's last option."

"That's why I brought you here," he joked.

"Savage," I said.

"What?"

"I can't believe I just said that. *Shit*. One of my freshmen says that all the time. I need to get out more," I said.

236

"That'll happen. Fourteen years into this profession, and you pick up a few things from these kids."

"I can't believe you've been doing this for fourteen years. Where did you start out?"

He told me the name of the school. "I taught Freshmen English there for seven years."

"What made you change schools?"

The waitress came over with our food. Wilson ordered another round.

"What happened?" I asked again once she left.

Wilson told me his story.

He had been very young when he walked into his first classroom with nothing but a box of printer paper that was supposed to last him the whole year.

It didn't faze him. He loved teaching. You could have given him a broken piece of chalk and a water-damaged copy of *Romeo and Juliet* and he would have moved kids to learn.

While I was bitching about my shitty projector or a laptop that froze more than an Eskimo exhibitionist, Wilson had taught with far less and managed to make it work.

He continued to talk about teaching and how much had changed since he started. He spoke with disdain of federal initiatives and the politics of education. I couldn't tell you anything about those topics other than the names of some of the laws, and you probably know them already. I just didn't care. My main focus was on being an effective teacher. I found the politics pointless. But Wilson's passion for education ran deep. He knew everything about the subject, it seemed.

He moved past his philosophical manifesto on education and focused directly on the events that led him to our school.

Politics.

It's unbelievable that you could be in a classroom, fighting to change lives, and know that you can't turn to some of your team members because of the political games they played. I knew all about that from my previous year. If you didn't make nice with your colleagues, whispers made their way to the ears of those who make the decisions.

The more Wilson talked, the more I realized how much my not being asked to return had nothing to do with my teaching. It was because I had refused to play the game.

Just like Wilson.

Wilson's problem had been his principal. His boss had been a little too handsy, a little too welcoming. And when Wilson had refused him, he found out just how miserable that man could make his life.

At the beginning of this story, I told you that teachers aren't "unfireable." That's true. If you wanted to fire a teacher in their first year, you simply didn't renew their contract. That's what had happened to me. It was the "diet" version of being fired.

But if a teacher makes it through the introductory period, barring them doing anything criminal, then firing that teacher becomes messy. It becomes work.

It was work Wilson's boss welcomed.

After he turned down his boss's advances, the principal began picking apart his class, showing up unannounced, criticizing his teaching, looking for holes.

He made Wilson's life hell.

When Wilson slipped up and showed a Shakespeare film without asking for permission slips, his boss pulled him into the office.

The two argued. It became heated. The principal had what he needed.

Wilson was asked to resign.

It was all too similar.

When you're angry, you say stupid shit, and I had said plenty at the end of my first year.

More food appeared and disappeared. Drinks emptied and exchanged. The fire still flickered over the unburned logs, and a distant audience of grandmas licked their lips in anticipation.

"That's bullshit," I said. "As if we don't have enough problems with the kids, you got to worry about the fucking casting couch."

"Teaching's mostly politics. I try to stay clear of it and focus on the kids," he said.

"I just want to teach this fucking novel. I want to feel like I can be successful, and then maybe I can stand back and feel some pride. And I know this sounds crazy, but maybe I can start to feel like a professional because I sure as hell don't feel like one now."

"One of my college professors told me that teaching is blue-collar work."

"Bullshit," I said. "I spent five years learning to be a teacher between my undergrad and my post-grad degrees. I'm not a fucking janitor."

"How many times do you pick up trash off the floor in your room? Make copies? Wipe down desks? Repeat directions endlessly? We're underpaid factory foremen. They get us at a rate for forty hours a week when we're really working sixty.

"You may be able to frame up those pretty pieces of paper and mount them to your wall, but at the end of the day, what we do is no different than what a janitor does. It's all the same."

I was annoyed. "Then why do it? Why not leave and do something else?"

"I've always wanted to be a teacher, ever since I was nine. When my classmates were out running around at recess or taking off when the bell rang, I was talking to teachers, asking them how to become one. Several told me not to, but I kept at it. It's my passion.

"You teach countless kids over the years. You impact lives. You gain a deeper understanding of the world. You learn life's value. No other job can ever do that."

"You ever think about doing anything else?" I asked, more for myself.

"Sometimes I wonder if I should've gone into law like my father, but it's not really for me. I've helped him with his work over the years. It's nice to have that insight, but it's not my passion. I know that I would've hated it after a while. It's empty. Teaching is the only thing of substance for me."

"Your father's a lawyer? What was that like?"

"Having grown up around lawyers, I can tell you that teachers work just as much as trial lawyers do."

"Really?" I wasn't sure I believed that.

"Easily. Think about it. Trial lawyers get a case, spend eighty hours a week preparing for it, then have downtime between that case and the next one before doing it all over again. Education is the same. Teachers put in continuous hours every day. We may get summers off, but most teachers work another job or teach summer school or plan over the summer. So it's really about the same amount of work, only with less money and far less prestige."

"When you put it that way, I'm so glad I chose this profession."

"We're not in it for the money," he said.

"What's wrong with wanting money?" I asked. "Why is it such a bad thing to not only want to make a difference but also earn a livable wage? That pisses me off.

"People look at doctors and lawyers, people whose primary job involves helping people, and think, wow. Impressive, they deserve their pay. But if a teacher speaks up and asks for money, all of a sudden you're a pariah.

"Why does everyone think we're supposed to be self-sacrificing messiahs? If I complain about the pay, my friends say, 'You get summers off.' But they don't realize that we all work way more than having a summer break justifies. And most of us work through our summers. And then you have people like you spending thousands of dollars on books just so they can do their jobs."

"That's why it's blue-collar work." He shrugged. "My mom never wanted me to be a teacher. She was embarrassed when I told her."

"No way." I didn't hide my shock.

"If I were gay, and came out to her, she would have handled that better than she did when I told her I was going to be a teacher."

"What? Why?"

"She thought it was beneath me. She sees teachers the same way people see janitors or garbage workers or someone working at the DMV: low-class civil servants."

"That's fucked up," I said.

"It may seem that way at first, but just now you said that you're overworked and underpaid. Is that any different? You have two degrees that get spat on as you scoop up trash and remind your students to take out their pens and paper at the beginning of every class. Why are you so upset with Period Nine?"

"Because they don't do anything."

"They don't do anything because they don't respect you. Would you agree that if your freshmen respected you, that they would try harder?"

"I suppose," I said.

"That's why my mom never wanted me to be a teacher. She felt that there's very little respect in it."

"Then why do it? Why not just quit and get a job that doesn't drain the life out of you every single day?" I was visibly upset, and I think he could tell. I know now that he was being honest with me. He wanted me to see education for what it was and not the glamorized version that gets advertised.

"Because we do make a difference. Maybe not as often as we'd like, maybe a couple of kids out of every year you teach will feel the impact of your actions. It'll be from something you most likely didn't realize, something you mumbled in class one day, tired and hungover, or maybe it'll be from a lesson you rushed to put together that somehow managed to click and stick with them over the years, or it could be from a quick conversation after class. Whatever the reason, your actions set them out on a different path. Most times, you won't notice any difference. They'll leave, and you'll mostly forget them. Then one day you'll get an email from a name you don't quite recognize. And as you remember, it'll all come rushing back, and you'll have this moment where you know you made an impact. You'll realize that *you* made the difference, that being a teacher *mattered*. It's a long-term investment, and you don't get back nearly as much as you put in, but you do get something back, something that only being a teacher provides."

"I don't like those odds," I said.

"Yes. You do. That's why you're in the game," Wilson said.

"No. I don't. I don't want to struggle year after year. It feels like I'm on the *Titanic*. The education system is a sinking ship. And we're all on board, running around with buckets, fruitlessly tossing spoonfuls of water back into the ocean. Every day is about survival, running around endlessly just to keep our heads above water. I can't do that forever."

"There are bad years and good years. Do you think *all* of your ninth-graders are horrible?"

"No, of course not. There are a few great kids in that class. They're just swallowed up by a lot of bullshit."

"And next year your eighth-graders will replace them. Do

you think that'll make it better?"

"True. And yes. I know technically we're not supposed to have favorites, but Sofía and Zooey are cool. There are a couple of others, too."

"They're awesome kids," Wilson said.

"They are...at least when they're not acting like typical eighth-graders."

"Are *they* worth it? Are *they* worth the frustration, the sacrifice, the effort?"

"My freshmen make me constantly second-guess being a teacher." I paused. "But my eighth-graders remind me why I became one."

"So they *are* worth it."

"I don't know," I said, leaning back in my chair. "Some days, yes. On those days, I leave school thinking I have the best job in the world. Some days, I'm unsure. And some days I want to scream until I cough up blood."

"If you're going to stay in this profession for the long run, you have to be prepared to gain nothing in return. You have to be ready for disappointment. You have to expect failure. Our job is people, and people always, in one way or another, let you down."

I leaned back as he spoke those words. Gazing into the fire, I wondered if I was willing to stay in a career with those kinds of odds.

"It's a broken system," I said.

"In a lot of ways, you're right, my good man."

We stood there in quiet for a moment until Wilson said, "So, are there any attractive women at this restaurant you work at?"

Laughing, I looked around at the drinking raisins that surrounded us and took a sip of beer. "Tons."

CHAPTER THIRTY

Same Shit, Different Day

"What are we doing today, Mister?" Charles asked.

He had discovered that I hated that question and decided to make sure he asked it every single day.

"Things and stuff," I said.

"Come on, Mister. Tell me."

"We're going to start off doing some things. And probably end up doing some stuff at some point."

"Ugh, Mister. Just tell me." He dropped his arms to his sides and pouted.

"We've been over this. Why would I waste time telling you what we're doing, then have to turn around, and tell everyone else all over again?"

"Whatever. I don't even care," he said as went and found his seat.

Joaquín walked in and asked, "Hey, Mister, what are we doing today?"

"Test corrections," I said.

"Cool," he said.

"Wait! You tell him, but not me? That's messed up," Charles said.

"I don't remember you asking," I said.

"Messed up. Real messed up," Charles repeated.

"It's because you're a ginger," Anita said. "No one likes gingers."

"People like gingers," Charles said.

"No," Anita said. "No, they don't."

"Truth," Joaquín said.

"Tell them that's not true, Mister." He looked at me.

"Sorry, busy," I said. I was pretending to read emails.

"Your mom likes gingers," Charles said.

"Nice one," Joaquín scoffed. "That may be true, but we all know that your real mother doesn't and that's why she left you behind a dumpster."

"That's cold," Anita said.

"Man, you're messed up," Charles said. "You know that?"

"You guys are still friends, right?" I asked.

"More like brothers," Joaquín said.

"He's more like a son to me," Charles smirked.

"I would kill myself," he replied. "I'd kill you first, then definitely kill myself."

"He's just mad because I know his mom." He paused. "Carnally."

"Charles," I said as the bell rang.

A few students rushed in late and took their seats.

"Why's Bob suspended?" I asked no one in particular. You weren't supposed to discuss those things with students, but as Wilson said, it wasn't your typical school. If everyone didn't already know, I would have been shocked.

"He punched Nemesis in the head," Anita said.

"Great. Now the kid's going to be even more brain damaged," Charles said.

"Charles. Enough. Not okay," I said.

"Why? It's not like Nemesis is here," he fired back.

"I don't care. I'm not cool with you talking like that about another student," I said. "Bob punched Nemesis?"

"He hit Nemesis so hard that the kid's head dented the wall," Anita said. "That's what I heard, anyway. And I haven't seen Nemesis today. Probably going to the doctor."

"I'm pretty sure a team of doctors couldn't fix that kid," Charles said.

"Charles."

"Agreed," Joaquín murmured.

"Is it true Clarissa tried to add you on Facebook?" Anita asked.

I sighed. "We aren't talking about that. But, since you brought it up." I looked out towards the class. "Everyone, listen up! Please. Please. Please do not add me on any form of social media. It's just weird. I have my own life, and you have yours...kinda. So, let's keep it that way."

"You have a life?" someone said.

I ignored the bait.

I had heard enough horror stories about people losing their jobs for posting on social media. I wasn't about to join them. I thought I had hidden my profile, but apparently I missed some setting or something. It had genuinely freaked me out, so I had deleted my entire account. Maybe it had been a slight overreaction, but either way, it felt better to get rid of it altogether. It was less to worry about it. My friends were upset, but they'd get over it. They weren't the ones who would have to deal with students finding a picture of them playing beer pong.

Meanwhile, my body still ached from the accident. I went into my bag for some Tylenol and saw the bottle of Xanax resting in there. My heart ached, but I shook the feeling off and left the pills in the bag.

I needed to focus.

Once I finished attendance, I stood up and went to the front of the class. "Today, I'm going to let you correct your tests from yesterday," I said. Just like before, I demanded that they read during the break; just like before, not many did it, and just like before, I had tested them like I said I would.

They were still pretty bad, but now I knew to let them fix their failures. It wasn't ideal, but it worked.

"Put everything away except your notes and a pen. You know what, you can even use the book. The only thing you can't use is your neighbor. You're going to correct your tests from yesterday. I won't lie to you. They were horrible. You'll see that when you get them. But don't worry, you get to fix them. When you're finished, you can continue reading," I said.

"I don't have a pen," Jeff said, strangely awake.

"Do you have a pair of scissors?" I asked.

"No? How would that help me?" he asked.

"Poke your finger. Write in blood," I said.

"Does anyone have scissors?"

"Sarcasm. Jeff. Sarcasm," I said.

"I'll give you a pair, but you have to promise to slit your wrists with them," Charles said.

"What the hell, Charles?" I asked.

"I'm just playing."

"You're so stupid," Jeff said. "Why would I slit my wrists?"

"You're right. That would mean you'd actually have to do something. And we all know how good you are at that," Charles paused. "It's a good thing living doesn't take much effort."

"*Pinche pendejo*," Jeff said.

"Charles, talk to me after class. Jeff, I know what that means," I said while handing back the tests. "No cheating. No phones. No bribing me with your mothers. No summoning the ghost of Mary Shelley in a demonic ritual to ask her questions. Charles, I'm talking to you there. We'll regrade them later."

"Why don't you ever grade the tests?" Chelsea asked, her

face coated heavy in makeup and glitter.

"Why would I do it when you can?" I asked.

"You're lazy."

"Work smart, not hard," I said. "Now, put as much effort into this as you do your makeup."

"Thank you, Mister," she said.

"I don't think that was a compliment," Joaquín said.

"Can I get a packet?" Kelly asked me.

"Kelly! You're back again! How've you been?"

She rolled her eyes. "I've been good, Mister. Sorry I was absent."

"I'm just glad you're here," I said.

At my desk, I began putting together the sub plans for when I would be at the doctor's the next day. The pain in my neck was constant but manageable. But that wasn't what bothered me. The thing was, I didn't want to be absent.

Setting up for a sub and dealing with the aftermath was work. There was always some problem. I knew this because I began my teaching career as a substitute. I would wake up every day in the morning around five a.m. to a robot telling me to fill a vacancy at a school. Some days were chill, but there was always an issue of some kind, a kid failing to follow directions or someone telling me to "fuck off and die inside a horse's ass."

I treated each assignment as a working interview, leaving my card when I finished along with a full, detailed report. Most times, subs are retired teachers looking for an easy way to double dip by leaning on twenty years of professional muscle memory. And rightly so. But for me, I had heard stories about how new teachers worked their way into a school by being a substitute. When I wasn't hired at the beginning of my first year, that's what I had to do. So, I understood the challenges a sub faced on a daily basis, especially at that school.

I was putting together sub plans when I looked up and saw Sallie gazing intently over her shoulder at her friend's test. I stared for a minute and contemplated the sight. It was an open book, open note, open anything except your neighbor revision of a test. It wasn't even the real test. And she was cheating. *Great.* I thought.

"Sallie. Sallie. Sallie!"

"What, Mister?"

"Really?"

"What?"

"You staring at her test and writing down the answers."

"Oh."

I walked over to her and took her test.

"What do I do now?" Sallie asked.

I crumpled up her test and threw it at the trash, watching it hit the rim and bounce off. "Read. Mediate. Think of how to cheat better in the future so you don't get caught? I dunno." I shrugged. "You do you."

The rest of the period passed relatively uneventful. My students retested, and I planned out how the rest of the quarter would go down. I had some ideas for projects that I thought were pretty cool, and I wanted to move away from reading so much and instead focus on more activities. I wanted my class not to suck so bad.

As time ticked toward the end of class, I stopped them to make an announcement. "You have a sub tomorrow. And I'm sure you've had plenty of teachers tell you to make sure you respect the sub. I'm asking you to do that now. The subs are here to help us out. I wouldn't be missing school unless it was necessary. Tomorrow, I'm going to the doctor—"

"Are you dying?" Sallie asked.

"Only on the inside," I said.

"It's from his accident, stupid," Charles said.

"Charles."

"You were in an accident?"

"Oh my god," Anita said.

"Anita."

"Mister—"

"It's not worth it." I rolled my eyes. "Yes. I told you this yesterday. Anyways. Please be kind and listen to the sub."

I stopped and let that sink in, looking out at them. Then I added, "Let me make myself very clear. If you step out of line tomorrow, I will walk you to the office myself and call for a meeting with your parents. I am not messing around here. I don't want to hear any negative complaints. Is that understood?"

They nodded.

But they didn't listen.

CHAPTER THIRTY-ONE

Gutted

I saw Wilson's car pull up on the other side of the gate to my apartment complex. I rushed down the small, freshly plowed stairs and felt the grit of salt beneath my shoes. A few quick steps had me down the path and out the gate.

A coat of street sludge from the on-again, off-again snow storms clung to the bottom half of his car, making the old, run-down Honda look older and more run down.

I felt the salt grime as I opened the car door and threw my man satchel inside before taking a seat, cradling my coffee thermos for warmth. Before he could put the car in drive, I asked him, "Any problems with the sub?"

"I wanted to talk to you about that." He cringed. "There were a few problems."

"Great. How bad? They tell her to fuck off? Or was it a fight? If it was a fight, it doesn't count against me. I wasn't there," I said. We had a running competition for who was the best at classroom management between us. He said he was better because, in all his years of teaching, he only had two fights break out in his class. I had more than that by the end of the first quarter.

"Worse."

"Worse than a fight? Did one of them take a shit on my desk?" With their usual responses to when I made them read, I was surprised I hadn't opened up the bottom drawer to my desk to find a big, nutty mound of shit with bits of torn up novel used for wiping paper resting on the top.

"No. Not quite." Wilson turned onto the main street. "Two students threatened the sub."

"Oh. Well, that sucks," I said, staring out the window. It didn't seem that bad.

"They threatened to stab her in the stomach and rip out her unborn child," he said.

"Wait. What?"

"She's pregnant. She ended up leaving halfway through the day because she felt uncomfortable, even after the two were sent to the office and then home."

"Are you fucking kidding me?" I held my face as my brain struggled to process what he had just said. I tried to fathom what could drive two fourteen-year-olds to threaten someone like that, to look at a pregnant woman and say *that*. "Which two?"

He told me.

"Why? Who the fuck says something like that?"

"Kids say stupid shit. Anyhow, they're both suspended."

"Yeah," I said. That was the cure-all, wasn't it? Kid bad: boom. Suspended. Would anything change? Probably not. Maybe. Hopefully. They weren't bad kids. "Fuck. I was gone *one* day."

"It happens," Wilson said.

"I feel responsible. If I had been there, they wouldn't have said that. That wouldn't have happened. Or if they were pissed, they'd have just said some stupid shit to me, and I'd have dealt with it." I was genuinely mad at myself.

"Don't think like that. You can't always be around, and you can't hold yourself responsible for their actions."

I gazed out the window in silence, still trying to process what he had told me. Word got around at that school faster than a fart in an elevator. Undoubtedly, kids had talked. I wondered how the others would react.

I turned my gaze to the interior of the car. It had seen some shit. The tan interior had faded years ago, and it was in need of a deep clean. The air inside smelled of cigar smoke, and there was a legit ashtray with the bud of a cigar sitting in the central console. I wasn't sure if it was the smell of the smoke or the news he had just told me, but I was getting a headache.

"Thanks, by the way, for giving me a ride."

"Stop thanking me. I said it wasn't a problem."

"Has anyone ever told you that you're too nice?"

"Only a handful of times. Do me a favor, though," he said. "Use the money you're saving on not paying for a new car, and please buy some furniture."

"I have furniture. I have one of those little ab ball thingies that you can sit on and do sit-ups. That's kind of like a chair," I said.

"That's an exercise ball. You need to get a mattress, buddy, and go from there," he said.

I thought about it, "You're right. In its current state, I couldn't convince Helen Keller to fuck me in there, at least, not without a few sit-ups first."

"A mattress would be a good start. And maybe one chair," he said.

"I'm never there," I laughed, "unless I'm sleeping. And besides, furniture means commitment, and I'm not sure if I'm ready for that, yet."

We talked about the weekend, and I shared some stories about the restaurant. Mostly brief descriptions about the hot, blonde bartender for his enjoyment or this one girl who I thought I was developing a crush on, a stunning brunette with a sense of sarcasm that put mine to shame.

"You should invite her back to...never mind. Go to her place for drinks and then fuck until you can't remember your ex's name."

"She's way out of my league," I said.

"Excuses," Wilson said.

"Anyways. I'm ready to get back at it today. I hate being out of the classroom."

"You're excited about testing?"

"Testing?"

"It was in the email," he said.

"I should start reading those."

"I miss the days when there was only one test you gave at the end of the year," Wilson said. "Every year, it feels like we give more and more of them."

"Only one test? Pretty sure we have four in September," I said.

"I think they cut back this year."

"You ever watch the kids take those tests? Their eyes glaze over, zombies clicking buttons, catatonic corpses searching for the right bubble to fill in; it's unnerving. They don't care, either. And after three days of doing them, I don't blame them.

"Plus, it's incredibly boring. We can't do anything. Well, we're not supposed to do anything. We're just supposed to sit there, waiting for it to end, watching them take a test. It drives me insane."

"I don't mind that, actually," Wilson said. "I use the time to reflect. What I don't like is that we're accountable for the results while none of our students are. Not to mention that no one knows how those tests work. If you ever want to anger an administrator, ask them how the tests work. And when they don't give you an answer, they can't because no one knows how they work, push them. It's a great way to get on their bad side."

"No one knows?"

"Not anyone I've asked. I can't even figure it out. Do you know?"

I shook my head.

"Exactly."

"It's retarded."

The car went quiet.

"I mean," I stammered, angry at myself for getting too comfortable.

"It's all good. What's talked about in the car stays in the car," he said.

I exhaled. "I just don't know, man. You got kids who don't give a shit about a test who end up randomly guessing because they don't care. They don't care because we can't grade them. We can only try and encourage them to care, which is bullshit. We have to stop what we're doing, stop everything, and give this stupid set of tests three times a year. And it's all because some asshole in a suit thinks that a test is the only way to improve education because it holds teachers accountable. It's fucking bullshit.

"You want to improve education? Instead of buying a bunch of tests, spend money on grade level books so we can teach without having to make photocopies every twenty minutes on a goddamn copying machine that never works. Maybe don't suck up nearly two weeks every year giving kids stupid fucking tests. Maybe back the fuck away, and let us fucking teach them. I *hate* when someone who knows fuck all about what it's actually like in the classroom tries to tell me how they think it could be better. I bet these kids would have those spineless cretins crying like little bitches before the bell rang."

"I'm with you there," Wilson said. "Quick side note, though. It's not that test. It's a different test."

"Oh," I said. "Still. Fuck all those tests. Which test is this one?"

"The language test. For English language learners. It was in the email. And we had a training about it last week."

"Last week?" Was I losing my mind?

"You sure you didn't hit your head in the accident? It was the one where you spent the whole time drooling over Ritz."

"I wasn't drooling," I laughed. "I have a thing for tall brunettes. What can I say?"

"Judging by your desire to shag Helen Keller, I'd say that two X chromosomes and maybe a heartbeat would about cover the extent of your tastes at the moment."

I laughed. "Maybe. Maybe it's time I take care of that itch," I said. "So, the language test is today?"

"Yes."

"Well, fuck that test, too. None of them make sense. Think about it. If a kid drops three grade levels in his reading and writing during the year, do you think it's accurate? Am I actually making my kids retarded by teaching them?"

"Well..." Wilson said.

"Fuck you," I laughed.

"No." He was chuckling. "They're not dumber from being in your class. They're just going through lulls. We all do it." He looked at the road ahead. "This doesn't look good." There was a wall of traffic on the highway, and he slowed down.

I kept talking. "Anyways, I didn't become a teacher to give tests. I wanted to help kids. I wanted to show them how literature could open their minds and give them a place to turn to when the world around them turned away.

"When I imagined being a teacher, I pictured these great lessons and projects and the most intense classroom discussions ever, the kind where you can look at the kids and see their eyes light up as it clicks.

"My favorite classes are the ones, and this happened at my school last year, they're the ones where you just sit back and let the class run itself, where they're thinking through the problems and applying what they've learned on their own. You stand back and watch them put it together for themselves. I want to do that here, but we're not there yet. I need them to do the reading, and then we can get there. But they keep fighting me on that, so for now, it's more tests than I care to admit. I hate tests. And I hate *those tests* even more."

And yes, I hated them because I did embarrassingly badly on them. Everything would jumble up in my head, and I'd struggle and second guess myself and walk away feeling stupid and useless. Having to give *those tests* to kids made me feel horrible, like I was complicit in gutting their esteem. It was disgusting.

I paused again, shaking. I was unsure if I wanted to tell him the truth, the reason why I almost didn't get hired back on as a teacher. But he had said, "What's talked about in the car stays in the car."

"When I was at my old school…" I hesitated. "I gave my kids an essay. It was hard. I realize now that it was way, way too complicated. I had fucked up. But instead of backing down, I went with it and tried to make it work.

"The problem was that we were running out of time. It was May, and we needed to take those tests, and they decided to make me give those tests. And that meant that I had three days where I would be stuck with my class in the computer lab instead of teaching them and helping them with their essays.

"I had already been told by my former boss that I would not return. I was burning through my sick days. I had been called out for flirting with my co-teacher. So, let's just say that my attitude towards my job was all but professional at that point. Having the tests dumped on me because no one else wanted to give them and because I was on my way out the door was like kicking me when I was already down.

"I didn't realize just how important they were for the school or the district. And during that week, I had discovered that I had miscalculated the time I needed to finish up the final semester. So when we were in the computer lab, I told them, in so many words, that if it were me, I would focus my attention on things that were actually graded."

"You told them to bomb the benchmark? That rumor's true?" He laughed. "That's incredible."

"Not exactly. I just said that my essay was far more important than tests that had no bearing on their lives whatsoever," I said. "I didn't realize that the school received funding based on test scores, not until later when the results came out. I didn't know that I could have hurt the school. Honest. It was my first year, and I didn't even start at the school until October. And even then, I felt like I was just thrown into the deep end, trying to figure out what I was doing.

"I went there to help them out, and they abandoned me. It was kind of a sick game. They had me, an English teacher, teaching history to fill a spot, paying me what you'd pay a long-term sub. They saved money on expenses and got a fill in until the year ended. Win-win. Meanwhile, I nearly went bankrupt, running my credit card into the red to keep the lights on and buy food.

"Around January, an English position actually opened at the school, but my former boss wouldn't put me in the slot because of the belief that any more change in that class would hurt the kids' academic performance or whatever. So, I stayed there, knowing full well that I wouldn't be able to come back the next year."

"I don't have words," he said.

"I was told I could keep my position if I started taking history classes at the local university. It was a little carrot my former boss dangled in front of me. I was broke. Beyond living paycheck to paycheck, I had nothing. And my ex-boss offers me my job for the next year if I paid more money for school instead of just switching me to the open English position.

"It made no sense to me. I never wanted to be a history teacher. I wanted to teach English. I had fought so hard to make it into a full-time position that I actually cried when my ex-boss agreed to make me a teacher instead of a sub. I actually cried. It sounds stupid. I know. But like you, this *is* my life. I wanted it for so long, and I finally got it...except, I didn't. It came with strings.

"I was a teacher, yes. But not of the subject I wanted. That was right across the hall. There was a little glass window in the front of my classroom where I could see my co-teacher in her classroom. I would go over to talk to her all the time, and yes, she was beautiful. And yes, I did flirt. I'm a server. It's what we do, but...I just wanted to be in there, around the books, in the classroom I had always wanted."

I paused and took a sip of coffee to clear my throat. "Naturally, I refused. When we had our meeting in April, after my last observation, I already knew I wouldn't be coming back. I thought I didn't care. I told my former boss that I didn't care. I wanted not to care. But I did. I felt played."

"You got burned."

"And so, I burned them."

CHAPTER THIRTY-TWO

End in Sight

There's your truth.

I could have kept my job, but teaching was only teaching for me if I was teaching English. Staying there would have been giving up. I would have been teaching, but not what I wanted. And if I did that, then what would be the point?

Stubborn. Arrogant. Shortsighted.

Call me what you will. I stood my ground and was forced to leave.

It was time to move on. I had to focus on what I had control over; my role as a teacher at that school.

Wilson gave me a ride in every day. In the car, I would pitch ideas to him, and he would give me tips on how to improve. And on the way home, I would vent the most horrible, vile frustrations, and he would hear me out. I could say whatever; it didn't matter. There was no judgment. "What's talked about in the car..."

And for better or worse, my work as a teacher continued.

Simply surviving the quarter wasn't an option. I needed it to be a success. I had put so much weight into teaching that novel, and it had taken me on a journey, but the journey wasn't over. The last discussion had been horrible, the final this time would need to be far better. If I could finish *Frankenstein* on a high note, then I felt like everything would have been worth it.

My life became work. Whether it was the school or the restaurant, I was busy. Wilson kept telling me that I needed to get laid, kept trying to get me to "hook up with that brunette from work you keep going on about."

And I would tell him, "Tomorrow."

Tomorrow.

The truth was that I hadn't told him what teaching *Frankenstein* meant for me. I hadn't explained the wager I had made with myself. And I hadn't finished what I had set out to do.

Eventually, Wilson gave up on it. Though occasional reminders floated to the surface when we went out for drinks after work.

With the money I was saving carpooling with Wilson, I did end up buying a bed, but my home purchases stopped there. Instead, I did what I said I would never do. I bought materials for my classroom. Little things, things to make my room seem less like a backwater treatment clinic in a small, forgotten town in rural Wyoming and more like a comfortable, English classroom. It wasn't much, a few posters, some new markers, a handful of graphic novels for my kids who struggled with reading.

It would never be as beautiful or as shiny or as new as that English classroom across the hall at my old school, but it didn't matter. There, in that room, I made something that was mine, that reflected me, something that made me proud.

Nearly two months had passed, and the final was fast approaching.

I'd be lying if I said it got easier the longer I worked there. The same bullshit that happened at the beginning continued to happen throughout the year. I just learned to handle it differently. That's not to say it didn't piss me off.

Student teacher does not handle apathy well.

I woke up students. I pulled kids outside to reprimand them or coach them. I took cell phones. I yelled at classes for not doing the work. I dealt with drama. I calmed crying kids.

That was teaching. Those things never changed. There were still problems. There would always be problems. They were just manageable now.

Wilson pulled his jalopy into a parking space behind the school. We left the car, still laughing about a joke I made involving an insurance salesman from Detroit and a midget with webbed fingers when we entered the building.

"You're sick," Wilson said chuckling. "You know that?"

"And you hang out with me." I shrugged, smiling and reaching for my keys. "I think that says more about you than me."

"I'm beginning to realize that."

The door banged open behind us.

"The bell hasn't rung yet," I said, turning around. I rolled my eyes when I saw Zooey and Sofía. "What are you nerds doing?"

"What's so funny?" Zooey asked.

"Grown-up joke," Wilson said.

"It's...an inside joke," I said, creating more laughter. I unlocked my door and put my stuff down inside. Everyone followed me into my room.

"You're ridiculous," Wilson said.

"You started it," I said.

"Pretty sure that was all you," he said.

"Are you two like BFFs now?" Sofía asked Wilson.

"What's that?" Wilson asked.

"You know, like Best Friends Forever. BFFs. How do you not know what that is?"

He laughed. "What are you crazy girls up to?"

"What's it like finally having a friend?" Zooey teased.

"I have other friends. Tons of other friends," I said.

"Oh my god, you guys are totally best friends," Zooey said.

Wilson waved and headed over to his classroom to get ready.

"Best friends forever!" Sofía called after him.

"Who's that?" I said. Then I looked down, "Oh, I didn't see you there."

She rolled her eyes. "I hate you. Don't try to show off in front of your bestie."

"You're just jealous because I have friends," I said. I started up my computer.

"I have friends! You only have the one friend," Zooey said.

"Loser," Sofía joked.

"People like me! I'm a likable guy! I've tons of friends," I said.

"How come you never talk about them?"

"Because they—" I paused and faked a frown "—they aren't real."

"So, now that you have Wilson, you feel like less of a loser," Sofía said.

"You're still definitely a loser," Zooey said.

"Coming from Dr. Loser, guest lecturer and returning alumni from the College of Losers, I'm not sure that's an insult," I said. I looked down at my suit and pretended like I saw something there. "Argh! I'm getting your loser-ness on me! Get out! Out! Out!"

"You'd be like the governor and the mayor and the president of Loserville," she said, rolling her eyes and trying not to laugh.

"Go on, nerds. Beat it." I shooed the girls away.

"Have fun with your BFF! LOSER" Zooey called out.

It was my turn to roll my eyes.

Wilson was a true friend. That was something I never had at my old school. Despite the fancy room, the new technology, and the endless stacks of resources, the one thing my old school didn't provide was friendship.

Students are fucking crazy. It doesn't matter where you teach. The things they say, the shit they do, the ideas they come up with, it'll blow your mind apart trying to process it all. And every school is different. The kids, the staff, the politics, the drama of education is multifaceted and ever-present.

And as sure as someone would walk into my classroom right after the bell rang or draw a dick on the board if I left the markers out, there were always moments that made me loathe teaching. But in the darkest moments of doubt, I would vent to Wilson, and he would have my back.

I was standing in front of Period Four again. "We are on the last chapter of *Frankenstein*."

"About fucking time," someone muttered.

"Really? I'm right here, and I have feelings," I said.

"Sorry, just feels like we've been reading it for-fucking-ever."

"It's taken longer than I had originally planned," I admitted.

"It's a good book," Joaquín said. "It's starting to slow down though."

"Well, we're about to wrap it up," I said.

"Not if you pay Joaquín's mom double," Charles said.

"Charles."

"Sorry, Mister."

"I hope you get ass cancer," Joaquín said.

"You guys ready?" I asked.

"Let's do this," Anita said.

"Jeff. Get off your phone."

"I'm not on my phone," he said.

"You're looking at your crotch, and you're smiling. Either you're on your phone, or you're doing something else. Both are inappropriate. Stop."

I took a deep breath.

It was time to finish *Frankenstein*.

CHAPTER THIRTY-THREE

Armchair Confessions

We stood there waiting in the dark for the door to open, spread out in a half circle like fans backstage after the show. Suddenly, light from the hall burst in as the door opened. We raised our pointed fingers from the darkness, and uttered in eerie unison, "We've been waiting for you."

"Oh my god." Sofía put her hand to her mouth and walked right back out.

Eighth grade erupted in laughter.

Sofía returned after a minute, missing the high fives, but not the trailing laughter. She found her seat, "Oh my god, Mister. You're so weird."

"You leave my class at your own risk," I said.

"I was thirsty!"

"Good thing you weren't pooping," Zooey said.

"Oh my god, that would have been embarrassing," Sofía said.

I thought about it. "I imagine that after about ten minutes, we would have sat down and never spoken of it again."

"That's what you think," someone said.

I had veered away from the idea that every minute of every day in every class needed to be some kind of vicious grind towards education. Throwing in a little crazy, remembering that I taught kids, helped me stay sane.

I was learning that you had to change it up, be unpredictable and keep the little bastards on their toes. Most importantly, I learned the importance of making them laugh.

The bell rang shortly after, and the kids trailed toward the door, some of them pointing out a finger and laughing on their way out. They were easily entertained.

Sofía bumped into Zooey. "Outta my way, ho!"

"You're a ho," Zooey said, bumping back into her.

"No. You're a ho." They began trying to tickle each other on the way out of the door, sending sudden screeches into the crowd of flowing students.

"Mister, it looks like they may fight," Aviana said as she was walking by. "You should do something."

"You're right." I dropped my hand down. "Round one!"

"What!?" Aviana said. "That's messed up. You're messed up, Mister."

"Go for the throat!" I called after them.

"*Mortal. Kombat,*" Alfred said slowly. "Do you know that game, Mister?"

"'Do I know that game?' he asks me," I said to an imagined audience. "Of course, I know the game."

The rest of the kids trailed out. As Alfred talked, I noticed that Brutus and Ezekiel stayed by the door, waiting. He was excited about a new PlayStation game that was coming out, and he was surprised that I knew what it was.

I looked towards his annoyed friends and said, "You should probably head to class. You don't want to be late."

"Your day would be unpleasant without us. Wouldn't it, Mister?" Alfred asked.

"It'd be like...eh. I mean, whatever," I said.

"No. You would be sad because then you would have to deal with your ninth-graders all day. This is because you know we are the very best," he said, still robotic as ever.

"You guys are okay. Most days." I smiled, walking him to the door.

"You should get more friends, Mister," Brutus suggested.

"That's what you keep telling me," I said.

He said something under his breath as he walked away.

While more kids were warming up to me, many still found me annoying. And kids like Brutus would slip in the cuts when they could. That was their nature.

"I hear you're starting fights, Mister." Ellen was back at my door.

"Gotta keep it interesting around here," I said, taking my spot out in the hall for duty.

"This isn't the Hunger Games," she said.

"That's not a bad idea." I paused. I looked down at her with a hand on my chin in fake contemplation. "That would give me fewer people to teach."

She rolled her eyes. "Rude."

"Hey, I'm just telling it like it is," I said. Little people moved up and down the hall with heavy backpacks bouncing as they bobbled on their way. I was surrounded by a sea of dark hair, hoodies, khakis, and multicolored backpacks.

"You know who I'd put in the Hunger Games? You." She stuck a tongue.

"Ooooh. Original," I said.

"No. No. Wait. You know who I'd put in the Hunger Games?" Ellen smiled. "I'd put the Broncos in because I know they'd lose. Go Seahawks!"

"'I'd put the Broncos in because they'd lose,'" I mocked back at her. "At least we were in the Super Bowl."

She shrugged. "You lost."

"And where were the Patriots, exactly? Oh. That's right." I grinned wide. "In the stands."

"Where were the Broncos? 43–8? They didn't even show

up," Ellen said.

"Oh, no you didn't," I said.

"Go, Seahawks!" Ellen said.

Someone in the hall yelled, "Go, Seahawks!"

"You're a Patriots fan!" I said to her.

She shrugged and walked away.

Aviana returned from dropping her stuff off in her math class and called me a loser as she walked by to the water fountain. I shrugged and looked at Wilson and Mack talking. We stood there making our presence known, waiting.

When she returned from the water fountain, I said, "You're the loser."

"No. You're a loser." she put the "L" to her forehead.

"You gotta be at least this tall—" I put my hand up near my eyebrow, which was a height she would never reach "—to call me a loser."

"You're just a freak of nature," she said.

"That's what my father used to tell me," I said.

"That's so sad," she said, making a frown.

"I'm joking!" I said, lying.

That was eighth grade. Joking about farts, teasing, and calling each other loser was the norm. You'd throw in a joke that only you or another teacher would understand just to keep your sanity, and then you went about your day.

"Get to class," she said.

"You get to class!"

"Oh. Yeah." She turned and went back to math.

The bell rang. And I disappeared into my classroom, thinking about what I needed to do to prepare for the day. I was organizing some papers when I felt the sudden buff of something soft slam into the side of my face. I jerked back. A stuffed owl rolled to the floor. It took a second to realize that Aviana had disappeared around the corner and back into Misako's class.

I picked it up ran after her. When I opened the door, Misako was writing an equation on the board. Her students were mostly focused, looking at her, copying down what she did into their notes. Aviana turned around in her seat and stuck her tongue out at me, fingers waving at the side of her head. I pointed to her and held up the stuffed owl.

"Can I help you?" Misako asked me.

"Nope. Just looking for someone."

"Is that my owl?" she asked.

"Nope. This is—" I stuck it behind me "—mine. It's a turtle. Sorry for the interruption." I closed the door and went back to my room.

Suddenly, Nemesis stormed down the hall screaming, "I only kiss girls! I only kiss girls!"

And with that, I disappeared quickly back into my classroom without making eye contact and began working on a presentation. Only a couple of minutes passed when I saw the academic counselor, Laws, pacing up and down the hall.

He looked confused, and when he saw me at my desk, he came up to my doorway.

"Do you have a second?" Laws asked.

"Sure," I lied. "What's up?"

"I'm looking for these kids." He handed me a paper with names highlighted. "Have you seen them?"

I looked it over, recognizing only one, a senior. "I have this one in World Literature, but that isn't until later. What do you need her for?"

"She keeps dodging me. That little shit isn't going to graduate unless she brings her grades up."

"I'll talk to her in class."

"Thanks," he said. But he didn't move.

"You doing okay?"

"No," he answered a little too fast as if that was his whole reason for stopping by in the first place.

I looked one last time at my incomplete presentation, then closed my laptop. "What's up?"

"I'm not doing well," Laws said, sitting down on a desk.

"What's up?" I repeated.

"I don't...I don't think I can do this," he said.

"Do what?"

"Work at this school anymore. I think I'm going to quit."

"What's bothering you?" I stood up and walked over.

"Everything," he said. "This job...it's...it's too much."

"You're thinking of not coming back next year?" I asked.

"No. I'm struggling if I even want to come back tomorrow," he said. In his eyes, I saw a familiar look of desperation, a look I had seen gazing back at me in the mirror too many times.

"What do you mean?"

"I dunno, man." He hung his head, letting his long unruly hair drape forward. A little older than me, he looked like a blonder version of Shaggy: skinny, clad in earthen colors, scruff on the face, everything but the whiny voice. "This job is nothing but paperwork, man. That's all I do. I run around, talking to asshole kids all day, trying to get them to realize that they're going to fail. None of them give a shit. I'm just wasting my breath. It's the same shit every single day."

"That's rough." *And familiar,* I thought. "I thought seniors would be easier."

"No. They aren't. They're the worst. So many are failing. I spend all day playing hide and seek with them only to have the same conversations. And then I get a fucking attitude from them like I'm the bad guy. They're the ones failing their classes."

"Don't take it, personal. They're just kids."

He ignored me. "This is not why I became a counselor. I wanted to help kids. Talk them through their problems, be there for them. Instead, I do paperwork. And when I'm not signing and printing forms, I'm talking about how many credits they need or some other garbage. I feel like a secretary. I've never done this much paperwork in my life. I've given up."

"Given up?"

"Yeah. I do what I can during the day, and then I leave. I don't take anything home with me."

"How many are failing?"

"Honestly, I couldn't tell you, man. I couldn't tell you. Enough to make my life more difficult than it needs to be."

"But they need to know if they're failing, right?"

"If I can't get to my paperwork in time, then I can't get to it in time. I let them know if I find out, but they're all old enough to figure it out without me. It's not like they're new to the concept of school. If they can't figure it out, then maybe another year as a senior would help. Either way, I'm not working at home."

"That's a little unrealistic though, isn't it? I know it sucks, but it comes with the job. Nimitz expects us to put in the hours. It's a challenging school, but we have to help each other out. We have to work together.

"I feel like a hypocrite telling you this because I felt the same way at the beginning of the year. I didn't want to waste time on students if they didn't care. I get that. I do. But as much as it sucks, sacrificing a little of your free time to do a better job makes everything easier in the end."

"I'm paid to be here until four p.m. That's when I stop. If they want me to work more, they should pay me more."

"Why not try it? Take the weekend to try to get caught up. It may make you less stressed. That's what I did." I had spent more than a weekend. I was using any free time I had.

"Have you been renewed for next year?" He ignored my suggestion.

"Yeah," I said. "Nimitz told me last week." Whether or not

I would return was another question. I would know after I finished the novel.

"He hasn't spoken to me. I think he's going to ask me to leave, and I honestly couldn't care."

"That sucks, man," I said. I knew that feeling all too well.

He was sitting there, staring into the carpet, that same brown carpet that held my tears on top of all its other stains. Finally, he said, "I need to find this dumbass."

"Victoria?" I laughed. "She's not that bad." I remembered something, "Though, one time she thought I was bringing the author of *Hamlet* into class to talk to them."

"Really?"

"I had to explain that he's been dead for over four hundred years and that his agent wasn't returning my calls."

"Wow." He pulled a strand of hair behind his ear. "How do you put up with that?"

"It was funny. She's a good kid. Probably just running around being a dumb senior. That's what they do," I said.

"I'm not happy here," he said suddenly. "And I don't think I ever will be. This school sucks. It's fucking horrible. Victoria's a senior, and you gotta put up with questions like that. I thought you hated it here?"

I sat on the desk next to his.

"I don't know. I did, at first. This school is challenging. These kids test you every single day. But it gets easier. It does. I guess I just try to find the fun in it, so it doesn't feel like a grind all the time. And I think once they saw that I enjoyed being here, their attitude changed. These kids have a wall up around them. I think it's because they're so used to people moving in and out of their lives. They want you to prove to them that you're going to stick around before they open up to you."

"My degrees should be enough proof. I put in the work to get to where I am. They should be grateful that I care enough to show up here every day. That's what they should respect."

"They don't care about that stuff. They care about what you're going to do for them. You have to show them you care."

"I thought you hated your ninth-graders."

"Teaching them is a struggle. I won't lie to you there. Every day is a struggle. But I don't *hate* them. They're just kids. And they don't really belong in a classroom like this. Most of them don't want to go to college. They want to do trade work, labor, stuff like that. And that's okay.

"I don't like that we push everyone towards college. I think having to go to college is one of the biggest lies we tell people. It's not for everyone, and it's not necessary. There's no shame in skipping it. Will learning how to write an essay improve Hunter's life? He's an artist. It won't do shit. How often do you write essays in your life? Never. If I wasn't a teacher, I'd never touch an essay.

"My ninth-graders are challenging because everyone's telling them that for their lives to matter, they have to be good at something they'll most likely never use and don't even need. There are better ways to teach these kids. Sadly, I don't know them. But they're out there. When they push back, it's the fault of our system, not the kids.

"So, you don't hate teaching them?"

"They're a pain in the ass, yes. But, no. I don't hate teaching them. I get frustrated because I'm responsible for how well they perform on some stupid test that proves nothing. I think that's bullshit. But, no. They annoy me, and I annoy them back. It is what it is."

The room went quiet again.

"It's frustrating," I said after a while. "And it sucks, and it makes me want to bash my head into a wall, but that's teaching. And when I'm furious, I grab a few beers with Wilson and vent until I'm exhausted. I go home. I sleep as much as I can. I hit the reset button. Then I come back and do it all over again the next day."

"So you're going to stick it out here?"

"What do *you* want to do? That's what matters here."

"I got this job because I wanted to help kids. I wanted to work with kids dealing with suicide, bullying, drug abuse, depression. Instead, I'm depressed. I'm tired of paperwork. That's not how I pictured helping them."

"We don't get to choose in what way people need our help," I said. *Or who needs it.*

He was quiet. And then he spoke up. "It's a losing battle."

"You're probably right," I said, "but we hold the line. And we keep holding the line because that's the only thing that matters in this crazy, fucked-up career. It's infuriating. It isn't fair. It sucks. But that's teaching."

"Do you think that what we do matters? Actually matters? Here? In this place?"

"I have to believe it does. Otherwise, I'll fall apart," I said.

"Yeah," he said abruptly and stood up. "Thanks for listening."

I nodded and went back to my shitty plastic chair.

When he reached the door, he stopped and turned around. "You're a good teacher. You belong here." He paused. "But I don't think I do."

And then he left.

I stood there in silence. The mood felt too somber, too serious for how early in the morning it was. I glanced at the owl lying on my desk, grabbed it, and walked out of my class. I turned the corner and slowly opened the door to Misako's room. She was still writing on the board. A few students turned towards me. I had one shot at this.

I hurled the owl screeching in a spiral that would have made Brady jealous and watched as it bounced off Aviana's head.

"Hey!" she shouted as it fell toward the ground.
Bullseye.
The class looked back at me.
"Was that my owl?" Misako asked.
"Wasn't me!" I said and then ran away.
They may have been little shits, but for now, they were my little shits.

CHAPTER THIRTY-FOUR

Better Late Than Never

"That's it?" said Sallie. "That was a stupid ending."

"What do you mean that's it?" I asked as I closed the novel, mildly annoyed.

"It's stupid. That's stupid. This whole book is stupid," Sallie said.

"Or. And hear me out on this," Joaquín said, "*maybe* you're the one that's stupid?"

"Fuck off," Sallie said.

"Sallie," I said.

"He started it," Sallie said.

"Only because you can't see how awesome that ending was," Joaquín said.

"How is it awesome? The creature just...what? Dies? Kills himself?" Sallie said.

"Let's talk about it," I said.

"You were probably too fucking stoned to remember anything about the book anyway."

"Joaquín," I said.

She rolled her eyes. "Whatever."

"Whatever? I'm getting a contact high from across the classroom."

"I like that the creature killed everyone," Charles said. "That's twisted. And no one could stop him."

Bob was laughing. Not at anything anyone said. He was just...laughing.

"That's it?" said Chelsea. "It's over?"

"I've never finished a book before," Sasha said.

"Wait. Really?" I asked.

"Nah. I mean like, I pretend to read them and stuff, but since you forced us to read this one, it's the first book I've almost ever completely read from the beginning. Kinda."

"Um, okay then," I said. "Did you like it?"

"Fuck no," she said.

"Well, I tried."

"I didn't like it, either," Anita said. "I mean, I liked the book, but not the ending. Walton's just going to let him walk away? He needs to go after the creature and kill him. He's a monster."

"Why? The creature's just going to kill himself, anyways," Joaquín said.

"But why kill yourself? He's like this super powerful being. He can do whatever," another student added.

"He had to kill himself," Joaquín said. "Frankenstein was his only reason to be alive. Everyone else freaks out and tries to kill him when they see him. It's not like he can rent a cottage in a village and live out the rest of his days herding sheep."

"I don't get the creature. It's like he just wants to be miserable. He didn't have to do all that stuff. He could have just gone off and did his own thing. Instead, it was like he wanted to be miserable," Anita said.

"Sometimes, misery gives people purpose," I mumbled.

"What?"

"Never mind," I said.

"What if he doesn't do it? What if he doesn't kill himself?"

Charles asked.

"He said he was going to," Joaquín said.

"And your dad said he'd come back home," Charles said.

"Motherfucker," Joaquín said.

"Guilty," Charles said.

"Gentlemen," I shouted. They apologized, and we continued.

"The monster is a liar. He killed a kid. It's not like you can trust him," Charles said.

"Interesting," I said.

"Oh, shit. Like, remember how Frankenstein said not to trust what the creature said?" Joaquín twisted his pen, the novel open in front of him. "What if he decided not to kill himself?"

"That'd be insane," Charles said, continuing to draw on his notebook. "He just runs around killing people for an hour and a half. *Frankenstein 2: The Sequel.*"

"He's totally going to do it," Anita said. "He's completely alone. He's miserable. Maybe if Frankenstein had made him a partner like he said he was going to do, then things would be different. He didn't, though. He's ugly and alone. He has to kill himself."

"Woah," Joaquín said. "You going to stand there, Mister, while she makes fun of Charles like that."

Charles said something back.

"Gentlemen," I said. "Anita, you were saying?"

"I was saying that the monster deserves to be miserable. He's a murderer. He needs to suffer. But really, he should have just been killed in the end. That would have made the ending better."

"Really?" Charles stopped drawing and looked up. "Why should he die? He's so fucking cool."

"Because he's a fucking monster," Anita said.

"Is he though?" I asked.

"A monster?" Anita seemed baffled. "Of course he's a monster. He killed a child. You kill a child, that makes you a monster."

"Why'd he kill the child?" I asked.

"To piss off Frankenstein," she said. "Why do you mean, why? You read the book. You know."

"Yeah. I've read the book, but I'm curious about what you think. There are no right answers here, just your interpretation of the text. So tell me, what pushed the creature to the point where he was okay with killing a child?" I asked.

"That one guy like shot him after he saved the little girl from drowning or whatever," Anita said.

"And those people freaked out on him," Joaquín said.

"He also had that baby mom drama with Frankenstein. You know, he made the creature and then took off without raising it. I know all about that baby mom drama," Charles smiled.

"Don't you say it," Joaquín said.

"You're going to be a big brother," Charles said.

"Mister?" Joaquín asked.

"Yes?" I was hesitant.

"Is it possible to get a girl pregnant if you still have to sit down when you pee?"

"Anyways," I shouted. "Back to the novel. We were talking about what made the creature a killer."

"Who cares? He killed *a lot* of people," Anita said. "You're going to have to try really hard if you want me to believe he wasn't a monster. I mean, he's the reason *everyone* in the novel is dead."

"Not all of them. Frankenstein fucked up too," Joaquín said. "He got his wife killed."

"See, the creature wasn't all that bad," Charles said.

I rolled my eyes.

"Marriage isn't that bad," Anita said. "And the creature

killed his wife."

"He warned Frankenstein first," Charles said. "And you're right. Marriage isn't that bad. I've got my heart set on one very special lady."

"Moving on," I said. "I really like where we're going with this…" I paused and glanced at Charles. "For the most part. And that brings us to our discussion for the final."

There were groans.

"Really, guys? Is that like a trigger for you? I simply say 'final,' and you all have a meltdown."

There were more groans and complaints.

"Wait. Let's try that again," I said. I whispered, "Final."

Groans.

"Creepy. Oh well, deal with it," I said.

"I thought you were trying to be fun. Tests aren't fun," Sallie said.

"It's not a test. I mean, yes. It's technically a test. But it's not like a test-test. It's a conversation. A discussion, just like we did before."

"Yeah, but that one sucked."

"That's because you weren't prepared. You know what to expect now. This one will be way better," I said. *Hopefully.*

"We finished the book, but we haven't finished the quarter. We still have a project and a final to get through over the next two weeks." There was more complaining. I talked louder. "We'll talk about the project tomorrow, but for now, I want to tell you the question for the final because I want you to be thinking about it over the next two weeks. Judging by how you've managed to discuss the end of the book so far, I think you'll like it. Our big question is: Who is the real monster in this story?"

The room went silent for a moment before conversations erupted.

"Wait. Wait. Wait," I put my hands up. "I know you all

want to have this conversation, and we will, but for now, I want you to put it in the back of your mind. Right now, we need to wrap up your thoughts on the book. So for the rest of class, I want you to reflect on your feelings and questions and write it all down in your notebook."

"Why can't we just talk about them?" Sasha asked. "Why do we always got to write shit down?"

"Fair," I said. "I get it. If I were you, I'd just want to sit here and talk about the book, too. But writing down your thoughts before we discuss it gives you a chance to make sure you don't forget anything. It also helps you organize what's going on in your brain."

"Are you calling me stupid?" Sasha asked.

"Um…no," I said.

"I'm just messing with you, Mister," Sasha said. "Gotcha."

"Right," I said. "Anyways. We just finished the book. You have a lot of ideas floating in your mind. So, for now, write down everything you can: thoughts, feelings, impressions, questions you may have. Whatever. If you think the book sucked, *great*, write it down, but be prepared to explain why."

"I think writing sucks," Sasha said.

"Cool beans," I said.

"So, do I have to do it?" Sasha asked.

"Yup."

"Why though?" Sasha asked.

"Because he likes to see us suffer," Sallie said.

"Bingo," I said. "See, you *are* learning!"

With some reluctance, they tore open their notebooks and started jotting their thoughts down. Some worked harder than others, some not at all.

And as a wheel goes round, it wasn't long before I was staring into the dead eyes of Period Nine.

"We're on chapter twenty-one," I said.

Books flipped open. Sighs flew out. Eyes rolled.

We made it halfway through the chapter. At some point during the class, Nemesis stormed out again. I snapped at Justin. Nimitz stopped by to pull Ted out at the end of the day and saw me reading to a class of dazed and confused students, trying to drag them to the end of the novel, frustrated, annoyed, and every other emotion that was naturally caused by Period Nine. And we still had two more chapters and then some until we would be finished.

Some things had changed.

Some stayed the same.

And when the final bell rang, I wanted them to get the fuck out of my class.

Student teacher does not....

I think you get it by now.

Wilson stopped by after the kids had cleared out. "You ready to go?"

"Yeah. Sorry, I was just thinking."

"You alright?" he asked me.

"No matter what I do with Period Nine, nothing changes," I said.

"That happens sometimes. You're doing what you can. You have to accept that you can only do so much and move on. It's okay."

"No!" I said, a little too loud. "No. It's not okay. I can't just write off an entire class. There has to be a way to reach these kids; there has to be something that I'm not doing."

"Slow down there, super teacher," he said.

I glanced up at him, almost sneering.

He saw the look in my eyes and walked over to my desk, taking a seat, "You can't save them all."

"This isn't about saving them all," I said.

"What's it about then?"

There was one thing left to tell Wilson that I hadn't told him, my wager. And so I told him the real meaning behind my decision to teach *Frankenstein*.

"That's why you're trying so hard," Wilson said when I finished.

"I'm sorry." I didn't know what else to say. The man had been spending over two months giving me rides to work, mentoring me, becoming my friend, and I had never once told him that I was thinking about quitting.

"I thought you were renewed," he said.

"I am, but what's the point of coming back if I can't teach."

"You can teach," he said.

"If I could, then why can't I reach Period Nine? They're going to fail the final. And who knows, maybe everything will be the same with my other classes, too."

"Maybe," he said. "That's just how it is."

"It's bullshit!" I yelled. "I come in here and try to care. I try. I start the day out in a great mood. I'm trying to be more friendly to my kids so they don't all think I'm some kind of monster, and that's great and everything, but they still hate my class. They still stare at me like they're dying inside. And I can't blame them.

"I go, and buy some shit and put it up on the walls in my room, and yeah, *great*. It's awesome. I'm trying. I'm *really* trying, but it's not enough. We're out here in a building that should have been torn down a decade ago. I've got shit seeping through the ceiling of my classroom, and I don't even —" Annoyed by the hard plastic chair beneath me, I stood up and kicked it so hard that it hit the wall and bounced onto its side. "I don't even have a fucking teacher chair!

"It's bullshit. Of course, they don't care. We teach in a shithole, Wilson. Look at this place. They don't care because no one cares about them. So, yeah. I got renewed. Big fucking deal. But if I can't teach here, like actually teach, not just do a job, not just make it through the day, not just survive, but actually teach, then what's the fucking point of staying?"

I leaned up against the wall next to my desk, refusing to sit back in *that* chair.

Wilson sat in silence.

"Laws came to me. He wants to quit," I said.

"That doesn't surprise me," he said.

"I talked to him. I told him what I thought you would say. I tried to talk him back from the ledge, but it didn't make a difference," I said. I told him what had happened, what I had said and how he had replied. "I doubt he'll be returning next year."

"That doesn't surprise me either," he said. "Laws was never going to be in education long."

"Why do you say that?"

"After years in this business, you just know," he said.

"And me?"

Wilson had his hands behind his head, leaning back, the emblem of the school t-shirt proudly gleaming on his chest. A smile spread over his face.

"What? What's funny?"

"You'll be around for a while," he said. "You're a stubborn sonofabitch."

I laughed a little. "Stubborn?"

"Yes, very stubborn. You could have just quit. At any point in the year, you could have just walked away. It's just a job after all. But you keep staying; you keep coming back. It sounds like Laws was looking for an excuse to leave. You're looking for a reason to stay. You're going to walk into that final looking for a way for them to succeed. You'll stay."

"And if I don't?"

He shrugged. "I didn't take you for a pussy."

My mouth dropped. Then I started laughing.

"Now, you want to go grab some beers or do you want to stay here and keep throwing shit around in your room?"

CHAPTER THIRTY-FIVE

Sniffing Markers

Wilson was right. I was a stubborn sonofabitch. I was determined to finish what I had set out to do at the beginning of the year. Only then would I sit down and decide whether or not I would stay.

The first obstacle was their presentations. Wilson had tried to taper my expectations as usual, and I shrugged it off as usual. I gave them more options, hoping it would inspire more people to do them. They also had the choice to come up with their own project, as long as I approved the idea first, but no one took me up on that offer.

It was a slight improvement overall. A little more than half decided to do them. I was putting in more and more work, but only a handful more were moved to action by it. And while better than before, I would need to see much better results from the final if I was going to stay.

There were a few of them that had stood out, despite my frustrations.

Kelly managed to come to class regularly enough to create not one, but two projects. And she wanted to present them both. Kelly said she knew that she couldn't receive two grades and that she would probably fail the quarter, but she wanted to make up for missing so much class. Later on, I found out why she was always absent.

Every student has a story.

Her presentation was incredible. She stood next to her giant cardboard cutout of the creature she had created and tried to sell him like a household product to an audience of somewhat attentive ninth-graders.

I stood and clapped for her when she finished.

She turned away, slightly embarrassed.

What can I say? I was proud.

But for those who surprised me, others had let me down. Joaquín had rushed his, overconfident from the praise I gave him in class. Charles didn't do one. Anita did well. Helen didn't. David and Cesar completed it. Barely.

And so it went.

In the end, I counted the trail of zeroes and grew frustrated. I took to the front of the class and berated them for not trying. I yelled at them for not caring about their future. I told them I was disappointed.

And then we moved on to preparing for the final.

I was in the middle of coming back from printing off a stack of papers during my plan when I ran into the school psychologist, Dr. Klein.

She called after me, and I turned around, holding a stapled forest in my hands.

"Can I talk to you about our little friend?" she asked.

"Which *little* friend?" I asked, annoyed. I hated that euphemism. It made me feel like I was on a kid's TV show rather than a teacher at a high school full of teenagers who cursed more than most sailors.

"Nemesis."

Even better. I nearly rolled my eyes but maintained composure. "Why?"

"We have a new strategy we'd like to use—"

"I gotta run to class. Email me," I turned and walked away before Klein could respond.

Nemesis had started skipping school more. And when Nemesis did show up, it wasn't long before the kid was bolting down the hall and straight to the principal's office.

Perón had rarely been to Period Nine. She said it was because of testing and promised to be in my class for the final quarter, but I wasn't sure I believed that. It seemed more reasonable that she simply needed a break. And I couldn't blame her.

But I could blame Nemesis.

Teachers aren't supposed to hold grudges, but I had. And the kid didn't make it difficult. When Nemesis did show up, I wondered how long it would be before I had to make that phone call. And every time the kid stormed out of my class, I sighed relief. Call me a monster, but I could only handle so much. You could've sat me down with that child all day, every day, for an entire year, and I would have failed.

Period Four started, and I broke them up into groups just like I had done at the beginning of the novel.

I dodged the mistakes I had made the first time, and while it wasn't a huge improvement, it was better.

"I want you all to be thinking about how important it is that the monster didn't have anyone to teach him social cues," I told my class. "Think about the creature's upbringing. Did Frankenstein have a responsibility to the creature? Or is the creature alone responsible for his actions? And what is the role that society plays in this novel? Remember, there are no right or wrong answers here. Just your thinking. You're going to use the articles I gave you to back up your ideas."

"What are social cues?" someone asked.

"Like, he was really fucking strange," Anita said.

"Social cues are clues you pick up on in a social situation, so you don't act weird. It's what keeps you from leaning back in your chair and farting really loud in class."

Someone laughed. Farts were always funny.

"Anita, why do you think he was strange?" I asked.

"Because he's like this giant monster who had spent weeks staring at a family through a hole in the wall. That's pretty much the definition of creepy. He can't possibly have been normal when he tried to talk to them."

"Excellent point," I said.

"I still don't understand what a social cue is," Sallie said.

"This is why you don't drink the bong water," Joaquín said.

"Joaquín," I said. Then I turned to Sallie. "If I walked up to you and I said, 'Hi.' Are you weirded out by it?"

"No."

"But if I do it like this." I stood beside her desk, looking sideways with a bizarre look on my face, lips pulled, back hunched, and said "Hi!" in a weird, raspy voice, a little too loud while waving like a penguin. "See the difference?"

"I mean, it's not that bad," she said.

"You must have some weird friends," I said.

"Sallie—" Joaquín said.

"Joaquín," I said.

"Mister, it's cool. I'm just trying to help," he said.

I hesitated. "Okay..."

"So, imagine you're walking home at night, and you see Charles, and he like, waves at you. That's normal right?"

"Yeah," Sallie said.

"You'd probably just wave back, right? And maybe you're like, 'it's after seven p.m. What's he doing out after his curfew? I sure hope he doesn't get in trouble again,'" he said looking over at his friend who was drawing something in his notebook. Charles snorted and muttered something under his breath. "Now imagine the same thing, but this time Charles in a van, and is like, 'Hey, little girl, you want some candy?'"

"That would be fucking creepy," Sallie said.

"That would be normal for Charles," Joaquín said.

Charles looked up from his article, "Hey there, little girl."

"Moving on," I said. "No one told the monster what was or wasn't creepy. That's what's important here. How do you learn what's creepy? How do you know what's okay or not okay to do in a certain social situation?

"You have this creature. He's been thrown into this environment that he doesn't understand. A place no one's prepared him for and he's expected to survive, to deal with it on his own.

"He has nothing. No one. And this means he messes up a lot along the way. Sure, he's got books to read, and he has an idea of what the world should be like, but he doesn't really have a clue. He hasn't really experienced the real world. And that's because there's a huge difference between what you read in books and how things actually are," I paused.

The kids stared back at me.

"The monster has this idea of perfection," I continued. "He sits there, daydreaming of being accepted. He creates impossible expectations. He puts too much pressure on one moment. He's staring at this family thinking, '*I want that. I deserve that. I need that.*' But it's not that simple. Life is never that simple. And when he tries to force himself into that family, they push away from him. And he's left feeling alone. Frustrated. Angry. So, he lashes out. He turns back to the only other emotion he's ever experienced: rage. He figures if he can't be a part of the world, then he will tear it down.

"Imagine how different the creature would have been if he simply had a friend. Imagine how much of a difference having just one person who cares about you makes. Think about it. Imagine how different this story would be if he had someone that showed him how to act, how to care, how to fit in. Imagine that."

There was silence.

"That's deep, Mister," Anita finally said.

"Does that help?" I asked after a moment.

"Yeah, I think so."

"Cool. I'll be around to help you if you need it," I said. I wasn't exactly sure I had answered the question.

"I'm going to wreck this, Mister," Joaquín said.

"Just like I wrecked your mom," Charles said.

Joaquín looked over at him and traced a finger over his throat.

"Nah brah, I don't like being choked; now your mother on the other hand—"

"Charles," I said.

"I'm just saying $20 goes a long way."

I stared at him.

"Sorry, Mister. I can't help what she's into," he said.

"You do realize that I'll have to talk to his mom in parent-teacher conferences next quarter, right? And the whole time, I'm going to have all these comments floating around in the back of my mind," I said.

"My bad, Mister," Charles said. "She's a nice lady. You should ask her out."

"Kill yourself," Joaquín said.

"We've been over this. I'm not dating anyone's mom."

Period Eight was about the same.

Except no one mentioned mothers.

I was writing some ideas and question stems down on the board in the back for my students while they were working in their groups when I turned around to see Mario with his hand raised.

"Mister, I got a question," Mario asked. "So, like nature is what Frankenstein would have done if he raised the creature in nature, right?"

"Not quite. Let me explain it." I went to the whiteboard and pulled out a marker. "So nature is..." I began writing out the definition on the board as hints of lemon-citrus scent poured into my nose. It wasn't one of my markers. Mine were all boring, bland, basic bitch teacher markers. Not that one. That one was scented.

"Hold on a second," Cesar interrupted. "Does that mean that..."

Cesar was asking me a question, but I didn't hear. I was engrossed. It was only me and that marker. Each breath drew in complex citrus notes blossoming around me like freshly squeezed orange juice.

I closed my eyes and inhaled.

There was a distant voice.

"Mister? Mister? Is that right?" Cesar was asking.

It was beautiful.

"Mister. Mister. Mister!"

I was lost in it.

"Are you...are you sniffing a marker?"

The world came back into focus as I suddenly remembered where I was. "What?"

"Did you just sniff that marker in the middle of my question?" Cesar shook his head.

"Huh? No. I—"

"Holy shit. You *were* straight up sniffing that marker," Mario said. "What the fuck, Mister? Are we that bad? You gotta go get turnt right here in front of us just to get through the day? Well, don't stand there hogging it. Pass it my way."

"It's scented!" I said.

"Sure it is," Mario said. "It starts with markers, and it ends with crack. That's a slippery slope, man."

I started laughing. I shouldn't have been laughing, but I was laughing.

"Fuck, now he's high," Mario said.

I kept laughing. "Sorry." Tears began to fill my eyes.

"You just had to do that right in the middle of my question?" Cesar asked. "This fool can't even wait until the bell rings before he takes a bump. Damn son."

"Is this what you do when no one's here? Huff markers?" Mario said. "Makes sense now."

I kept trying to justify it, but it only made it worse. "It's scented! I wanted to know—" still giggling "—the smell."

"I'm sure that's what Scarface said too," Mario said. "What's this smell like? Then just plants his face in a mound of powder like he fell off a ski lift."

"I give up," I said, shaking my head, still laughing. I walked over to my desk, sat down on my hard plastic chair, and tried to compose myself.

CHAPTER THIRTY-SIX

The Moment of Truth...Again

Wilson had spent the whole morning giving me every strategy he could think of to make sure my day would be successful. He was still going on when we pulled up behind the school, the car crinkling over gravel as we stopped.

I was in a hurry to get started. I grabbed my stuff, opened the door, and took off towards my classroom.

"Wait!" Wilson called after me. "Can you help me carry something in?"

"Yeah, give me a second to set my stuff down," I said.

When I returned, he was standing out in the cold by the back of his car with the trunk open. I walked over.

"Thanks, my good man. I can't carry this in by myself."

"What is—" I saw what was in the trunk. I looked at Wilson, then looked at the box.

"Well, it seemed to bother you," he shrugged.

I was beyond words.

"Help me bring it in, will ya?" he said.

We lugged the big box out of his car and into the building where we set it down in my room. Wilson turned to leave. "Where are you going?" I asked.

"I bought the thing. You can figure out how to put it

together," he laughed.

I slid down next to the box. "Thank you. Wilson."

"Don't mention it," he said. "And good luck today."

"Anyone ever tell you that you're too nice?" I said.

"Once or twice." And with that, he went into the hall where he turned to usher students back outside the building.

I looked at the box.

Wilson had bought me my very own teacher chair.

Near the end of the year, I was standing in the gym for our final assembly.

The bleachers had been extended into the space. Students lined the rows, organized by class. Across from them, sat empty metal chairs. A projector idly flashed blue on a screen, waiting. Next to the projector stood the principal and two assistant principals, waiting. Parents and families sat in chairs that lined one wall of the gym, waiting. And the staff stood on the other side, shifting awkwardly, and mumbling to each other, but also waiting.

What may have looked like the culling, was our high school assembly. Soon the screen flickered from a deep blue to a fancy picture of the school (which was saying something) with the words "Honor Roll" at the top.

Nimitz held up the microphone and spoke.

Back in my classroom, the desks were in a misshapen circle, yet again. I had covered the back board with possible ideas and questions to ask during the discussion. On their desks, rested the various handouts and notes they had prepared for the debate.

I sat in my comfy, black and grey, swirly teacher chair, swinging slightly from side to side, with a clipboard resting on one knee, waiting.

"You having fun there?" Anita asked.

"You ready?" I asked with a slight smile.

"Education is a gift no one can take away from you. Its value cannot be measured. You are all here because you value education.

295

It's easy to forget the importance of that gift and put off what you should be working on today until tomorrow. But there are those here who value education every day. Today, those are the ones we celebrate.

I took a deep breath and said, "Who is the real monster in Mary Shelley's novel *Frankenstein*?"

"Sometimes, we need to be reminded just how important education is.

"I've worked in this field for a long time. I went to school in this district, at this very school. When I graduated high school, I worked as a security guard at the main campus while I studied my way through college. Once I earned my degree, I turned in my security guard badge for a teacher's badge and taught at that school.

"I worked there for many years, but I knew I could do more. And so I went back to school; I studied more. And after I earned my degree in administration, I turned in my teacher's badge for my thermos and the stern look I give you all every day." He smiled.

Anita started, "I think the real monster in *Frankenstein* is the creature because he's the one that killed all those people. He decided to murder William. He did it out of revenge. In the article..."

"But even as a principal, I am still reminded every day how important education is. Every summer, my wife goes to Africa with the people she works with at her clinic.

"For those of you who don't know, she's a nurse. She works with a plastic surgeon. She helps people out who've suffered horrible tragedies. She sees suffering every day. It's unthinkable, the things some people have to go through.

"The doctor she works with is one of the best. This man could operate with a spoon; he's that good. And every year, they take a trip to Africa.

"I think the real monster in *Frankenstein* is Frankenstein because he had the opportunity to be a father to the creature, but he gave it up," Joaquín said.

"They operate on people who have cleft palates. If you don't know what a cleft palate is, it's what happens when the mouth doesn't form properly. When these kids are born, there's a space, a gap, so these kids can't close their mouths all the way.

"The real monster in *Frankenstein* is society," Paris said, "because they turned their back on the creature instead of helping him. When the creature tried to talk to the De Lacey family..."

"It's not common in the U.S. because the surgery to fix it is quick and easy. But it's a different story in developing nations. In the places where my wife goes, kids are forced to grow up with this condition. Imagine living your life like this, where people see you and look away. Remember that these are kids.

"According to that documentary we watched, there is scientific evidence proving genetics can make people violent. Frankenstein made him, so he could have used pieces that had genes that would make him violent," Cesar said.

"She tells me about all these kids that line up for this surgery. They've been living with this disability their whole lives. They suffer constantly. And not only do they have to deal with the deformity, but people won't even speak to them. They won't even look at them because they believe their deformity is a curse.

"I disagree," Emily said. "The monster was a monster because Frankenstein didn't raise him. He didn't act like a father. He just left him there, walked out on him. That's why he became a killer."

"The people in these villages turn away from children. They're forced to grow up in insolation.

"He would have been a killer, either way," Ricky said. "He was seven feet tall and super strong. You can't be that powerful and not be violent. It was in his blood. It was in his nature."

"They live like this for years. And every year my wife goes to help. And every year she comes back with stories. This year, she told

297

me about this little boy.

"He didn't have to do it," Charles said. "He wanted to kill. What he went through sucks, but he's the one that did it. He chose to be a murderer. He's the real monster."

"This little boy walked twelve miles to get the surgery. It took him two days to get to the site where they were operating. This little boy walked all the way there and then waited in line. They eventually operated on him. And afterward, they hand him a mirror to see his face. Do you know what this little boy does? When he sees his face the first time after the surgery?"

"What about society? They treated him like he was a piece of trash. He kept trying, but they just didn't care. It didn't matter what he did because he was so fugly," David said.

"He just starts crying. These big old tears start to roll down his face. And people are confused. They don't understand why he's so upset. They're afraid that he doesn't like it. And so my wife goes up to him and asks him what's wrong.

"No way. The creature framed that one girl. And he like murdered William with his own bare hands," Sallie said.

"She asks him what's wrong; she asks him if he's okay. And he says, 'yes.' And then my wife asks him why he's crying. And the boy turns and looks at her and says, 'Because I can finally go to school.'

"Do you think Frankenstein should be punished for what the creature did?" Emma asked.

"It turned out that if you had a cleft palate in that village, they wouldn't let you into school. He had to wait twelve years, but finally, finally, that little boy could go to school.

"I think nurture plays more of a role in how you handle situations," Mario said. "If no one tells you how to act, like if he doesn't have a mom there to smack his hand when he does some dumb shit, then he's going to grow up doing dumb shit," Mario said.

"And that's why we're here. Education is a gift. What you do

here matters. It's easy to forget that. But it matters. There will be moments when you struggle to focus, struggle to study, struggle to do the work. And when you experience those moments, remember today. Remember the people who stood up in front of you today and know that it is possible.

"You're saying that parents should get in trouble if their kids commit crimes? That doesn't make sense," Clarissa said.

"The awards ceremony is one of my favorite moments as an administrator because I get to congratulate you on all the hard work you've done so far. I know it's not easy. For me, football was easier. Studying took a lot of work, but I never stopped believing how important my education was.

"What are you talking about? You can't blame society for what the creature did. They were scared. It's not their fault," Kiera said.

"It isn't easy. You'll have to make sacrifices on the road to your success. But those sacrifices will improve your lives. Those sacrifices will define who you are and where you will go.

"If you look in the book, you'll see how messed up the creature is. Look at what he does. He murders Frankenstein's wife just to make him miserable," Selena said.

"I know everyone in this room. I've met your families. I know where you come from. I know why you're here. We're a family. We're here for one another. We're here to build a better future. And that future starts with you.

"Frankenstein pushed him to do it. He could have just walked away. He could have just made him a companion. He wanted him to be a monster," Sasha said.

"I'm proud of each and every one of you," he said. He looked out at the classes before him, nearly 200 kids staring back at him in total quiet. "Each one of you matters. Each one of you is part of our community. You're part of this family. Our school. Remember that.

"No one just decides to be a killer! Look at everything he went through. In that article…" Kate looked through the pile of papers on her desk. "In that one article..."

"And with that, we'll begin by calling off the names of those students who made Honor Roll," he said, turning to Ritz and handing her the microphone.

It wasn't perfect.

But, it was better than before.

CHAPTER THIRTY-SEVEN

Talking Shop

The final parent-teacher conference of the year was only for those kids who were going to repeat the ninth grade. We gathered in my room at the end of the day near the end of May and for three hours told families that their children would return as freshmen the following year.

Kids cried. Parents shook their heads in silence. And we, as a team, told the truth. We pulled no punches.

A certain sense of sadness was still in the air when the last family left. We sat in the room, saying nothing, sitting motionless as the heavy metal doors down the hall clicked shut.

"Who's coming out tonight?" Mack finally asked the room.

In exchange for staying late, Central Admin had given us the next day off.

"You in?" he asked me.

"I'm in," I said.

"I know Wilson's in. Who else?" And with that, he coaxed us back to life as eventually everyone agreed to go out.

As I packed up for the weekend, I thought about how it must feel to fail a grade. It was something I had never experienced, to know that your entire year had been wasted and that you'd have to return and do it all over again. I felt for them. They weren't bad kids. They were just... complicated. After all, every student has a story.

I thought about that as I locked up my room and went into the hall. Wilson was still in a meeting with some parents, so I headed into Mack's.

His room was cluttered. Tables and chairs packed tight into a space much smaller than mine. His walls were barren with heavy scratches in certain places. Some of the wallpaper had been stripped, and looking closely, I spotted a tiny penis someone had drawn there. And in a far corner, there was a broken bookcase with no shelves, books haphazardly stacked inside.

"You okay?" he asked. He was packing up for the weekend.

I didn't normally come into his room.

"Yeah. Just kind of bummed I guess."

"I feel you," he said.

"Does it get better? These meetings."

"What do you mean?"

"Telling a kid he's going to repeat, does that get any easier?"

"No. But most of them know it's coming. It just sucks because it doesn't feel real for them until we tell them and by then it's too late. They had to look at us and accept the fact that despite all the chances we gave them, they failed, and they have only themselves to blame."

I nodded. "If you had asked me in September who would fail this year, I would have picked out every kid we talked to today."

"That never changes." He turned off his computer.

"It sucks."

"It does. I'm just as frustrated as you are. I think we all are. Over the years, I've gotten pretty good at handling it, though.

But frustration is part of this job."

"What's it going to take for that to change?"

"You can't change it."

"I thought about quitting this year," I said suddenly.

He stopped what he was doing and looked at me. "You bring a lot to this school. You've got a lot of energy. You're optimistic. You genuinely care."

I shrugged it off.

"No, don't act like you don't. I see you constantly trying to come up with ideas to make it better. You did well this year, and you're good for this school." He looked at me right in the eyes. "And it's why you need to leave."

"What do you mean?"

"You're my kid's age. So, I'm going to talk to you like I would talk to him. If my son told me he wanted to be a teacher, I'd tell him to quit being a jackass and wise up. I'd tell him the system was broken. I'd tell him to get the hell outta here with that nonsense and choose something else.

"Every year, I think of quitting. Every year I fight the urge to follow through with it. You bust your ass, and then you watch these yo-yos drop the puck. It kills me.

"I'm too old to get out of the game now. I've given too many years to teaching. But you, you're young. You could easily choose a different career. It may set you back a bit, but eventually, you'll be way better off."

"Yeah?"

"I've been doing this for twenty years. It never changes. You'll be better off finding a job where you're appreciated. Get a job that pays well, one that ends when you walk out the door on a Friday afternoon. You'll be much happier."

I leaned up against a desk in the room, thinking about what he said.

"You ready, my man?" Wilson called from the hall.

"Yeah. Good to go," I said.

"Mack, you coming?" Wilson said, peering in from the hall. He was so happy that he looked like a kid.

"Of course. But you better keep those fucking shots away from me."

Wilson clasped his hands together loudly and grinned. "Here we go, boys!"

"This fucking guy," Mack said.

I nodded at Mack and then turned to leave with Wilson.

We drove over to our usual after-school spot, a steakhouse that had a sports bar in the back. It was a place just classy enough for a handful of teachers to get wasted. Shiny, light-brown wood covered every surface, and flat-screen TVs hung from nearly every wall. There was also the odd creeper wearing flannel and a trucker hat sitting in the corner. And among a few of the tables sat much older women who looked like they had just crawled out of the neighboring trailer park. Not the sexiest of places, but the beer was cheap and so was the food.

The elementary teachers were well into their drinks as we pulled a few more tables together to expand upon the helter-skelter, lattice work of employees working their way towards wasted.

Paige took a seat. Wilson, Mack, and I followed.

As soon as the server came over, Wilson ordered. "One Jack and Coke and five shots of Jack, please."

"There goes pacing ourselves," I said.

"This ain't Dart Night, Wilson," Mack said. Then he turned to me with a grin. "Oh, you never told me what happened on Dart Night, by the way."

"That's because I barely remember," I said. "I went out with Wilson. We were just having a beer after work and a burger. And Wilson tells me that he has to play darts later. So, I'm thinking he's going to drop me off and do his thing because I'm not, to use his words, 'ready to hang.' But, he actually asks me if I want to come with him, and I'm thinking, cool. Finally.

"So, we get a ride to where he plays darts. And I meet his team. And these motherfuckers are just doing shot after shot after shot. And it's a Thursday. So, I'm thinking, fucking hell. This is going to suck in the morning. The last thing I remember is seeing the receipt. It was, I shit you not, this fucking long." I spread my arms out on the table. "And it's just: shot of Jack, shot of Jack, shot of Jack. I didn't bother counting.

"I'm fucking wrecked at this point. And thinking, alright, I'm out. But no. We go to another bar and keep drinking. I got a cab home at like two a.m.

"I wake up on the floor of my apartment between my bed and the bathroom, feeling like death, and I crawl into the shower for two hours. I think I fell asleep in there.

"Then 7 a.m. rolls around, and I still feel like someone had ripped out all my insides and scattered them across my apartment. I basically hobble to the 7-Eleven down the road and grab some Pedialyte. Wilson shows up shortly after to pick me up.

"And this fucker is just as happy as can be. He's smiling, in love with life, telling me he never gets hangovers. And I feel like someone's poured nail polish remover into the back of my skull. I'm incapacitated. Done. I'm being tossed back and forth between wanting to vomit and feeling like my brain might actually implode.

"We get to school, and I go to make copies. And that's when I walk by Tate. He's standing outside his class while his fifth graders go grab backpacks or whatever, and he asks me how it's going, but then he sees my face. And he goes, 'rough night?' I manage to utter two words, 'Dart Night.' And he says, 'I guess that explains why you reek of booze.'"

"So, I go back into my classroom, and I'm just trying to

have a low-key day when Sofía comes up to ask me a question. When she reaches my desk, she just pauses and makes this weird face before saying, 'Mister, you smell like my dad.'"

"Oh no!" Mack said.

"It was rough. I just turned my desk to block off the kids from coming to talk to me and had them work on their essays," I said.

"I had to see if you could hang," Wilson said.

"I wanted to hang myself," I said.

"Let me know when you're ready to go out again."

"I think I'll pass," I said, laughing it off.

"You and everyone else who's gone to play darts with the man," Mack said.

"I don't even think I picked up a dart the whole night," I said.

"You're welcome to come out next week," Wilson said to Mack.

"Fuck no," Mack was laughing. "My wife almost killed me last time."

The waitress came by shortly with our drinks, and Wilson began handing out shots to all of us.

"Cheers everyone," Wilson said.

"To some damn good colleagues," Mack said.

"To our family," I said.

"Oh, stop with that mushy shit," Mack said.

"To family," Paige said.

"To family," we all said.

I set the glass down, coughing.

"See, you're getting used to it," Wilson said.

"It tastes like someone throat fucked me with a burnt log," I said, cringing.

"No more parent-teacher conferences this year," Paige said, unfazed by the shot.

"I hate them," I said.

"I don't get that," Wilson said. "I love them."

"What?! No. Everyone hates them," Paige said.

"Not a fan," Veal said.

"See, you're the weird one," I said.

Someone mentioned something about Nemesis.

"I'll talk about anything or anyone, but Nemesis," I said.

And so we talked shop. We talked about what teachers talk about, the kids, our classes, crazy shit that happened, politics. Fresh drinks came and went, and our big group splintered off into cliques.

It wasn't like the conversations I had had in the car with Wilson. In the car, there was no filter. I could vent and not worry about being politically correct, not worry about the status quo. I could be myself, get my frustrations out of my system, and move on. It was different at the bar surrounded by all the other teachers. And as if to reaffirm this, throughout the night our eyes would catch, and we'd nod or toast and then we'd go back to BS'ing with the people around us. Teaching may have been trench warfare, but Wilson was my brother in arms.

"In a few more weeks, I'll be sipping margaritas by the pool, soaking up that sweet sun," Paige was saying.

"You already have plans for the summer?" I asked.

"The same thing I do every year. Tan by the pool; read a few books; drink more than I should." She elbowed me in the side. "You'll get used to it. Summer's where the magic is."

"It's crazy to think that the year's almost over. It's been insane," I said.

"You did have a bit of a rough spot there," she said, sipping her beer.

"Teaching is a lot different than I thought it would be," I said.

"How so?"

"I got into teaching because I liked reading. Then I came here," I laughed.

"I'm the same way, but you teach freshmen. I get them when they're Juniors and Seniors. They're much cooler at that age. But you're also new. It'll get easier," she said. And then, as if she sensed my doubt, added, "You're doing fine."

"How'd you survive?" I asked.

"I reminded myself every day why I got into teaching in the first place. I wanted to make a difference. And that's never easy. When it's the hardest, that's when you know you're needed most. Some years are rougher than others, but I love what I do," she said. "I hear you're coming back next year."

"Yup," I said. "And I have a few new ideas for *Frankenstein* next year. Nimitz told me he found a bit of funding to get more books, so that'll help. And I want to see what my eighth-graders can do. They're pretty cool. Weird, but cool. It can't be harder than this year was."

"I'm glad you're sticking around." She turned towards Khus. "He's coming back!"

"That's good to hear," she said. "Cheers!"

We clinked glasses.

"Laws didn't get renewed," Khus said. She was the middle school history teacher.

"Laws?" I asked.

Veal sat down next to us with a fresh drink. "What are you all talking about?

"Laws," Paige said.

"Oh. Yeah, that wasn't good," Veal said.

I know what that feels like, I thought.

"Nimitz gave him a choice. He asked him if he was willing to come back and work harder next year. Laws said he was done. He's going to finish out the year though. So, that's good," Khus said.

"Then what?" I asked.

"Who knows?" Khus said.

There was an awkward pause.

"Are your kids any better?" Paige asked me, changing the subject.

"You're just worried because you're going to have to teach some of them next year," I said, smiling.

"From all the stories I've heard about them, I'd be an idiot not to be a little worried," she said.

"They're the hardest class I've ever had, but it's only my second year. The ones that passed shouldn't give you any problems. They're some pretty cool kids in there."

"Gentlemen. Ladies," Shanahan said as he walked by. "Drink up. The festivities begin tonight. No excuses! There's no work tomorrow, so I expect a bunch of bad decisions tonight." He winked at Veal. Shanahan was another force of nature. He had been coaching high school football since before I was born.

"I can only have one," Veal said.

Shanahan frowned. "Come on, gorgeous. We're all going to get wild tonight. Mack even promised that he'd dance, if we get him drunk enough."

"I heard that," Mack said from a distant table where he was chatting with Wilson.

"How's your other job?" Paige asked.

"Same old, same old. It's a restaurant. Nothing too exciting," I said.

"How much longer will you work there?" she asked.

"A little longer."

"Don't work your life away. You're young. You gotta go out. Get laid, man."

"I'm not in any rush," I blushed.

"No. He's too busy crushing on some girl at his restaurant that he's too scared to talk to," Wilson said as he returned.

"This bitch," I said.

"Oh, shit," Mack said. "Chicken?"

"Wait. What's this I hear? You're too big of a pussy to ask a girl out?" Shanahan said squeezing my shoulder. The man was powerful, never mind the fact that he was pushing sixty.

"It's just a work crush," I said.

"Who is she?" Shanahan asked.

"It's complicated. And boring. You know what's better? Wilson, why don't you tell him your story?" I said with a wide grin.

"Wait. What story? What story is that?" Shanahan asked. Suddenly eyes turned towards Wilson.

"That's right, motherfucker," I said, nodding at Wilson.

"Not a bad choice of words," Mack said, laughing. Wilson joined in, and I followed.

"Wait. What? I'm missing something?" Shanahan asked.

Mack leaned over and whispered into his ear.

"I don't believe it." His mouth fell open. "I don't believe it."

Wilson really did go all in on parent-teacher conferences.

I watched as Wilson and Mack pulled Shanahan aside. I couldn't see his reaction, but I imagined it was something similar to what mine had been. Shanahan returned a few moments later, dying, tears welling up in his eyes.

Some moms really are hot.

When he finally regained some composure, he turned to me. "And you knew this? He told you?" He looked at Wilson. "You told the New Guy?"

Wilson was handing out another round of shots. "He was the first one I told."

CHAPTER THIRTY-EIGHT

The Last Day of School

Someone had stolen my laptop.

"They're probably halfway to Mexico by now," Wilson said.

"All my stuff was on there," I said. We were sitting in my room, talking during lunch.

Whoever had stolen it had also taken a sign that was hanging on my wall and placed it on the spot where my laptop would have been. The parents had made the signs for Teacher Appreciation Week and handed them out to all the teachers. It said, "Teachers are candles cast into darkness. They give from themselves to light up the world." Or some shit like that.

"Whoever stole it had a sense of humor," Wilson said.

"I'm not even sure why they would take it. They'll get maybe fifty bucks for it," I said. "I can only hope that they try to turn it on and watch it load. To know that someone else had to deal with that piece of shit would make me happy."

"Look at it this way, at least you'll finally get a new one," he said.

"Just let me be angry for a few minutes."

"And they didn't take your chair. That's a silver lining."

He shrugged.

They had taken other stuff though: two more computers, twenty iPads, and even a set of Legos from our classrooms. The police had investigated in the morning and had left before lunch.

"True," I said. "I don't really care about the computer. I care about all my work from the year that was on there." I was spinning the sign on a finger as I leaned back in the chair.

"You've got all summer to come up with new stuff," Wilson said.

I gave him a look.

"We'll work on it together. Beers on me."

"Has anyone ever—"

"Yeah, yeah." Wilson threw a hand up in protest and then sat on top of one of the desks.

I went back to emptying my desk into a box for the summer.

"Wait, wait, wait. Don't forget that." Wilson reached forward and grabbed the purple folder off my desk and handed it to me.

"Right," I said and tossed it in on top of the rest before closing up the box with tape. I put the box with the rest of them off into the corner of my classroom. Back in my chair, I gazed about my room, still twirling the sign around my finger.

"What are you going to do with that?" he asked.

"This? This can fuck off," I said, tomahawking the sign into the overstuffed trashcan by the door, missing entirely.

"You sure you don't want to keep it?"

I gave him a look.

"Okay, okay," he said, putting his hands up in mock protest.

"Maybe they'll break my bookcases when they move them, then I can get new ones."

"They won't move those. To be honest, I think your bookcases were probably here before they put up the building," he said.

"Damn," I said, looking out at my room. It was back to its original condition except now I had posters, student artwork, and little, fluttering butterflies covering the walls. On top of one bookcase rested the giant cardboard cutout of the creature that Kelly had made. I had begged her to keep it. I wanted it to gaze out at my students for the years to come, hinting at what waited for them there.

Wilson took off when the bell rang, and I waited for the final period of the day.

They had rearranged the schedules for the last day of school; so, I had my eighth-graders one last time before the summer break. That was much better than finishing off the year with Period Nine. Most of them hadn't bothered showing up, anyway. I had spent one last period in the morning talking to Emma, Ricky, and Kate while waiting for the bell to ring.

It had been alright.

Eighth grade hung about the room and talked to each other, sharing stories of the summer, playing games on their phones, and asking me annoying questions. When I noticed there were a few minutes left, I went to the front of my class. "Listen up, before you leave, I need to tell you something."

The room went silent except for the sound of Brutus kicking a soccer ball back and forth.

"Can you stop that for a second?" I asked.

"Sure, Mister," he said as he continued kicking the ball.

I walked over. "Give it here."

He rolled his eyes as I took the ball and threw it out the open window.

"Really, Mister?" he said. "You think I'm not going to get that?" Suddenly, he ran out of my class with Ezekiel close behind.

"What was I saying?" I asked

"You said you wanted to tell us something?" Zooey said.

"Oh yeah. We've come a long way. It's been a crazy year. I stayed up late last night trying to figure out what to say before you left. I knew what I wanted to say, but I wasn't sure how to say it.

"At the beginning of the year, Wilson told me that you were all amazing. I didn't see what the big deal was. Not at first, but now things have changed. It's been a good year, not perfect, but a good year. We have a lot of work ahead of us, but I'm excited to continue on the journey with you. One way or another, you all belong here."

Alfred looked down. "Not me, Mister."

"No. Everyone in this room right now belongs here. We're one big, dysfunctional family. This class has been the highlight of my year. It sucks that someone stole my laptop with all my lesson plans on it, but that just means I'll have to make sure that my class is better than before. I'm glad I get to teach you again next year."

Brutus and Ezekiel walked back in.

"What did we miss?" Brutus asked.

The final bell rang.

"Have a great summer."

I watched them all leave.

"Have fun with your bestie!" Sofía called out on her way out.

"Let's go, bitch," Zooey said, dragging her friend away.

I rolled my eyes. "Go home already."

"You're going to miss us this summer!" Zooey said.

"What's your name again?" I asked.

There were no lingering goodbyes, no hugs, no one stood on the desk and said, "O Captain! My captain!" They merely left as the bell rang. A few of them called me a loser, but that was about it.

I remembered what Wilson had said, that each school was different. They were slowly opening up to me, but it would be a process. In the meantime, I would be what they needed me to be.

I followed the kids outside. The sun was unbelievably bright, and the air was hot. The promise of summer sauntered about with the scent of warm grass as they all sprinted away. I stood there by the railing watching as kids talked with friends, played soccer, and walked home with their siblings.

Teaching *Frankenstein* had been a success, at least, in its own way. I had finished the book. My kids had improved. And I was determined to return and teach it again the following year. I leaned over the rail and took the school in for the first time. It really was one big family. Deciding to teach the novel wasn't a test for my kids; it was a test for me. I had been searching for a reason to stay, and for the moment, I had found one.

"You want a cookie?" Mario appeared next to me with a container full of them.

"Sure," I said, grabbing a big chocolate chip one.

"Don't smell too many markers this summer, Mister," Mario said.

"I'll try to cut back. But you know me, I've got a problem."

"Your head is really shiny in the sun; it's blinding me," he said.

"I wanted to thank you—" I looked down at him "—for letting me know you were there. I wouldn't have seen you and might have stepped on you."

"You know, Mister," he said, "your class kinda sucked at first, but it was alright in the end."

"You know, Mario, you were kind of a shit-head at first," I smiled, "but you turned out to be pretty cool in the end."

He held out a hand, and I shook it.

"I'll catch you around, Mister. Have a good summer."

"You too."

And with that, he walked away to join the rest of them.

CHAPTER THIRTY-NINE

Epilogue

"You ready to head out?" Wilson asked.

"Yeah. I think so," I said. I was back in my room swaying slightly from side to side in my chair.

"Working tonight?" he asked.

"Yeah. I'm not feeling it though. My heart's here right now," I said.

"It grows on you."

"You doing anything over the summer?" I asked.

"No big plans," he said. "What about you?"

"I suppose I should do some planning for next year," I said.

"You should get out. Go on a date. Take that one girl camping. Please, do something, anything with that girl. I can't listen to you spend another year going on and on about her."

"I have a mattress now, so it's more like glamping at this point," I said.

"Glamping?" he asked.

"Glamour camping...it's when—" He gave me a look. "You know what, never mind," I laughed. "You ready to head out?"

317

"If you are."

We talked all the way to the restaurant.

When he parked, I grabbed my stuff and opened the door, but before I left, I turned to him. I had something I needed to tell him. I hesitated. "I can't teach forever. I can for now because it feels like it's the right thing to do, but I know the moment we walk back into that auditorium this feeling will change. I know that when I sit there looking out at all the other teachers waiting for the year to begin, knowing that we have to sing our stupid little songs one more time, I know that I'll hate teaching just a little more. Then the year will start up, and the chaos will ensue, and we'll get lost out there in the trenches. But everything that room stands for will stick with me, and eventually, I will leave. It may not be next year or the year after, but I know I will walk away from all of this."

"I know," he said. "But until you do, I'll be around, my good man."

I nodded and closed the car door behind me. After he left, I turned to face the restaurant. The air was hot and smelt of garbage. There was nothing I wanted to do less than enter that building. I wanted to go home, crack open a beer, and think back over the year and how much everything had changed. But that's not how it was.

Sweat pooled beneath my arms as I stood there looking at that building. I gripped the bag that hung from my shoulder, feeling the weight of my work clothes inside, but I couldn't move. I wanted to stand there, still, holding onto the feeling that day had brought me.

I am no longer a teacher.

When I tell that to most people, they immediately assume it was because of the kids, but that's not true.

The kids were the best part. They had their problems sure. Every student has a story. They may have been ungrateful often, and they may have fought me constantly, but through it all, they made me laugh, and they gave me hope. They made me feel like I had a purpose, that I mattered.

Teaching *is* trench warfare. You hold the line. Some days you gain ground, other days you lose it, but either way, you keep fighting. And sometimes, when you're fighting for so long, you forget who the enemy is.

Politics killed teaching for me.

I watched as politics chewed up Wilson and spat him out. And when he walked away from education, my passion for teaching trailed behind.

I soon followed.

But we had two more years together before that happened. Two years of lunches, car rides, bullshitting, and yes, even darts. And for two years, we held the line, brothers in arms.

I'd like to think that we changed lives, but as I said, it's still too early to see the payoff. Maybe one day I'll know.

I gripped my bag tight, took a deep breath, and moved towards the door. It opened suddenly in front of me, and I moved out of the way, the sounds of a busy kitchen and garbled half-conversations quickly shut off as rapidly as they appeared with a loud clang as the door closed.

She stood there, staring at me. I felt my heart flutter the way it always did when I saw her.

"What are you doing all dressed up?" she said.

I watched as she undid her hair, and it fell flowing past her shoulders. I don't know if my eyes ever left hers as I stumbled to find my words. "I'm a...I'm a..."

"Spit it out," she said, chuckling.

"I'm a teacher," I finally managed.

"Oh, are you now?" Her eyebrow raised.

At least for the moment, teaching had its benefits.

CHAPTER FORTY

Afterword

Are you up for a little homework?

If you have time, write an honest review on Amazon or Goodreads. Teachers deal with unbelievable obstacles every day. Awareness can help bring about change.

Until next time.

Vj

09/03/2018

Made in the USA
San Bernardino, CA
10 May 2019